MADELEINE went up the spiral staircase. *Deadly lady*, she thought. Ah, yes, but *who* is the deadly lady? Is it Lola, or Lyla . . . Clarissa . . . or perhaps the mythical Penelope Marsh? But no, the deadly lady was, of course, Madeleine's alter ego, the elusive Madge, who showed herself to every one but Madeleine.

Fawcett Gold Medal Books by Joan Dial:

SUSANNA

LOVERS AND WARRIORS

DEADLY LADY

DEADLY LADY

by

Joan Dial

FAWCETT GOLD MEDAL ● NEW YORK

Readers may write to Joan Dial:
c/o CBS Publications
Fawcett Gold Medal Books
1515 Broadway
New York, New York 10036

DEADLY LADY

Copyright © 1980 Joan Dial

Published by Fawcett Gold Medal Books, a unit of CBS Publications, the Consumer Publishing Division of CBS Inc.

ISBN: 0-449-14348-1

Printed in the United States of America

First Fawcett Gold Medal printing: July 1980

10 9 8 7 6 5 4 3 2 1

DEADLY LADY

by

Joan Dial

FAWCETT GOLD MEDAL • NEW YORK

Readers may write to Joan Dial:
c/o CBS Publications
Fawcett Gold Medal Books
1515 Broadway
New York, New York 10036

DEADLY LADY

Published by Fawcett Gold Medal Books, a unit of CBS Publications, the Consumer Publishing Division of CBS Inc.

ISBN: 0-449-14348-1

Printed in the United States of America

First Fawcett Gold Medal printing: July 1980

10 9 8 7 6 5 4 3 2 1

I hate and love
You ask how that can be?
I do not know, but know it tortures me.

Catullus

CHAPTER 1

Madeleine stirred, shivering. She opened one eye and squinted at the strangely unyielding body that lay beside her. She put out her hand to touch him, and pulled it back. His flesh was cold, almost rigid.

The sheet was rolled into a snake, wrapped around her ankle, pulling her leg close to the lean frame of the man. Panicked, Madeleine tore at the sheet and twisted free.

She was wide awake, her heart pounding. The room was swathed in a ghostly dawn as she fumbled with the switch to the swag lamp that hung over the bed. It clicked on, flooding Dean's face with a garish white light. His eyes stared straight ahead, his skin had a gray pallor, and there were tiny bubbles along his lower lip.

Madeleine sprang from the bed, her feet sending the braided rug skittering across the tiled floor. She was naked and trembling. A scream was trapped in her throat.

Nightmare and reality blended as Madeleine struggled with a deluge of conflicting thoughts. As always in moments of stress, two distinct voices were at war in her head.

He raped you and you killed him. But I came willingly—how could it have been rape? *You changed your mind, resisted, and he wouldn't take no for an answer.*

There was a gaping hole in her memory about exactly what had happened. One minute she saw Dean forcing a dry and painful entry into her resisting flesh, and the next she was convinced it had all been a dream. *Only in a dream would Madeleine have strength enough to fight Dean and win.* No! Stop it! her rational mind screamed. You're thinking of yourself in the third person again.

Forcing herself to look at the body on the bed again, Madeleine saw his hands frozen in the act of clawing at his stomach. On the dresser was the cardboard container from which they had eaten supper. The red stain of the *salsa* and the stale smell of the heavily spiced remnants of enchiladas brought the bile back to her throat.

Her clothes were in a wrinkled heap on the floor. She snatched the blouse, remembered where she was, and shook it vigorously. A small brown spider fell to the floor. When she attempted to button the blouse, her fingers refused to obey her brain's command. So she grabbed her jeans and yanked them on. She scooped up her car keys from the dresser and stumbled outside. Madeleine took a deep breath of the chill air and then locked the door behind her.

Her Volkswagen was parked in front of the motel room, streaked with moisture from the mist that had drifted up from the beach. A high storm tide was sending plumes of spray over the dark rocks.

To the east a silver band of light marked the horizon. *His body will be discovered before I can reach the border. There's nothing to do but ask for Lucien's help.*

Madeleine glanced longingly at her car. She wanted to jump behind the wheel and put as much distance as possible between her and the horror in the motel room. Instead she hurried past it, in the direction of the motel office.

A dark-eyed maid came slowly to the door in response to her insistent knocking. "Señora?" she asked, her eyes full of sleep.

"I must use the telephone. *Teléfono, por favor.*"

"*Sí, señora.*" She pointed to the desk.

8

Madeleine twisted a long strand of dark hair and tapped her foot anxiously as she heard the distant whirring signals. Had the maid cared to observe she would have seen an intensity in Madeleine's deep-blue eyes that fully reflected her distress.

"Hola?"

"I want to place a call to California—Laguna Beach," she stammered in English, forgetting what little Spanish she knew.

There was a long pause, more clicks and the whirr of machinery, then a different voice announced, "The circuits are busy. We will call you."

"Wait!" Madeleine shouted. "You don't know who I want to call. Listen, I want Lucien Cornell. Area code 714 . . ." She gave Lucien's unlisted number.

"Sí. Gracias."

Madeleine replaced the receiver and said to the maid, "Señorita, we want to stay another day. But please don't disturb us. My husband wants to sleep. No maid service today, OK? Look, I'll pay for the extra day now."

The dark eyes regarded her blankly as she dropped a twenty-dollar bill on the desk.

Madeleine paced up and down outside the office for an hour, glad there was no one about at the early hour. Part of her wanted to run, but the other more cunning voice at the back of her mind warned that certain precautions must be taken first. Lucien would know what to do. When the phone rang shrilly she crashed into the office door in her haste to reach it.

Sarita's cool voice was already on the line. "I thought it would be you calling at this ungodly hour. He's still asleep."

"Get him up. Put him on the phone, Sarita. If you keep me waiting, I swear I'll . . ."

"Calm down. Here he is."

"Penny? Where are you, princess?" For once the bored indifference was reassuring. She usually balked when he insisted on using that name, but now Madeleine didn't care. She needed his help.

"I'm in Baja, at a motel on the beach, just north of Ensenada. It's called—oh, I don't know what it's called. But you'd better come for me. I need you. Desperately."

"What happened? If you can give me a hint, I'll know whether to bring the fire brigade or plenty of boiling water."

"Please don't make light of this, Lucien. It's happening again. *The same thing that happened in London*. Oh, God! What shall I do?"

His voice changed from the bored drawl to brisk command. "Don't do anything. I'll be right there. Go back to your room and wait for me."

"I can't. . . . That's where he is." Her voice sank to a terrified whisper.

"You must. Throw something over him. What's your room number? Keep calm. I'm on my way."

She held the phone for half a minute after the receiver clicked down at his end of the line.

An hour later his silhouette fell on the drawn curtains of her room. Who else on the West Coast would be wearing a hat? she thought irrelevantly. He'd probably flown down in his Cessna.

She flung open the door and fell against the fine gray worsted jacket, smelling the faint hint of musk that always clung to him. He rewarded her with his straight-lipped smile, the thin black mustache barely moving. He was suave and slightly amused, as always.

The thought crossed Madeleine's mind that she could have confessed to the worst depravity known to humanity and Lucien would not only have come to her aid, he would have applauded the act. How many times had he told her that superior intellects made their own rules. More than once she had wondered what dark streak in her own personality had drawn him to her.

"Close the door, princess."

There was a station wagon parked next to the Volkswagen. The driver had backed into the space and she could not see his face, but the license plates were Mexican.

10

Lucien gently disentangled her clutching arms and walked over to the bed. Delicately, with his index finger, he hooked the corner of the sheet she had draped over the body. Madeleine turned away as he studied the face beneath, then ripped the entire sheet away to expose Dean's naked and vulnerable body.

"Have you had anything to eat today?"

Madeleine did not turn around. "No."

"Drive into town. Buy some *pan dulce*. Then take it down to the beach and eat it. I'll come for you when we're finished here."

"I'm not hungry. Are you going to call the *policía?* Will they put me in jail right away? Oh, Lucien—" The tears came in great frightened gulps.

Lucien crossed the room swiftly and enfolded her in his arms. She wanted to pull away because he seemed to bring the smell of death with him. "You're going to do exactly as you're told. I have only one question. What is the last thing you remember last night?"

She looked away from his searching dark eyes. "We made love," she said defiantly. Madeleine could see the disgust in his face. She was silent, hating him and needing him, envious of the bored aplomb, the sophistication of nearly fifty years of life and experience. He was unaware that she had learned his age, that she knew he was closer to fifty than the forty he admitted. The taut tanned skin, athletically lean body, and coal-black hair untouched by gray gave the appearance of benevolent genes rather than careful maintenance.

Madeleine did not remember driving into town. She picked up a tray and tongs in the *panadería* and selected half a dozen sweet rolls, paid in American currency, and drove back to the rocky beach below the motel.

The sun had burned off the mist, but there were few people on the beach midweek in October. She broke up a roll and scattered the pieces among the gulls. Their comrades came shrieking in from the offshore rocks to join in the feast. The receding tide left sand dollars and glistening amber seaweed that popped beneath her sandals.

Yesterday she and Dean had walked the same sand, giggling and teasing and pushing each other into the chill surf. The sudden whim to come to Mexico with him had been more to escape all of the problems crowding in on her than because of any real interest in Dean himself. She had not really known him. He was young and strong and laughed a lot. Somewhere in his background was Vietnam and vague show-business aspirations.

At the time she had assured herself coolly that a romantic interlude was just what she needed. Hadn't Lucien just returned from a weekend in Palm Springs with a ravishing actress—and didn't he look rejuvenated for it? Madeleine's life was more celibate than a nun's, which was probably why she had begun to awaken in the night filled with erotic and vaguely sinister longing. Dean appeared to be the answer to what ailed her.

He had scorned her suggestion that they buy Mexican insurance before crossing the border. She blanched visibly when he told her to stop on a Tijuana streetcorner to buy tacos from a street vendor whose wares lay beneath a hovering cloud of flies.

"I bet you won't drink the water either," he teased when she shook her head to his question as to whether she wanted a taco. "In Ensenada we can get shark-meat tacos. Boy, are they good," he said, pulling a crumpled Mexican bill from his jeans pocket as he stepped out of the car to the cracked and dusty sidewalk.

The inevitable crowd of ragged urchins and desperate-eyed men hawking gaudy pottery quickly surrounded them. Madeleine remained in the car. After a few moments the crowd was so thick and their pleas so shrill that she was not at first aware of the man with whom Dean was in quiet and rapid conversation. He was a powerfully built Mexican wearing an embroidered white tunic over immaculate white ducks. She noticed first, however, his shaved head and almost theatrical drooping mustache and goatee, which reminded her of the deliberately fierce and flamboyant badges of professional wrestlers.

She was emptying her purse of change, distributing it to the children, when Dean returned to the car. He shrugged off her question about his exotic-looking friend and instructed her to turn onto the toll road to Ensenada. When they had traveled beyond the desperate poverty of the cardboard shacks on the outskirts of Tijuana and were feasting their eyes on the breathtakingly lovely coastline, Madeleine remembered that she had not actually seen Dean buy or eat any of the vendor's tacos.

Dazzling beaches flashed by, and the majestic Pacific stretched out endlessly. Sparkling surf danced on dark rocks in deserted coves. She lost herself in the beauty of picture after picture, seascapes framed in her windshield.

Then they were at the motel, and she experienced a moment of panic when Dean opened the door to their room.

Of course she knew he expected to sleep with her. She wanted it too—wasn't that why she was here? She wanted casual sex, didn't she? She wanted to drop the charade of faultless grooming, designer clothes, insulated surroundings, programmed conversation. The pretense of being someone she was not.

She wanted to let that other Madeleine loose—the one who awoke in the night from fevered dreams, or who fought the sudden desire to tear off her clothes and scream obscenities at an audience of very proper matrons. Not even Lucien, who relished debauchery in private, would have considered behaving in public in the way Madeleine sometimes imagined. The capricious whims both repelled and fascinated her.

She liked being with Dean, who was not awed or even particularly impressed by her background. To Dean she was nothing more than an attractive woman. There was something very ordinary in the way they related. Madeleine liked the feeling. It was like being able to get away with murder. . . .

That was the problem, of course. Why must she always think of sex and death together? Lucien called it the *petite mort*—the little death. That was it. She must forget the other.

But when it came down to it, she couldn't. Dean's arms were around her and the hardness of him was probing her thigh and his tongue was inside her mouth when she pushed him away and muttered something about taking a shower.

He shrugged and waited while she stalled. *I'm too serious about getting into bed with a man,* she thought. It isn't that big a deal, is it? Everyone does it. If I could just be as casual about it as he is.

Just as casually, he offered her the choice of a joint or various capsules. She refused, requesting wine instead. He laughed and said the influence of her sugar daddy was showing.

"Sugar daddy?" she asked.

"That's what they called them in his generation." When she still looked blank, he added, "Your sponsor, Lucien Cornell. Doesn't he always have the dusty wine bottle brought for his inspection? Sniff the cork, savor the bouquet, or whatever the hell they do with it?"

She had flushed, and defended Lucien. "I'd still be an itinerant nobody if it hadn't been for Lucien. He's like a father to me." *Besides, there is a hidden side of me that envies Lucien.*

"He's also forced you into a role you don't enjoy. Churning out purple prose when you'd rather paint."

"Painting is just a hobby. Writing is my profession, and I'm not ashamed of my books."

"Oh? Then why do you use a pseudonym?"

"Lucien felt Madeleine Delaney was too long and would dominate the book cover."

"OK, babe, it just seems strange to me that you'll talk easily about your painting but freeze up at the mention of your books."

She thought, Oh, Lord, I must be more careful or I'll give the game away.

"Watch out you don't wind up with a senile old millstone around your neck, pretty lady."

Protesting that Lucien was stronger and healthier than most

men half his age had produced a scuffling about the bed as Dean demonstrated who was or was not healthy.

When he became aroused again she began to fight him in earnest. "No! Stop it! I've changed my mind—let me go," she screamed and beat on his chest.

At first he just laughed and tickled her, unzipped her jeans, managed to get her blouse off. When she slapped him in the mouth his mood changed swiftly. "What the hell . . . why, you rotten little tease—" The rest of his howl of fury was lost in the ringing of her ears as he slapped her. Then he was pinning her to the bed, his knee going savagely between her thighs.

After a while it hurt more to resist than to comply. Red waves of rage raced across her brain, and she lay still while he thrusted and twisted and groaned, his sweat dripping on her. In her imagination, it was she who had control of things. Her hands had strength, and they squeezed his throat until his bloodshot eyes bulged. He was as helpless as was she at this moment.

"You frigid or something? You shoulda had some pot," he said when he rolled off her.

It wasn't supposed to be like that, she thought numbly, as she lay there in pain and humiliation. Dean was pulling on his swim trunks, whistling, as though nothing had happened. It was even worse than the last time . . . nearly two years ago.

Had it been that long since Tony? She had loved him with all the passion and abandon of first love, but he, too, had taken her in pain. And the following day he, too, was dead. Her head throbbed again.

She dropped down on the cool sand, digging her fingernails into the dry grains. A small olive-skinned boy was playing in the tide pools, leaping from rock to rock. He smiled at her.

Smiling back, she waved for him to come closer and offered the paper bag of *pan dulce*. He said, *"Muchas gracias, señorita,"* and politely took a broken sweet roll.

Under Mexican law, I am guilty until proved innocent. I could spend months in jail before even coming to trial for just being on the scene of a mysterious death.

15

The Mexican boy looked up the beach and then raced away. Lucien was coming toward her. His dove-gray suit and matching hat, polished leather shoes, and silk shirt all looked incongruous on the untidy beach. But no one would have laughed at the man wearing them. In the sunlight the network of fine wrinkles on his face was more noticeable.

"Are you ready to go home?" he asked as she rose to her feet and went toward him.

"What about Dean? What killed him?"

"The doctor believes he died from natural causes."

"But he was young and healthy."

"Even the young and healthy can die from natural causes. Come, we must be on our way. I have the plane waiting."

"But won't I have to tell my story to the police, or the coroner, or someone?"

"I've taken care of everything. There is no reason for Penny's name to be linked with his. Fortunately he signed the register 'Mr. and Mrs. Jennings.' You really must try to stay home for your little romantic adventures, my dear. It is too much of a coincidence—you accompanied your friend Tony to England, and now this incident in Mexico."

"I can't believe Dean died from natural causes. Are you sure it wasn't an OD?"

"Was he an addict?"

"Not really. He smoked a little pot."

"And that, of course, doesn't count. It isn't like being a little bit pregnant, is it? Although that too is possible with your generation. Abortion on demand. Gratification without thought of consequences." He seemed oblivious of the fact that he was a fine one to speak of morality. But then Lucien was surely the inventor of the double standard. He was as complex and diverse as the myriad of companies he controlled in the international conglomerate that had made him a millionaire.

She was silent, staring at the vastness of the Pacific, still partly in shock from Dean's death, trying to grasp what had happened. Lucien's bullying and her own acceptance of it were

16

less important than the sudden rush of events shaping her life. She thought later that Lucien would not have spoken to her in such a manner under normal circumstances. Her quick temper when she felt her rights were being threatened and her refusal to be intimidated by anyone or anything had been the traits Lucien himself had most admired in her.

"Come on," Lucien said, more gently. "I'm taking you home."

As Madeleine tossed in restless sleep that night, the nightmare returned. First the iron bars materialized, and with them unbearable fear. A shadow fell across the cage. She was on her knees, trying to hide, held fast by an unseen bond. The dark figure was grotesque, filling the small space she occupied, trying to engulf her. It wavered and hovered, descended on her shrinking flesh like a cloud of insects. She felt the icy touch of evil, and she was screaming soundlessly, writhing in agony, lashing out at a shadowy adversary who remained just out of reach.

She sat bolt upright in bed, breathing rapidly, bathed in perspiration. The familiar silhouettes of her room came gradually into focus. A breeze fluttered the curtains on either side of the French door. She got out of bed and went to the small deck beyond, drinking deeply of the night air. She wanted to be fully awake. Too many times she had remained in bed after the dream, fallen asleep, and been caught once again.

The Pacific was silver and serene in the moonlight. The salt tang of the air was spiced with woodsmoke. The fire Lucien had lit must still be burning. He had been kind to her in a soothing, fatherly way, all evening, as though trying to make amends for his earlier abrasiveness. He had cooked dinner, dined with her, and insisted on staying until she was drowsy enough to fall into a sound sleep.

A glass of milk, Madeleine thought. That's what I need. And I'll sit in front of the fire for a while. Must think.

The staircase curved down to a slate-flagged entry hall. What time was it? The fire, still burning brightly in the living room, sent orange light dancing across parquet. She stopped abruptly on the threshold. A dark figure stood in front of the fire, its back turned to her. For a moment the panic of her nightmare rose again. Then the figure turned and she saw the proudly arrogant tilt of the head, the high forehead and slightly pointed chin.

"Lucien," she said, letting out her breath in a sigh of relief. "I thought you'd gone home. What time is it?"

"The bewitching hour. I was worried about you and not particularly tired myself, so I stayed down here while you slept. You had a terrifying experience. I was afraid it might bring back your recurring nightmare. Is that what happened, or couldn't you sleep, Penny dear?"

"I wish you would stop calling me Penny, at least when we're alone."

"Come and sit by the fire. Better hang up that coat—it cost a fortune." She'd chosen instead of a robe the fur coat she was too embarrassed to wear in public. "Why does the name still upset you? It's really better for you to use it all the time."

"Because every time *you* call me Penelope Marsh I feel as though I've lost my own identity."

"And that troubles you greatly? My dear child, how many girls your age have fame and fortune? Surely you feel some gratitude to dear old Penelope for that? Look at you, standing there dripping sable, surrounded by priceless antiques in a million-dollar beach house. You are free to come and go as you please . . . wined, dined, feted, adored, admired and sought after."

Madeleine dropped the sable coat to the nearest chair and went closer to the warmth of the fire. She looked up into his sardonic eyes, the unconsciously cruel lips curling slightly to reveal strong white teeth. In the flickering firelight the chiseled cheekbones and hooded eyes, beneath the bold sweep of black brows that almost met in the middle, were thrown into sharp relief. "Lucien, please . . . you know I'm grateful to you. I just wish I could be myself when we're alone. It's hard enough putting on the Penelope act for the rest of the world."

He reached out to brush a long silken strand of her hair back from her brow, and his fingers lingered for a moment, leaving behind a cool imprint. "You've had a trying day, haven't you, princess?" he asked softly. His voice was low and resonant and seemed to vibrate in her ear. "I thought it better to take your mind off what happened. But perhaps I was wrong. Perhaps we should have talked about the man who died."

"The second man who died," Madeleine said in a small strangled voice.

He drew her into the circle of his arms and held her like a frightened child. "Don't think of it. You merely came into their lives just as they were ending. Pure coincidence."

"What shall I say if someone asks me about Dean?"

"Nothing. You last saw him on the beach here. You did not go to Mexico with him. Just that." He paused, looking down at her with his intense dark stare. She wanted to pull her eyes from the mesmerizing grip, but could not. She was relieved when he spoke again. Lucien's silence was somehow more threatening than other people's rage. "Will you be up to addressing the women's club tomorrow, princess? No questions. I've insisted there be no questions. I shall go with you, of course. . . . Penny, dear, are you listening?"

"Madeleine is listening," she said. "Lucien, it would make far more sense for *me* to call *you* Penelope. After all, you do write the books."

"You're tired, that's all. Come on, I'll take you up to bed and brush your hair until you fall asleep."

"Perhaps you ought to read me a chapter of Penelope's latest romance. That should put me to sleep faster."

"Now, now. Don't be nasty."

"Have you finished it?"

"Yesterday—while you were en route to Mexico. I believe Penelope has really outdone herself this time."

CHAPTER 2

There were only two men present at the women's club luncheon—Lucien, seated beside Madeleine on the dais, and the young man who sat alone at the back of the room. Even if he had not been the only male in the confused blur of faces, he would have caught her attention. He had an air of quiet strength, a sense of compelling honesty, as well as aloof reserve. His features were rugged, his eyes steel gray. His light-brown hair had deep-bronze undertones and was sun-streaked about the temples. He looked out of place in the salt-stained jeans and fisherman-knit sweater he wore. He was a paradox from twenty feet across the room. Madeleine felt his presence as surely as she felt the warmth of the sun on the window behind her.

She forced her eyes back to the page in front of her and continued reading in her slightly husky voice. "... Clarissa cowered, trying to cover her nakedness with trembling hands. Did he hear the fear in her voice? 'I will never willingly submit to you.'

"He laughed, a chilling sound without mirth. His lips came down on hers, burning and devouring as his tongue forced her teeth apart and his hands fondled her breasts. She felt the hard strength of his body, his erect manhood probing her thigh as insistently as his strong fingers now forced her legs apart. The great swelling touched her most private place, and she moaned, both wanting and hating him."

Madeleine glanced up, pausing as Lucien had instructed. The circle of women listened raptly. The fisherman at the back of the room grinned at her. As she caught his eye, he winked solemnly. *He knows that I didn't write this! But how can he? Who is he?*

"Sir Giles was poised on the brink of possessing her completely, and she was powerless to prevent him. 'You won't return to face Madame Guillotine, never fear,' he whispered, his voice strangely gentle all at once. 'You are too fair a doxy to lose your head.'"

Glancing up, Madeleine saw the fisherman watching her now in a puzzled way. She felt hot under the silk dress and stumbled over the next words she read. She could almost feel Lucien frown at her side. *Don't look up again—concentrate on the book.*

After a few minutes, Madeleine forgot the audience and the quizzical-eyed young man at the back of the room. She was Clarissa, fighting desperately for her honor, hating the way Sir Giles dominated her, yet longing for him to overpower her, to bring forth within her the same all-consuming passion that infused his being.

There was an excited babble of voices as she returned the manuscript pages to the kidskin briefcase. The brim of the lacy straw cartwheel hat shadowed her face, creating exactly the aura of mystery that Lucien wanted. Her dress was pure white, virginal, simple, a drift of pure silk.

"You will forgive Miss Marsh," Lucien was saying. "She is exhausted."

"Where do you get your inspiration?" a voice close to her asked. There was a slight hesitation, a shyness to the question.

Madeleine turned her head so quickly the circular hat connected with the face of the man who had moved swiftly to her side. He held a copy of the previous Penelope Marsh romance.

"Would you autograph it for me? My name is Simon Tanning. How about something like 'To Simple Simon from Mad Madeleine'?"

She managed to keep calm, her face frozen in a smile. How did he know her real name? "You've done your homework, I see," she said, scribbling the Penelope Marsh signature. There was no reason to panic, really. He was probably connected with the publishers.

But he immediately dispelled that theory when he said, "I'm puzzled why Madeleine Delaney bothered with a pseudonym. Your real name is much more intriguing."

"There were reasons," Madeleine said, attempting to evade the question. "Are you a member of this women's club?" She turned innocent blue eyes to his and smiled a slow smile. Her heart was beginning to thump erratically.

He stared at her for a moment, struck by the luminous quality of her eyes, and answered without thinking. "I came because your social secretary wouldn't put through my calls. I came to ask you what happened to Dean Jennings."

The book slipped from her fingers and fell with a soft flutter to the carpeted floor.

By the time Simon Tanning had picked it up and his quizzical eyes were again searching her face, she was ready for him. "Later . . . meet me on the beach near Smuggler's Point. It's a private beach—you'll have to walk up from Hidden Bay. I can't talk now."

The words were barely out when Lucien moved to her side. "Come, my dear, many of the ladies are waiting for your autograph. And you, my good man, are you a reporter? If so, I will be happy to answer your questions."

Madeleine managed to flash Simon Tanning a warning glance before Sarita deftly steered her toward the table bearing copies of Penelope Marsh novels.

"Who is the handsome gorgeously muscular hunk?" Sarita asked with a predatory smirk. "How positively cheeky of him to crash the women's club lunch." Sarita was a petite blonde, her hair a perfectly tinted shade of platinum. Her green eyes glittered like pale beads, and she managed to look down her aquiline nose disdainfully, although Madeleine was two inches taller than she.

Madeleine murmured vaguely.

"I saw him whispering to you," Sarita persisted. "If you're not interested, I am. There's a definite animal magnetism under that unkempt appearance that I would like to investigate."

There was no time for Madeleine to reply because one of the women approached with a book to be autographed.

As she stood in the sunlight, signed books automatically, and gave noncommittal answers to questions, Madeleine again pondered why Lucien had not allowed Sarita to pose as Penelope. Sarita had been Lucien's social secretary for nearly ten years, and she deeply resented Madeleine's presence. Lucien explained to Madeleine that he had written the first historical romance for a lark, never expecting it to become a best seller. He said if Sarita were passed off as Penelope in press interviews, someone might remember she had been hired as his secretary. Besides, he said, he needed Sarita to organize his household, his office, and his life. He added privately to Madeleine that he wanted Penelope Marsh to be a more alluringly mysterious creature.

"A dark-haired, magnolia-skinned beauty with deep-blue enigmatic eyes . . . and a ghostly aura . . . like yourself, my dear. Once we have stripped you of the hippie trappings, dressed and groomed you, taught you what is good taste and what is not, you will do very nicely." He did not add that Sarita's beauty was as blatant as her sexuality and the mid-Atlantic accent she affected.

Madeleine never believed it would last nearly three years. She expected at any time that Lucien would announce to the world that he was Penelope Marsh, not the vague young woman who fielded questions uneasily and retired behind Lucien's urbane screen at the first hint that someone was peeling away her carefully wrought facade. But he had not. He was content to reap the financial rewards. Madeleine supposed he had had his fill of acclaim in other fields, since he had not turned to writing until he was forty. Previously he had been a brilliant chemist who rose to become the head of a company called Agri-Chem. With inherited family wealth he acquired several other companies, and, eventually, Agri-Chem merged with other small companies to become a large corporation with international tentacles. He had written several books in his own field and a somewhat convoluted mystery novel before turning to historical romance.

"You are so young to write so knowledgeably about life," someone was saying. "And the research for your books must be overwhelming. I really felt, when reading *Captive Desire,* that I was right there in Colonial America."

She loathed the compliments more than anything else—no doubt, she told herself, because they were unearned. Or was she merely jealous of Lucien's success? His books were riveting and unputdownable, after all. Even Madeleine herself enjoyed reading them and devoured his manuscript pages as they came from Sarita's typewriter. Perhaps, she thought as they made their excuses and departed from the meeting, if I achieved success in my own right, as an artist . . .

Her head had begun to ache. She was anxious to be home and out of the dress and bra, the hot sticky pantyhose and high-heeled sandals. Her face felt stiff under the application of makeup, and the false eyelashes weighed on her eyelids like dead spiders.

Climbing into Lucien's Rolls-Royce, she pictured herself freshly washed, the hair spray shampooed from her long hair. She'd slip into a halter and battered shorts and walk barefoot on the beach.

Simon Tanning. She remembered she must meet him. Her head pounded again.

"What did the good-looking women's club gardener say to you?" Lucien asked, displaying his uncanny knack of reading her thoughts.

"Was he the gardener?" Madeleine asked in surprise.

Lucien shrugged his shoulders. "Gardener . . . or possibly the gamekeeper?"

"Gamekeeper?"

Madeleine drew a blank, but Sarita giggled and glanced over her shoulder at the passengers in the back seat. "He was very muscular-looking. Lucien is thinking of the gamekeeper in *Lady Chatterley's Lover*. Big, hulking brute. There was something very sexual about that man at the club."

Lucien frowned. "Pay attention to the road, if you please, Sarita. It is not necessary for you to interpret my remarks, nor to add editorial opinion."

Sarita turned the Rolls onto the Coast Highway and headed south with only a slight tensing of her hands on the wheel displaying her discomfort.

"I really don't know who the man at the club was. He just had me autograph one of your books," Madeleine said, looking straight ahead.

"How about dinner tonight?" Lucien asked. "You were a good girl this afternoon, and I'd like to reward you." His tone was careless.

Madeleine dug her fingernails into the leather seat. "I have a headache. I thought I'd go to bed early."

"Then I'll send Sarita over with a tray of goodies," he said with elaborate indifference.

"Please don't bother," Madeleine began, but she knew it was useless. She leaned back and closed her eyes. Immediately the image of Simon Tanning burned into her mind.

He watched her walk down the steep cliff trail. She moved with infinite grace, lost in her thoughts. The long legs swung easily, bare feet found the soft sand between the rocks. Her arms and legs were tanned, and, surprisingly, so was her face now the layer of makeup had been removed. Her hair blew about her shoulders in a dusky cloud. She wore frayed shorts and a faded halter and looked ten years younger than she had at the women's club luncheon.

Surely, he thought, that lovely creature couldn't be involved in Dean Jennings' rotten business. What would have been the point? She was obviously wealthy and successful. Perhaps that

25

was the answer—a cheap thrill for a bored have-it-all, done-it-all? She didn't look that type. Perhaps she wanted to write a novel—but no, she wrote historical romances. They were surprisingly well-researched adventures filled with passion and romance and showed a lively imagination.

She looked up and saw him waiting. Luminous blue eyes met his, and he saw the fear there for a second before she assumed the cloak of careful composure.

"Hello, Simon Tanning," she said, her voice low and well-modulated. She smiled, showing even white teeth, and the smile lit up her eyes. He felt a slow ripple pass down his spine.

There was a long vivid green streak running down the side of her halter, matched by another daub on her bare arm. He studied it with interest and, following his gaze, she said, "Oh . . . it's paint. I was finishing a sea-scape."

"I thought you were a writer, not a painter."

"Painting is just a hobby," she said apologetically.

"No need to be defensive about it. I think it's great that you're multi-talented as well as beautiful. What the hell did you see in a creep like Dean Jennings?"

The flush spread slowly up her cheeks, and the color enhanced her eyes. "I didn't really know him very well. I don't know how I can help you find him. I haven't seen him since . . . since that day I met him on the beach."

"I thought you went to Mexico with him."

"He told you that? Is he a close friend of yours?" The veil was still there, but there was an edge to her voice. "He did say something about Ensenada—No! Don't!"

Tanning stopped, puzzled. "Don't what?"

"Don't walk any further. From this point on, the beach is visible from Lucien's house. I turned down a dinner invitation and I wouldn't want to hurt his feelings by showing up on the beach with you."

He dropped to the cool sand, sitting cross-legged. She stood looking down at him uncertainly.

"OK, Madeleine. Let's stop playing games. I saw you and

Dean take off down the San Diego freeway in your red bug. At least I assume it was your bug. It did seem a bit incongruous for the rich lady author to be driving a '71 VW, but I figured it was probably your incognito car. Like, for when you wanted a little fun and games on the side." His voice was gentle, despite the accusation.

"On the side of what?" She looked out to sea, watching the red sun splash the horizon with gaudy splendor. A sandpiper darted after a retreating wave.

"You know what I mean."

"I gave Dean a lift to Oceanside. I was visiting a friend there. I just dropped him off."

"And he hitched a ride to the border? Did he say he was going to Ensenada—you're sure? Not Tijuana?"

She was staring at the darkening sea and suddenly gave a little exclamation and splashed into the water.

"Hey—wait—what are you doing?" He scrambled to his feet.

She was at the edge of the white surf, and the wave curled and broke as she dived under it. She came up holding a shiny black bundle in her arms. He went to meet her, getting his shoes and socks wet. Lying limply in her arms was a sea lion pup.

"Is it alive?" he asked.

"Barely. There's a lifeguard who has been taking care of them. We've had several injured sea lions washed up because of the storms last week. This one must have been separated from its mother. I don't know . . ." She cradled the small creature to her breast and set off toward the trail to her house.

"May I come with you?" he asked.

"No."

"May I see you again?"

"I've told you all I know."

"I'd like to see you—get to know you."

"You'd be wasting your time."

He watched her climb the cliff, bearing her burden with tender care. Surely, he thought, someone who cares about a little sea creature would also care about people—at least enough to refuse to be part of Dean Jennings' traffic in human misery. Simon put aside the thought that Madeleine could have dived for the sea lion as a means to distract him and end the interview.

Madeleine sat bolt upright in bed. The spinning images of her dream receded as her bedroom came into focus. There was moisture on her brow, between her breasts, on the palms of her hands.

The accusing dead faces were still there, superimposed over the silhouettes and shadows in her room. She blinked furiously, trying to make them go away.

Out of the darkness came remembered whispers, so real she could hear the words again. "No, Madeleine, you aren't going to stop me now. It's time you learned you can lead a man to a point of no return. Christ, I've got a pain in my gut. I've had frustration pains before, but never like this. I'm sorry, sweets, you're going to accommodate me like it or not—"

His dead face floated mistily about the room. She buried her own face in her hands to shut out the image, along with the pain and anguish love had caused her.

CHAPTER 3

Sarita was cool and efficient, ticking off items on her notepad. ". . . then lunch with the organizers. Except for meeting the literary group on Thursday evening, that's about it for this week. You'll have all the time you want to smear paint on your canvases in the loft. It's also about time for you to make your monthly visit to . . . you know where."

"The sanitarium," Madeleine supplied for her. "And the patient I visit is my mother."

Sarita studied her notepad. Her light-blond hair was arranged in S-waves and carefully casual curls, but did not move in the breeze that sent the window curtains fluttering like sails.

Hair spray, Madeleine thought. A sticky lacquer that keeps every hair in place. Why do I dislike her so? Because she in turn dislikes me? Is that too childish of me? Her brain is probably as neatly in place as her hair, every thought in the right little compartment.

Sarita looked up. "Lucien asks again that you refrain from driving into town wearing shorts or jeans. I'm also to mention getting rid of the Volkswagen beetle."

Madeleine smoothed her denim shorts against her tanned thighs and rose from the breakfast table. "Tell Lucien I'd rather not. The bug is all I have left to remind me I was once Madeleine Delaney, would-be artist and free spirit."

"It surely must remind you also that the patient who now has every luxury in that expensive desert sanitarium was then incarcerated in the state asylum." Sarita's narrow nostrils twitched slightly as though an unpleasant odor assailed them.

"Asylum? Do they still use that word?" *They fed her through a tube up her nose. The woman in the next bed laughed and laughed. The orderly said another patient had done something terrible to her. They couldn't be everywhere, all the time, could they?* "All right, Sarita. Report back to Lucien that I've been reminded that when he found me on the beach I was broke, hungry, and probably on the verge of a nervous breakdown myself. Is the bug still in Mexico? I didn't think about it when I left in Lucien's plane."

"It's here. But you shouldn't drive it. Lucien feels it might be a link to the man who died there and we should get rid of it."

"He told you about Dean?"

Sarita looked at her pityingly. "Of course. He tells me everything."

"I want to end the masquerade, Sarita. Did he also tell you that?" *I feel trapped and desperate. The nightmares are worse . . . especially since Dean.*

"You can't just abruptly stop being Penelope Marsh. We need time to cancel engagements, and make other arrangements. You gave your word to Lucien, and he asks so little of you." The resentment was in her voice again, and the unspoken thoughts hung in the air, *What does he need you for? You need him more than he needs you. Do you want your mother put back into the ward at the state hospital?*

Madeleine read her thoughts very well, and the panic came welling up again. She couldn't put her mother back in the state hospital—nor did she want to join her. But nightmares and sleepwalking did not add up to mental instability, did they? The decision she had reached in the desperate hours preceding the dawn had to be acted upon, and there was no way she could keep it secret. She said carefully, "I've been thinking of doing something about my . . . insomnia."

"Oh?" Sarita was instantly quivering with curiosity.

"I thought maybe I should talk to a psychiatrist, perhaps get into some kind of therapy."

"Good idea. Shall I make an appointment with one for you?"

"I'll choose my own, thank you."

Madeleine picked names at random from the phone book. She made an appointment with the fourth psychiatrist she called; the other three did not make house calls. His name was Regis Vaughan and he could stop by for a brief visit the following day. He arrived at precisely the appointed time. Regis Vaughan was about Lucien's age, but white-haired and fatherly in a way that Lucien would never be. He wore deceptively casual slacks of fine wool and a mismatched cashmere sweater over an open-necked shirt. He was a walking advertisement for the joys of clean living, trim and healthy-looking with a springy step. He smiled and offered his hand. Madeleine led the way up the stairs to her studio.

"You don't mind if I work, rather than lie on a couch, or whatever you usually require? The light is just right."

His steps fell silently on the polished wood stairs leading to the attic. Looking back, she saw he wore running shoes.

"Excellent idea." Vaughan felt this was an unconventional way to interview a new patient, but decided against the usual method of face-to-face confrontation. He might learn more this way. He had sensed something during their phone conversation that made him wary. "I want you to be completely relaxed. Besides, I'd like to see your paintings." He had an engaging smile, reassuring without being clinical.

"In lieu of the ink-blot test, perhaps?" she asked. She was instantly sorry she'd said it. She did not intend to be flippant.

He made no comment as she threw open her studio door. The sloping roof had been filled with skylights, and the profusion of glass gave the impression the semicircular room was a clear bubble floating over the endless sea.

She told him everything she wanted him to know, quickly and dispassionately, focusing on the nightmares, the sleep-

31

walking, and the memory lapses. Briefly she outlined her personal history, and then, because she had to, she told him about Tony and Dean.

He listened intently, occasionally interjecting an incisive question that searched out more than she intended to reveal so soon.

"And your relationship with Lucien Cornell?" he asked when she finished.

"A business relationship. He pays me to pose as Penelope Marsh." She paused and added guardedly, "I suppose we're friends, too. He's kind to me."

Surely, she thought, I wouldn't have been able to bear the masquerade—even for Mother's sake—if Lucien had not been such a supportive friend.

It was not in Madeleine's nature to let someone else arrange her life. She had always been fiercely independent, but Lucien had made the transition painless. It was a shock to her to suddenly realize she had come to depend on his judgment. Had she cast him in the role of her missing father, a role easily filled by the only man she had known well who had never made a sexual overture?

Occasionally, when Lucien looked particularly handsome, Madeleine had been disturbed by her reaction. She wondered if she should tell the psychiatrist of the times when she had seen Lucien, dashing and urbane in a tuxedo, whispering seductively to some beautiful young woman. Madeleine felt at those times, a strange blending of envy, anger, and erotic arousal. She decided against such an admission.

Regis Vaughan waited for her to elaborate on her business relationship and friendship with Lucien. When she did not, he said, "You say you were with your mother when she discovered her sister's body. Were you a small child when your aunt committed suicide?"

She nodded, resisting the urge to tell him that childhood trauma was too easy an answer.

He was studying one of her seascapes, a slight frown knitting his brows. "This is good. You've caught all the turbulence without making it too awesome." Almost without a break he added, "Tell me how you feel about your mother."

Madeleine picked up a can of spray varnish and waved it in front of a half-finished canvas on her easel. "She's the most beautiful woman you've ever seen, but since the suicide she's been enclosed by an impenetrable screen."

"Catatonic?"

"Yes. I suppose so."

"Do you remember finding your aunt's body?"

"She was sitting up in bed, her hair streaming about her shoulders, her eyes wide open. She was wearing a negligee, and when we went closer we could smell her perfume. My mother began to scream. I thought she would never stop. But she did, and hasn't uttered a sound since."

"How do you feel about your father?"

"I haven't heard from him for years. He's in Australia, I believe. In the beginning he sent money. We went to his sister in Santa Barbara, and she had Mother committed."

"After your father's sister died, you dropped out of college, hit the hippie circuit. Did you ever take drugs?"

Madeleine shook her head angrily. "My aunt died of an overdose of sleeping pills. I've always been terrified to take even an aspirin."

She chose a sable brush from the jar of turpentine and shaped the bristles carefully between her long tapered fingers. Her hands were trembling. "Besides, my mother and aunt were Christian Scientists. My father tended to ridicule their beliefs, but I never could bring myself to use drugs. Because they'd been right, you see—drugs killed my aunt."

"Tell me more about Tony Waring."

She dipped her brush into the cobalt blue on her palette and made light strokes in the dark tunnel of a wave on her canvas. "A few months after I came to work for Lucien, Tony came to take photographs for a magazine article. He was devastatingly handsome . . . charming, older, and sophisticated. I was overwhelmed by him. It sounds silly now, but I fell in love with him at first sight." Her eyes misted in remembrance.

Regis Vaughan was silent, waiting.

"At first it was fun—pretending to be Penelope Marsh. I even enjoyed the clothes and parties. Then I began to feel like a cheat, taking a bow for someone else's performance. By the time I met Tony it had begun to pall, but I couldn't bear the thought of putting Mother back into the state hospital, and I knew I couldn't afford to keep her in the sanitarium on a waitress' or file clerk's pay. I especially hated pretending to Tony, and told him the truth about my relationship with Lucien. Tony said he loved me, and not the pretend personality. He was going to England on assignment and wanted me with him."

"Did he propose marriage?"

"Yes. But I asked him to wait until we were safely over there."

"Why 'safely'? What were you afraid of here?"

"I don't know why I said that. Anyway, we flew to England. The first night in London we took a hotel room and made love. I awoke in the morning to find him dead. I panicked, packed my things and got out of there. I took a train to Stratford-on-Avon . . . it seemed a touristy thing to do. Lucien found me almost immediately. He had arrived at our hotel just after I left."

"How did Lucien know where you were?"

"When I asked him that, later, he said that Tony had asked Sarita to make the reservations. Lucien often travels in Europe, and he rescheduled a business trip because he was worried and felt Tony was taking advantage of my . . . naiveté. He found Tony and called a doctor. It was food poisoning, acute salmonella. I guess I was lucky to be alive, because we'd been together every minute, eating the same food."

She was silent, remembering how many times she had promised herself she would return to England and read the entire transcript of the inquest she had not attended. Perhaps there was something there, a fragment of hope that Tony would have died no matter what. But there had never been an opportunity to go back.

"And how did Lucien find you in Stratford?"

"He didn't—I called him at his London hotel. I read a brief item in the newspaper that there would be an inquest on the body of an American found in a hotel room by Lucien Cornell. Lucien kept me out of it."

"Did you feel you were running away from something when you went to England with Tony? Do you ever feel you must run away from something, without knowing quite what it is?"

"No. I told you. I was in love with Tony."

"But even before he came along, didn't you miss your former . . . shall we say, nomadic life?"

"Dr. Vaughan, earlier you said I had hit the hippie circuit. Now you imply I lived like a gypsy. Neither of these assumptions is correct."

"I'm sorry. It was the impression you gave. Go on about Tony."

"There isn't anything else." She was slashing her painting with a palette knife, ruining the division between sea and sky. Her eyes showed rage and the knuckles of her hand were white as she clenched her fist about the slim wooden handle of the knife.

"Salmonella poisoning, you said," he prompted, watching her carefully.

The palette knife snapped in her fingers, the blade separating from the handle. She spun around, her eyes like bruises in a face drained of color. When she spoke her voice was high and strained, unlike her normal slightly throaty voice.

"You're a doctor—I don't have to tell you what happens when someone gets salmonella poisoning. I'll leave it to your imagination what kind of state I was in when I woke up in bed with him."

"You're sure he was dead?"

"He was dead. Terminal shock due to severe salmonella poisoning and resulting dehydration, they said at the inquest, Lucien told me."

She dropped the broken palette knife, moved to the window, and stared out unseeing. "Are you going to be able to help me? I just want the nightmares and sleepwalking to stop—and the little memory lapses. I lose bits of time, somehow. I'm afraid of those missing pieces of my life. I'm not sure exactly how long I was in that hotel room with Tony. I'm not sure exactly when I left for Mexico with Dean. I'm not aware of it happening, but all at once I find I've forgotten what I did for several minutes . . . or hours."

"Yes, I'm sure we can trace the cause. You must try to be patient, however. It will take time. Tell me, what kind of work did you do between leaving college and becoming Penelope Marsh?"

"You name it. I loathed most of the jobs I had. And all of the bosses."

"You've been with Cornell almost three years. I take it you are happy with your present position?"

"I'm here because he pays for a very expensive sanitarium for my mother. I hate playing the part . . . the deception . . . I hate not being myself. There isn't enough time to do all the things I want to do—my painting, especially. I want to be my own woman again, in control of my destiny, but not at Mother's expense."

There was a crash from the room below, and a lilting voice exclaimed in Spanish.

Madeleine said, "It's Josefa. Lucien's maid. She comes over here two or three times a week to clean the house. Look, I want to speak to her, and I'm getting a headache. Could we stop now?" It was painful talking about her life. She hadn't realized how difficult it would be. His questions seemed harmless enough, but she thought he could perform some magic, erase the symptoms as one might erase a word on a page.

"Of course. I'll come back in a few days. How about Thursday?"

"Make it Friday. Thursday I go to the sanitarium to visit my mother. She never knows me, but I like to go on the same day each month, just in case she somehow expects me. I'll walk to the door with you."

The house presented to the street a blank stucco wall topped with red tile, in the Spanish style. The area between house and street was filled with giant cacti, bristling with spines. There was an interior atrium, cool and moist with ferns and fuchsia, offering a sharp contrast. Regis Vaughan followed Madeleine through the atrium. She opened the wrought-iron gates leading to the street at the same moment an ancient jeep stopped at the curb. Simon Tanning was at the wheel.

He smiled his shy smile. "Hi. How's the sea lion?" He turned off the engine and picked up a box from the seat beside him. "A gift for our sick friend," he explained, lifting the lid. A neat row of slightly smelly fish lay inside, head to tail.

"Goodbye, and thank you, Dr. Vaughan," Madeleine said.

Vaughan's hazel eyes carefully examined Simon Tanning, his gift of fish and decrepit jeep, before the soft-soled shoes moved noiselessly toward the Mercedes parked in the driveway. Once inside his car he scribbled into a notebook:

Psychogenic amnesia (injury ruled out). Since hypnotic amnesia unlikely, consider hysterical amnesia. Paramnesia? Does she remember as genuine events only imagined or hallucinated in fantasy or dream? Korsakoff's syndrome? Somnambulist. Creatively intelligent. Childhood trauma.

When the Mercedes glided away, Madeleine said to Simon, "I asked you not to come here. If you hadn't shown up at the exact moment I was showing him out, you would have stood here all day. There is no way to get in. Visitors must be expected and know how to attract attention by means of a secret intercom."

"Then it must have been fate that brought me at the right moment," Simon said earnestly. "Please don't keep me in suspense about our sick friend."

"Dan, the lifeguard I told you about, didn't hold out much hope. I'll tell you how to find him, and you can deliver the fish yourself. He keeps the sick sea lions in a pen on the beach. Come in and I'll draw you a map."

He followed her through the atrium, into a tiled hall with

massive Spanish furniture and cool gloom. "Why don't you just install a moat and drawbridge?" Simon asked conversationally at her retreating back.

"Don't need them. All of the windows face the sea, and, as you know, we're a long way from the nearest access road to the beach. A would-be intruder would have a difficult time breaking in."

"I've been up all night reading Penelope Marsh books and can't find you or your thoughts in any of them."

"What makes you say that?" she asked sharply. The unexpectedness of the comment had caught her off guard.

"I don't believe a woman wrote those books," he said quietly.

She pulled open a small drawer in an antique hallstand and extracted a pencil and pad. "Go on."

"Every heroine is brutally raped, yet apparently enjoys it and usually winds up marrying the man who raped her."

Madeleine looked away quickly, afraid he would see in her eyes her own aversion to that aspect of Lucien's novels. She said, "You'll find all the current crop of historical novelists— at least the best-selling ones—use the same formula. Are you accusing them all of being male writers hiding behind female pseudonyms?"

"I haven't read any of the others," he confessed. "But I still say Penelope Marsh is a man. Apart from the rapes, there are other things that give the author away. Things only a man would think of or say. Who is it—Lucien Cornell?"

She kept scribbling a map and directions and did not answer.

"I have to conclude it's Cornell. I checked at the library at UC Irvine to see if he'd written anything under his own name. The listings show he wrote several textbooks on chemistry, years ago. He also wrote a mystery. I guess historical romances by women sell better than those by male authors. But Lucien's were so popular every newspaper and magazine in the country wanted articles and interviews. He's never been married, although his name has been linked with some of the most beautiful women on earth. Not having a wife to pose as Penelope

Marsh, he hired you. Offhand, I'd say he was probably getting a great deal more out of the arrangement than you are."

She flushed. "What do you mean by that?"

"He isn't locked in a gilded cage."

"You haven't the vaguest idea what you are talking about. May I suggest you mind your own business?" She was angry that he had put everything together so quickly and tidily. She was also acutely aware of his physical presence. Her fingers shook as she tried to hurry with the map. She could feel his eyes examining her, knew there was a chemical attraction between them. No! It was too soon!

He studied a picture on the wall beside the hallstand for a moment. "This one of yours?"

"Hardly. That's a Dali."

"I don't know much about art—" he began.

"But you know what you like," she finished for him, on safer ground.

"I was going to say that an artist has to be closer to full awareness of the senses than anyone else. To feel intensely—creatively. To be able to reflect all the passion of life in a motionless picture. Such a gift could only belong to a person capable of a superior relationship with another human."

She raised her eyes and held his in a long questioning glance. He could not tell from her expression if she was receptive or just amused.

He flushed. "I was trying to tell you I've never met anyone like you. I'd like to get to know you."

A shiver of apprehension went through her, and she wished she had never met him. His sheer physical presence would be hard ever to forget.

"I'm sorry," he said. "But you're very beautiful. Intriguing. Why would a warm-blooded, lovely woman shut herself away from the world, then break out briefly with a creep like Dean Jennings?"

She thrust the sheet of paper into his hand. "Just drive north on the Coast Highway. Anyone can direct you to Dan's beach."

"Ah! A Madeleine Delaney original. I shall treasure it always." He folded the scribbled map reverently. "Could I see one of your paintings before I leave? I couldn't find you in a Penelope Marsh book—perhaps I'll find your essence in a painting?"

She hesitated. "There's one in the living room. Over the fireplace."

She watched him cross the living room in a few long strides. She could not help but compare his swift and decisive progress with the silent padding of the recently departed Regis Vaughan and the slightly mincing walk of Lucien, who usually entered a room as though expecting to find the sewers of Tijuana backed up there.

"Of course," Simon said softly. "I'd like it better if there were a sailboat on the horizon. The loneliness of your ocean is almost unbearable."

"Are you a boat lover?"

"I do own a boat. Will you come sailing with me?"

"No." *I can't! You're too attractive. I'm afraid of where it might lead.*

He was wondering what it would be like to make love to her in his boat on a giant ocean swell, and could not meet her gaze. Dimly he heard himself ask her to have dinner with him. He was afraid that he sounded like a petrified schoolboy.

"I can't. Besides, you're having dinner with a sick friend. If you don't hurry the dinner will spoil."

He smiled, his teeth white against his tanned skin. "Could we meet again? Your terms—anywhere, anytime? I'd like to be your friend." His hand drifted tentatively in her direction, lightly brushing her arm.

She drew back as though his fingers were on fire.

At that moment a disembodied voice spoke from the general direction of the hallstand. "Lucien here. Someone press the button please. Penelope . . . Josefa? Hurry, my arms are breaking."

Madeleine jumped, visibly.

"Your jailer is here," Simon remarked. "It is he, isn't it? He writes the Penny Dreadfuls."

40

Madeleine smiled, in spite of her discomfort. She raised her hand to flip a switch on the hallstand. "It's open, Lucien," she said into an unseen microphone. "You're just jealous of his success," she said to Simon.

A small dark-skinned woman bustled into the room. "Is the señor, *sí?*" She was vividly pretty, with teasing eyes and a quick smile.

"Yes, Josefa. Would you go and help him? He's bringing dinner." Madeleine looked at Simon. "You really must go now. I have business to discuss with Lucien."

"May I call you in the morning? Will the icily polite Sarita put me through? Please—I want to get to know you. It is nothing to do with Dean, I swear. I'm attracted to you, and I want to pursue it."

Lucien came through the door from the atrium, taking short precise steps. He carried a yachting cap and a cheesecloth-swathed tray. His navy-blue blazer gleamed with brass buttons, and his gray flannel slacks gave no hint there was flesh and bone beneath them. A silk cravat was wrapped about his neck and tucked into his shirt. Josefa hurried along behind him bearing a wicker-wrapped wine bottle and a long French loaf. Lucien stopped abruptly when he saw Simon.

"I'm not sure if you were ever properly introduced," Madeleine said. "Lucien, this is Simon Tanning. Mr. Lucien Cornell." She relieved Lucien of the tray and started toward the kitchen. "Mr. Tanning was just leaving," she added.

Simon offered his hand, which was ignored as Lucien held the door open. "Then we must not detain him." His eyes were black, hooded. Except for the tanned skin, Simon thought, he'd make a perfect Count Dracula. Lucien's nostrils twitched slightly, and Simon wondered if he smelled of the fish he had brought for the sea lion.

"I trust, young man, that you have not been making a nuisance of yourself? Miss Marsh has a great deal of work to do."

"I've been here no more than five minutes, admiral," Simon replied, allowing his eyes to drift briefly over the impeccably tailored blazer and slacks. "And you know what they say about all work and no play."

"When I saw the jeep, I thought the workmen had come to repair the patio. What a disappointment." Lucien's eyes moved from Simon's worn denims to the kitchen door as Madeleine reappeared. "Do go and change for dinner, dear. My Beef Wellington cannot wait another minute." There were tight lines etched into the skin between his eyes.

"Goodbye, Mr. T," Madeleine said. "I hope your sick friend is better."

Lucien closed the door firmly behind Simon. Madeleine was glaring at him. "Was it necessary to insult a guest of mine? Or to command me in that tone of voice? Perhaps you should share your Beef Wellington with Sarita instead. I'm sure she'd be happy to change for dinner. I'm comfortable as I am."

Lucien raised a perfect black eyebrow. "My apologies, princess. I believed he was an unwelcome guest." He laughed softly. "How lovely you are when you're defiant. I've always admired your spirit. You're the only woman I've ever known who is not afraid of me. Come, don't be angry. You know you can't resist my Beef Wellington. And I've made some of those *petits fours* you love."

Madeleine's rage subsided before his persuasive plea and the tantalizing aroma of perfectly cooked food.

The soundless scream echoed down all the corridors of her mind. She saw only the black bandage over her eyes. Ready, aim, fire. . . . Her fingers touched something. Wet, sticky. Cold slime.

She was trying to stand up, but her limbs were held fast. The more she struggled, the farther she sank into the dark pit. She was going under the surface, slowly disappearing. Were the hands helping her escape, or pushing her farther down into that evil mass? The hands were on her body, holding her down.

A nightmare . . . is it a nightmare? She forced her eyes open.

The sound of the surf broke through the numbed, gradual return to wakefulness. She was cold, shivering. Her nightgown clung wetly to her body. There was a clump of seaweed near her face, smelling of long submersion in the depths of the sea. Now in a sitting position, she saw she was on a dark and deserted beach.

She stood up, teeth chattering, and wondered at the dexterity of a somnambulist who came down a shifting cliff trail without cutting bare feet on the sharply pointed rocks.

She picked her way carefully back up the cliff to the house. She had awakened before to find herself in another part of the house. This was the first time she had actually gone outside. She did not dare think that it might be a dangerous sign.

CHAPTER 4

Madeleine found Simon's note tucked into the hallstand drawer the following morning. He had obviously written it before coming to the house, perhaps with the intention of leaving it in the mailbox, she reflected as she studied the brief message:

My phone number and address, Madeleine. Please call me, any time, for any reason. I've a feeling you could use a friend.

She memorized the phone number and tore the note into small scraps. The address was an apartment in Costa Mesa, fifteen miles up the coast.

She frowned. Friend? She didn't have any friends. She had Antoine, her art teacher, who came to give her lessons twice a week. He was a volatile Frenchman given to extremes of mood. She sometimes felt he retarded her artistic progress more than he helped it. Then there were Sarita and Josefa, to relieve her of all chores. Lucien himself, of course. And now the psychiatrist, Regis Vaughan.

There was also Ramón, the Mexican gardener, a leanly handsome young man with the eyes of a martyred saint. There had been times she wished she were more adept at portraits. Ramón would have made an excellent subject.

Her circle was a small one, but she was kept busy—there really was no time for anyone else. This morning Antoine would come. She should apply another coat of glaze to the canvas in progress, but a golden sun beckoned over the southern horizon and the sea was an inviting blue-green. She went up to her room and put on a swim suit. A spray of fine sand fell to the carpeted floor. She stuffed her discarded clothes under the dust ruffle of her bed, just in case Lucien came looking for her. He despised untidiness.

Outside, she shivered as the cool air enveloped her. Ramón was cutting back the bougainvillea, and he smiled as she appeared, his tortured eyes lighting up. *"Buenos días, señorita. Is a beautiful day, no?"*

She smiled back. *"Muy bueno,* Ramón. Why don't you stop traumatizing that vine and come swimming with me?"

"Too cold—and the señor would send me back across the river. What is traum . . . traum . . . ?"

"Cutting. You're hacking it to death."

"Ah! Is necessary. Good for blossom."

"Ramón, if Antoine arrives before I get back, tell him I won't be long. OK?"

"Sí, señorita." He watched her run gracefully across the

deck, bare feet skimming the brick patio, until she disappeared through the gate leading to the cliff trail. Ramón sighed deeply and slashed another branch from the bougainvillea.

The sand was cool beneath her feet. She took a tentative step into the water, gasping as the 60-degree shock raced from toes to brain. The late-October sun was low over the sea, sparkling and shimmering on the bursting spray as waves rolled and broke. She dived through the first wave, came up to gulp the warm air, went down again to the bottom to allow a second to thunder over her head to the beach.

She opened her eyes in the misty green and silent world, picked up a large sand dollar lying on the bottom, and broke the surface again. Simon Tanning was sitting on the beach, watching her. He was dressed in faded denims and a sweater.

"Where is your towel?" he asked as she splashed toward him.

"Must have forgotten to bring one. I brought you a present." She handed him the sand dollar, and he turned it over in his hand, smiled, and slipped it into his pocket. He pulled off his sweater and offered it to her. "Use this—you'll freeze."

"No I won't, because I'm going to race up to the house. Sorry I can't invite you. I have an art lesson this morning. 'Bye."

He caught her wet wrist, not roughly. "You found my note?"

"Yes." His chest was beautiful, firmly muscled, a shading of red-gold hair accentuating the planes and hollows. She forced herself to look away.

His hand went under her chin, tilting her face upward. "You feel it too," he said softly. Before she realized what he was going to do, he leaned forward and kissed her lips lightly. "You're salty," he said. "You taste of the sea and all its mystery." He was as surprised as she at his temerity.

She stared at him, feeling she ought to protest, or at least offer some sort of smart remark. She did neither, but pulled her wrist free and sped back up the cliff.

Antoine was waiting for her in the living room. He was

unusually silent, considering she had not been there to greet him. He stood near the heavy Spanish trestle table, nervously tapping his fingernails on the rough wood. He was a small, wiry man with an ageless look, olive skin, graying dark hair and matching beard.

"Antoine, I'm sorry I kept you waiting. I won't be a minute. Do you want to go on up to the studio while I change?"

"I have already been up there," he said in a low voice. His eyes searched her face. "What 'appened last night?" When he was agitated, his French accent returned.

She was shivering. "What do you mean? Look—I must get out of this wet suit. I'll be up in a minute."

"I will wait *here*," he said firmly.

"Suit yourself. I'm too cold to argue." She ran up to her room, leaving a trail of salt water in her wake. In the steamy comfort of the shower she thought about the look on Antoine's face when he asked his question.

I awakened to find I'd walked in my sleep again . . . that's what happened. But how would Antoine know anything had happened? She had not seen him for over a week. Her mind groped back to last night, to yesterday.

Regis Vaughan, the psychiatrist . . . and Simon . . . and Lucien. Lucien was a gourmet cook and often cooked dinner and brought it over to share with her. He refused to cook in her kitchen because it did not boast all the fancy crocks and food-processing machines he owned.

They had dined, discussed the new Penelope Marsh book and its promotion campaign. Lucien had been charming and amusing. He had not reproached her about anything, had not even mentioned Simon. Nor had Lucien wanted to know about her session with Regis Vaughan, although Sarita must have told him about the psychiatrist.

Madeleine had been so grateful and relieved that as Lucien was about to leave she had impulsively placed her hands on his cheeks and kissed him lightly on the lips. "Thank you for everything. I wish—"

Lucien's finger went to her lips instantly, silencing her.

There was a momentary flash in his dark eyes, mocking, taunting, as was usual when he disapproved of something she did or said. He was only slightly taller than she, and for a second their breath intermingled, then she stepped backward.

"I'm sorry," she said quickly. "I know you don't like people touching you."

"You are not 'people,' my dear. Have I not comforted you like a father, many times in the past? I merely wanted to stop you from saying what you were about to say. You were going to wish I were twenty years younger, or express some such mundane thought."

She felt her color rise. She had not been going to say that. She had been about to say she wished she could have known him as a friend, without being obligated to him. It was not the first time he had supposed she would utter some banality. She felt sometimes that Lucien believed everyone under thirty went around mouthing clichés or murmuring, "Oh, wow!" She felt a stirring of resentment. Damn him for his arrogance.

There were times when she wanted to humiliate him, and there were times when she wanted to be like him, not giving a damn about anyone or anything. And both of those goals were impossible for her.

Lucien had been everywhere, done everything, and was bored with it all. She thought about him as she lay awake that night, because she didn't want to think about Simon Tanning with his shy smile and clumsy eagerness. When she finally slept the nightmare came back.

She turned off the shower, remembering the shock of finding herself on the dark and deserted beach. She pulled on her jeans and a sweater. Detouring through the kitchen, she had a quick glass of orange juice and a couple of bites of a sweet roll. Antoine did not like to be kept waiting.

He was pacing the living room. As soon as she appeared, he said, "Why you do this thing?"

"What thing?"

"You pretend you do not know? You want me to think I

imagine it? Very well. Come. We will go and look together. Then tell me why."

Puzzled, she followed him up the spiral staircase to the studio. He flung open the door and stepped back, gesturing for her to enter.

She took one step into the room and stopped, her breath caught in her throat. Every canvas was slashed to ribbons. Paint was splashed over walls and floor. Brushes lay like broken twigs in forlorn piles. The legs of her easel were splintered, and it tottered, ready to fall. The canvas she had been working on was face down on the floor beside the easel. Broken glass was everywhere. Every window had been shattered, and the chill ocean breeze swept the room.

"Why you do this, *chérie?*" Antoine asked. "This terrible rage. This is not the way—"

She spun around, turning her back on the carnage. Her heart was pounding against her ribs, and her meager breakfast began to rise uncomfortably in her throat. She pushed blindly past Antoine and stumbled down the stairs. She collapsed on the bottom stair.

Antoine's footsteps came slowly after her. "You do not remember doing it?" he asked more gently.

She shook her head silently, not looking up at him. "Yet you were alone here last night, were you not? And there is no way anyone can get in with all of the fancy wires and buttons and locks. And even . . . even if someone did get through the electronic barrier, you would have heard him smashing wood and glass. Did you hear anything?"

She shook her head again.

"I did not call the police. I thought first we tell Lucien."

"No!" She was on her feet, her eyes wide with fear. "Please, don't tell Lucien. I'll clean it all up. Perhaps I walked in my sleep. I used to, you know. You're right, Antoine. I must have done it, since I'm the only one who ever goes up there. And I have been very upset lately. . . . Antoine, would you go now? I'll see you next week. You won't tell Lucien, will you? Promise?"

The day went by in a blurred haze. She spent the morning cleaning the studio, making endless trips down to the trash container in the garage with the mauled remains of three years' work. The only picture that had not been destroyed was the small seascape hanging in the living room.

As she carried the last of the debris through the breezeway she told herself that sleepwalking was common. *But violent acts of vandalism are abnormal.* She didn't need a psychiatrist to tell her that.

Her mother's a loony. Her mother's in the loony bin. Go away, Madeleine, you're weird. We can't play with you. The taunts of the children came echoing down the years, followed by Aunt Cilla's voice, stilled long ago by death.

"Let's just hope it isn't hereditary. You walked in your sleep again last night, Madeleine. I'm afraid you'll go outside. Your mother kept going outside. If she hadn't, then the neighbors wouldn't have known, and we wouldn't have had to put her away. . . ." *Put her away, put her away.*

"Now, Madeleine, it isn't my fault the children are mean to you. God knows I tried to keep her in the house. They'll say worse things about you if you don't stop walking in your sleep. I'll have to do something to stop you from going outside in your sleep. Perhaps we should tie you to the bed." Madeleine blinked away the disapproving ghost. She rushed back into the house, poured herself a tumblerful of wine, and gulped it down. The room swam slowly about her head and she clutched the table for support.

A languorous haze descended, and she shrugged her shoulders. The psychiatrist would explain it to her. But what if he wanted to commit her? No! Don't think of that.

Was it possible, she wondered as she felt her way cautiously toward the staircase, that she was perfectly normal in the daylight hours and just had a problem after dark? A quick image of werewolves and vampires flitted across her mind, and she hiccoughed and giggled foolishly. She said, "Excuse me," to the empty landing.

Her bedroom was floating mistily in the distance, and she

was weaving unsteadily toward the nightstand bearing a white telephone.

The telephone was actually an extension connected to Lucien's line. He had decided it would be easier to control prying callers by having all calls routed through Sarita. To prevent visitors to Madeleine's house from unwittingly giving away the existence of the extension phone, there was no outside line other than the one through Sarita's multiline telephone.

Madeleine picked up the receiver, dropped it, apologized into thin air, and then said to Sarita, "I want to make a call." She paused, trying to remember Simon Tanning's number.

Sarita's voice was cool and impersonal. "You sound a little fuzzy. Whom do you want to call? Yes, I got the number—but whom shall I ask for?"

Madeleine drew a deep breath. "Sarita, just dial the number I gave you. I'll stay on the line."

"Yes. Of course. Just a moment."

There was a pause, and then the distant whirring of the phone. Madeleine hung up on the fifth ring. "Why am I calling him, anyway?" she asked aloud. *Because something electric happens every time I see him. And I want to see him just once more before . . .*

An hour later she called again. The wine still lay heavily on her senses, and she had to speak slowly, to be sure she did not sound utterly ridiculous. "Simon, I'd like you to come over. No, not dinner. I want you to eat before you come. And don't eat anything here, even if I offer it to you. Just bring a bottle of wine. I'll be waiting out front for you and I'll show you where the intercom button is."

A moment after she hung up, the phone rang, startling her. Her heart began to thud again as she picked it up. Sarita's voice came insinuatingly across the wire. "You hadn't forgotten you promised to address the group in Long Beach tonight, had you?"

"I'm not going, Sarita," Madeleine said, hearing her own voice as though from far away. "I just stopped being Penelope Marsh."

50

"Great timing, Madeleine. Lucien had to go out of town, and there's no way I can reach him. He'll be gone a couple of weeks."

Madeleine groaned. "OK, I'll go tonight. But cancel all the other appearances."

"But next week—"

"Cancel everything," Madeleine repeated firmly.

"I'm afraid I have to go out in a little while," Madeleine told Simon when he arrived. "But I wanted to see you. Could we talk? I'm not sure how to handle this. I've never invited a man over before."

Simon smiled happily, held up a bottle of Burgundy, and asked if it was all right. "Madeleine, I'd have walked all day for a chance to spend five minutes with you."

They went into the living room, and Madeleine found glasses while he pulled the cork from the bottle.

She sat down and surveyed him over the rim of her glass, thinking that she would like to paint his portrait. Would it be possible to portray the power of those shoulders and arms, the gentleness of the hands, that eager, questing light in his eyes, and the disarming honesty of his mouth? "I suppose women call you constantly," she said. "You probably should do something about that comfortable air of security you put out, or someone will take advantage of you."

He raised his glass in a silent toast to her. "I'm not sure how to respond to that. I'd like to be *your* protector and have *you* feel secure with me. But I guess you hardly need one." He glanced about the room. "I feel a bit overwhelmed by your affluence. You've acquired more on your own than any man will ever be able to offer you. But I suppose that's an old-fashioned attitude. I didn't mean to sound like a male chauvinist."

She studied him, from his earnest eyes to the way he leaned forward in his chair, eagerly awaiting her reply. His shoulders bulged under a clean but slightly threadbare jacket, and his shoes were old but well shined. He held the wineglass carefully, as though afraid of breaking it. Before he had entered the room, the furniture had appeared massive, oppressively so; now it was perfectly scaled to his size. He dominated the inanimate objects around him while reassuring the human element. She thought fleetingly that she would never have a nightmare again if she could fall asleep in his arms.

"Don't be overwhelmed, Simon," she said gently. "None of this is mine. All I truly own is a set of sable paintbrushes and an old VW bug. You were right. I just work for Lucien. He is the real Penelope Marsh."

"You're a talented artist. Have you sold any of your work?"

She shook her head. "Not yet." She thought of her smashed studio and shivered.

"What is it?" Concern leaped into his eyes.

"Nothing. Someone walked over my grave."

"Madeleine, I don't want to pry, but if you'd like to tell me what's troubling you—"

"Why do you think something is troubling me?"

"I feel it. You're tense, as though waiting for something to happen. You . . . aren't afraid I'll make a pass? Believe me, I won't spoil my chances of getting to know you."

She smiled. "No, Simon. I'm not afraid of you. And you have every right to assume I'm troubled. That phone call of mine must have sounded strange, to say the least. But now you're here I'd rather not talk about it. Tell me about your boat."

"When I've finished the repairs I'd like to take you sailing on her. She's called the *Viking*. I didn't name her that. I bought her secondhand and didn't change the name."

Madeleine thought it was a perfect name—both for the boat and for Simon. He did remind her of a Viking. He was big, strong, and valiant. "I'm afraid I have to leave," she said. When his face fell, she added, "We could go swimming tomorrow, if you like."

His eyes lit up again. He looked at her, wanting to devour her, afraid he was embarrassing her by staring. She was so beautiful he felt an aching sense of unworthiness. He should be questioning her about Jennings, examining everything she said with suspicion. Instead, all he could think of was his fierce urge to drive away whatever demon it was that haunted her lovely eyes.

She told him the following afternoon that Lucien would be away for a time and that when he returned, she was ending the Penelope Marsh masquerade. "I'm going to make it on my own, as an artist. I'll probably have to take a job for a while, but I was thinking about what you said—about my being in a gilded cage with Lucien. I honestly don't know why I've stayed so long . . . well, I do. Because of my mother."

He waited, not wanting to pry, and on their next meeting she told him that her mother was in a sanitarium. Learning that Madeleine had been her mother's sole support for years, Simon admired her even more. He knew he was falling in love with her and couldn't fight the emotion, despite the doubts and questions he had about her.

For Madeleine's part, in Simon's presence she felt young and carefree for the first time in her life. They walked on the beach, swam in the chill winter surf, shared a bottle of wine in front of a roaring fire, and talked endlessly. Bit by bit she felt secure enough with him to reveal pieces of herself and her life. He never pressed for more than she was willing to tell. Nor did he question her adamant refusal to eat with him. When she was ready, she would explain.

Simon told her he was an orphan. As a small boy he had lived on a boat with his father, who had been a fisherman before he was killed in the Korean War. "I had a teacher once, a geography teacher," Simon said, "who made us draw maps of the Far East all the time. He kept telling us that was the part of the world to watch. He was an old man and described it as the Yellow Peril. When I had to go to Vietnam, I thought about my father's being killed in Korea, and I thought about that teacher."

"You must have been very young when your father was killed," Madeleine said.

He nodded. "I lived in foster homes after that."

"You don't live on your boat now, though. The address you gave me is an apartment complex."

"I did live on the *Viking,* but she was badly damaged. I'm rebuilding her."

"Vietnam must have been terrible for someone like you."

"How did you know?" he asked. He had not told her the experience of war had left him with a horror of violence of any kind.

She placed her hand on his arm and looked up at him sympathetically. "Because you're a gentle person, Simon. I've never known a man as gentle as you, not only in your manner, but in the way you think."

She's perceptive, Simon thought, and gentle herself.

He wanted to put his arms around her and to kiss her. Yet some instinct warned him not to move too quickly. They had not kissed again since that first time on the beach. But the memory of those brief seconds had kept him awake and thinking about her far into the night.

Almost two weeks went by before Madeleine took matters into her own hands. As he was leaving one night she stood on tiptoe, pulled his face down to hers, and kissed his mouth. He caught her to him in an embrace that was firm without being crushing and returned her kiss with all the fervor of his awakening love. When he released her she said, "Simon, the last two weeks have been perfect. I can't tell you what they've meant to me. That day I called you, I'd had a shock, and I was afraid I was losing control of my life. But I've known such peace with you that now it all seems like a bad dream."

She clung to him, feeling the comfort of his strength and nearness, aware that it drove away the nameless terror that stalked her.

"Madeleine, I love you." The words were out before he could stop them. He had made the declaration so often in his imagination it seemed the most natural thing in the world.

He felt her withdrawal in her tensed body, in her indrawn breath. "Simon, you don't know me well enough."

He silenced her protest with his lips, but she pushed him away. "You haven't asked me about your friend Dean Jennings lately."

"He wasn't my friend. He was involved with a vicious traffic between here and Mexico. What are you trying to tell me?"

"Tomorrow night," she whispered, not looking at him. "I'll tell you then why we can share only friendship, why we can never love or make love."

CHAPTER 5

The soft gray mist that shrouded the beach shifted occasionally to offer ghostly glimpses of the dark sea beyond. A foghorn wailed.

Reflected firelight flickered on the window as Madeleine stared into the blankness of the fog. Simon stood behind her. He reached under her sweater, his hands gently stroking her bare breasts. The flesh yielded, molding beneath his fingers, and the rise and fall of her breathing was in pliant harmony with his caresses.

She did not move. He pressed his lips to the back of her neck, finding the warm skin between the silken strands of hair.

The air smelled of the sea, flavored with woodsmoke, and

the elusive fragrance of desert willow blossom emanated from her hair.

"I'm frigid," she said abruptly. "You're wasting your time."

"Let me decide that." His hands followed the contours of her body, sliding downward to touch her hips, circling to find the soft mound below the taut stomach muscles. He felt her body tense against him, and his own desire swell and grow.

"I may be insane," she said in a small flat voice.

"Mad Madeleine," Simon murmured, all of his concentration in his fingers and lips, wild with the wonder of being this close to her.

She whirled around to face him. "Don't call me that!" Her eyes were wild with terror.

The fog rushed from his brain. "I'm sorry. I thought you were joking. You can call me Simple Simon, if you wish, by way of revenge." He was filled with panic at the thought that their delicately constructed relationship might crumble. In his own aching need of her, had he misunderstood the look in her eyes, the unspoken longing conveyed by her touch?

Madeleine was trembling. Until that moment his presence had been comforting in a way that no other had ever been. She knew she had invited intimate caresses, wanted them. Now she was again filled with terror.

She loved him. She wanted to say, "Simon, I love you." But that distant voice mocked her. . . . *What will happen if he makes love to you?* It was suddenly important to find out. She had once seen a film of a black widow spider mating and then destroying her mate. Why did she think of that now?

"Simon, hold me. Please, I'm afraid."

For a moment she looked into his face, at the hope and eagerness written there. Poor foolish Simon, blindly infatuated. The thought did not seem to be hers, it came from far away. She felt a twinge of pity and a momentary urge to send him away.

She told him about Dean and Tony, sitting on the floor in front of the cozy fire. She tried to dissuade him, warn him that she was dangerous. All he could say was, "Madeleine, I love you. I promise I won't die."

Her fingers closed around his hand. "When I was a little girl I used to watch the trains on the sidings. The coupling and uncoupling. They came together with a great crash of shining steel. I used to think that's how it would be when I found the man I would love."

"Did you love Dean, and the other one, in England? And were you disappointed because it wasn't a clashing of steel?" He pulled the coffee table closer and poured wine. The Burgundy glowed deep red in the firelight.

She stared at the color of the wine, holding her glass up to the light. "I loved Tony. But he betrayed my love. I didn't know that until after he was dead, but it didn't hurt any the less. It's too painful to talk about. I didn't love Dean. Dean was . . . it's hard to say. An act of defiance. I wanted to misbehave and felt Dean wouldn't expect too much from our encounter and wouldn't be hurt by it. Oh, God, Simon, they both died, and all I can think of is that I couldn't bear the shattering of the myth. The myth of a glorious, all-encompassing love."

It did exist, Simon told her, and it would for her. He took away her glass of wine. "I don't want you to think about other men anymore tonight." He leaned forward to kiss her.

Her lips began to relax, parted slightly, but her body was tense and unyielding in his arms. "Madeleine, you're so beautiful. Please, don't shut me out."

His lips slid to the sensitive column of her throat, and she felt a tear slip down her cheek. She trembled as he pressed a trail of kisses toward the soft swelling of her breasts. Tenderly, reverently, as though she were the most fragile of flowers and he wanted to savor each petal, he waited for the unfolding of passion, controlling his own rising fever of desire.

Madeleine's hands went slowly to his back, feeling a slight spasm in his rock-hard muscles as she touched him. She nestled closer to his vibrant body, feeling a velvet mist obscure all of her inhibitions. She allowed a sweet surge of longing to sweep

her toward that slow-burning fire of passion where he lingere
so patiently. The feelings aroused in her by his lips and hi
touch drove away all thoughts until she was mindless with th
need for fulfillment, knowing that with Simon it would be a
expression of love for him.

The mist fled before the sunrise. Sunlight entered the roo
through the open door to the hall, like a golden highway. Th
window framed a bright-blue sea.

He was awake, lying there and watching as she opened he
eyes. He smiled and kissed the tip of her nose. "Who are you
lovely Madeleine? Who were you? And who are you goin
to be?"

She nestled closer to the encircling warmth of his arms
"You're alive . . . and warm," she murmured sleepily.

"More than that. Ardent." He picked up her fingers an
pressed them to the warmth of his lips.

She opened her eyes and looked at him, blinking in th
brightness of the morning. "Who am I?" she repeated indig
nantly. "I thought I told you all there was to know about m
last night."

"You told me all you wanted me to know, sweetheart," h
said in a passable imitation of Humphrey Bogart.

Madeleine smiled and closed her eyes as he kissed he
remembering all the sweetness of the night. She had bee
right, all along. It *was* like the steel clashing of the trains—
definite and final and irrevocable, sending vibrations down th
track and echoing throughout the land. "I love you, Simon,
she said when his mouth released her lips.

"And I love you. Worship you. Adore you." He punctuate
each declaration with a kiss, then rolled over so he was abov
her, looking down at her with his eyes filled with love an
longing.

She sighed and pulled him closer. They had made love o
the living-room floor last night, and then, so naturally ther
was neither hesitation nor awkwardness, they had gone up t
Madeleine's bedroom. Falling asleep in the pleasant tangle c

Simon's arms and legs, Madeleine knew she need not fear the coming night.

His lips were touching her as gently as the morning sunlight, and she felt the mind-numbing passion sweep through her again, more intense than before, because her body remembered his and yearned for their joining. Last night they had journeyed into an unknown realm, but this morning they wanted to rush joyously toward a dear and familiar plain.

A disembodied voice spoke from the head of the bed, shattering the tenderness of the moment. "Lucien here. Push the front door release button, Penny."

"Damn," Simon said. "He even installed an intercom in here? Don't answer. He'll go away."

Madeleine was tense, her desire gone as swiftly as it had arisen. "I must go down to him. Please understand. You can stay here. I must find out what he wants. It must be important. He never comes in person this time of the morning."

Simon uncoupled himself reluctantly and watched as she uncoiled her long slender limbs. She pulled on a robe, lifting her hair so that it fell like a dark waterfall down her back. "Don't move a muscle," she said. "I'll be right back."

Lucien's lips were set in a tight line. The neatly clipped black mustache was a shade darker than the cashmere sweater he wore. "You let me down, princess," he said reproachfully. "Sarita says you had her cancel all of your appearances for the two weeks I've been away."

"Lucien, I was going to come and see you today. I have to go back to being plain Madeleine Delaney. No more Penelope Marsh. I can't go on with the pretense any longer. I can get a job and support Mother. Perhaps it won't be so elegant a sanitarium, but . . ."

Lucien's face was composed except for a pulse that beat erratically in his temple. "There is an ancient jeep parked in the street. I take it the owner is here. What do you know about Simon Tanning, Madeleine? I take it he has told you all about himself? What he does for a living, for example? Or did you merely measure his muscles and surmise that he would be a

good bedmate? That's all you want of a man, isn't it, my dear
A big strapping fellow with all of his sensibilities in his gen
italia. I would have thought you would have been more hes
itant, so soon after finding the miserable beachcomber dea
in your bed."

Madeleine felt a blaze of anger. "How dare you judge me
You don't own me, Lucien. I'll be out of your hourse an
your life today."

"With Simon Tanning, I presume?" he asked caustically
"Who has shared your bed and does not have to prove himse
in any other arena?"

"For God's sake, Lucien. It isn't one of the seven dead
sins anymore."

"Do you think I give a damn about sin? I'm concerned onl
with discretion. What a little fool you are. Let me repeat m
earlier question. Do you know who he is and what he reall
wants from you?"

"None of this is your business anymore, Lucien. I'm no
going to argue with you. I'm leaving—"

"How much have you told Tanning about your little ex
cursion down to Mexico with Jennings?" Lucien interrupted
an ominous softness in his voice now.

"Nothing—I—"

"Don't lie to me. I never lie to you."

"All right. I told Simon everything."

Lucien drew in his breath sharply. He glanced in the d
rection of the staircase. "Then you've told everything to
private investigator. I trust you're satisfied."

CHAPTER 6

The two-hour drive to the sanitarium in the tiny desert town was never a chore. Even in the heat of summer, Madeleine preferred to take the un-air-conditioned VW and the leisurely route that wound through the small towns of San Diego County. With a golden October sun hanging low over the horizon, the drive was a blessed pause in the turmoil of her life, a time to reflect.

She always made a point of remembering her mother as she had been, not as she was now. Madeleine remembered a childhood of love and laughter. The weed-engulfed house near the railroad was the social center of the dusty truck-stop town.

As a child, Madeleine had been convinced that her mother and aunt were really angels, astonished to find themselves in mortal bodies. Fluffy golden hair like haloes framed two cherubic faces. Identical robin's-egg-blue eyes, large as saucers, regarded the world as though it were a newly opened oyster containing the rarest of pearls. Lola and Lyla had never been separated from the moment of their conception. Even when Lola married Kevin Delaney, Lyla moved in with them.

Kevin was a "traveling man," and Madeleine's memory of her father was of whirlwind visits, impractical gifts, bearlike hugs, and shrieks of laughter from the twin sisters. He was a tall, black-haired man with a weatherbeaten face and devilish blue eyes. His presence filled their small house with bawdy jokes, footstamping songs, and the unashamed expression of his love and physical need of his fragile golden-haired wife.

Madeleine rose early on the mornings her father was home from his travels. She would creep silently into their bedroom just for the pleasure of seeing her mother and father sleep, all entangled with one another, Lola's fluffy golden curls pressed against the dark hair of Kevin's chest, her delicate white fingers like pale stars against his black head. Brawny arms held Lola firmly in a protective embrace, while a thickly muscled leg was draped carelessly over her slender hips. Their expressions were always rapturously content. Madeleine felt sorry for Lyla, who slept alone in the narrow room between what was referred to as the "master bedroom" and the "nursery."

When the boisterous Kevin Delaney was home, it always seemed to Madeleine that her Aunt Lyla's expression was one of haunted sadness. After Kevin departed on his mysterious quests, which were called Being on the Road, life would go on as before. The two women never lacked companionship. Every evening there would be neighbors dropping in, tunes played on guitars and banjos, songs sung over glasses of home-made wine and cans of beer.

Looking back on her early childhood, Madeleine realized that the twin sisters lived like genteel spinsters, except when Kevin Delaney was around. They were gracious hostesses, confidantes to broken-hearted young girls and dispirited matrons, bandagers of scraped knees and healers of bruised egos. They moved quickly to aid the sick and lonely. There was little money, but Madeleine was never aware of anything lacking in her life.

She accepted the fact that her mother's attitude toward her only child was somewhat vague. Madeleine supposed that this was because Lola "mothered" the whole town. Still, it was unsettling at times to see Lola's eyes register bewilderment, as though trying to remember who she was. Then Lola would mile and say, "How like your father you are, Madeleine dear. You'll be a heartbreaker when you grow up, just like him."

"But I want to be like you," Madeleine would protest. "Dainty and gentle, like you and Aunt Lyla." *Then Daddy will love me. How can he love me when I'm dark and gangly and not tiny and golden like you?*

The tinkling bells of her mother's laughter would ring out and Lola would pat her cheek and lean close for a kiss. The fragrance of her perfume always lingered after she drifted away to give her attention to someone else. Essence of violets, the same fragrance that Aunt Lyla wore that day they found her propped up in the middle of the big double bed in the "master bedroom," deep in the sleep from which she would never waken.

The details of that terrible day had never been clear in Madeleine's mind. Even when it was happening, she thought it was a nightmare, disjointed and blurred. At first she thought her father was there too, but then she remembered he had gone on the road again. Then she thought perhaps Aunt Lyla had done this before, only that time she wasn't dead, she was just pretending. It was all very confusing.

Her mother had crushed up a pill and given it to her in a glass of warm milk, telling her it would make her sleep. Her mother had explained carefully that sleeping pills were very bad and were against their religious beliefs. Then her eyes had become frighteningly empty and she added that sometimes it was necessary to blot out by artificial means what could not be dealt with in any other way.

The pill had produced terrible nightmares. Madeleine awakened to find herself clinging to the draperies in her room, her feet on the narrow window ledge.

Sometimes, when she tried to remember the exact sequence of events, she thought that after she had been given the sleeping pill and climbed up on the window ledge in her sleep, Aunt Lyla had still been alive. But if that were so, why then would it have been necessary for her mother to give her the pill, to make her sleep and forget the terrible shock she'd had?

Then, too, her mother had screamed and sobbed when they found Aunt Lyla asleep with her eyes wide and staring. People came rushing to hold Lola, because she was thrashing about the room. Yet the Lola who crushed up the pill and put it in the milk was quiet and calm, despite the agony in her eyes. The passage of time had become telescoped in Madeleine's mind. Days had passed, yet she was aware of only fragments of hours.

During that frantic time, Madeleine was buffeted from one neighbor to another. In the battered "sample" case her father had once given her, she carried her toothbrush, comb, change of underwear, and a clean blouse, as well as her most treasured possessions—a box of crayons and a bundle of old brochures. The brochures had plain white backs, suitable for sketching.

Kevin Delaney was subdued and grave when he came for her at last. His eyes were more guilt-ridden than devilish and avoided her questioning gaze. He shifted his feet nervously.

"Lola isn't herself, Madeleine," he told her. "Losing Lyla . . . well, it was like she lost a part of herself, I guess. I'm going to take you both to my sister in Santa Barbara. She'll look after you while I'm on the road."

"I didn't know I had an aunt in Santa Barbara," Madeleine said, surprised.

His eyes darted about the room, and there was a long pause before her father replied. "Yes. Well, she's much older than me, see," as though this explained it all.

Madeleine was entranced by Santa Barbara. Its Spanish stucco and red tile roofs spilling down the hills toward a topaz sea, the bright blossoms amid soft green foliage, and the taste of salt in the air, all opened her to a beauty she hadn't known existed. She gazed at the vastness of the Pacific, mesmerized, and knew she could never bear to live in a dust-cloaked inland town again. Her hands strayed longingly toward the attaché case containing her crayons and sketching brochures.

The woman with whom Kevin left his silent and empty wife was a white-haired old lady of stern demeanor. She seemed

64

old enough to be Kevin's mother at least, rather than his sister. Her name was Priscilla Dougall. Madeleine assumed she must at one time have been married to a man named Dougall, but there was no mention of him. Madeleine was instructed to call the fierce old lady Aunt Cilla. Lola was put in the charge of a white-uniformed nurse of gargantuan proportions.

Lola did not speak, nor laugh, nor cry. She would only eat if someone held a spoon to her lips. After a few days she began to wander aimlessly about the house until restrained by the white-garbed Amazon. Then one day Lola walked through the front door and almost under the wheels of a passing car.

Madeleine was at school when Aunt Cilla had her mother taken away. She returned home one afternoon and was told brusquely, "Your mother is too sick for me to handle. She's gone to a hospital where they will look after her. No, you can't visit her right now. You would just remind her of the bad experience she had."

No matter how many times Madeleine begged and pleaded, the answer was always the same. Visitors were not allowed. When Madeleine was sixteen she threatened to go to the police if Aunt Cilla did not tell her where her mother was incarcerated. Tight-lipped, Aunt Cilla took her on that first nightmare visit to the state hospital.

Seeing her mother in a ward inhabited by a milling crowd of wild-eyed women was an experience that kept Madeleine awake long after the visit. Some cried softly, others tore at their clothes and hair. Several were curled in the fetal position on their narrow beds. One woman screamed continually until white-jacketed orderlies came and removed her.

Lola sat quietly, contemplating a blank wall. Her eyes and face were so devoid of expression that Madeleine did not recognize her. The once-glorious golden curls had turned to wisps of white. Madeleine hugged and kissed her, cried and shook her, but the frail body was limp as a rag doll and the robin's-egg eyes were blank.

Aunt Cilla stood silently for a while and then said, "You

can see it's useless. She doesn't know you. Come along now, or you'll upset the others."

Madeleine visited her mother regularly after that, and the visits were despairingly similar. When Madeleine graduated from high school, Aunt Cilla surprised her by offering to help with college expenses. Madeleine promptly asked that instead they use the money to place Lola in a private sanitarium.

Aunt Cilla's lips compressed tightly. "She's fine where she is. And if you have any ideas about private care in the future, I suggest you think about something other than an art major. Your mother is not an old woman, and her case is hopeless. You'll be paying for her care for a lot of years. But not with my money."

When Aunt Cilla died, Madeleine learned that neither she nor her mother had ever been objects of the old woman's charity. Kevin Delaney had sold the house by the railroad and given all of the proceeds to Cilla. He had also sent money regularly until he was swallowed up by the great continent of Australia. An endowment policy had been taken out to provide for Madeleine's education.

Aunt Cilla's final illness all but wiped out their financial assets, and Madeleine dropped out of college and began the first of a succession of mind-numbing jobs—waitress, sales clerk, file clerk. She rarely lasted longer than a month or two. She would be caught daydreaming, or hiding out in the store-room with a sketchpad and piece of charcoal in her hand. Or there were days when her mind and body rebelled against the imprisonment of an artificially lit building when sunshine filled the heavens outside, or amorous employers made the job unbearable.

Madeleine braked suddenly as a giant tumbleweed bounded across her path. She was beginning the slow ten-mile descent to the desert floor. Painted hills beckoned in the distance. As her car followed the mountain road she glimpsed the shimmering sands of the great valley far below, like a silver lake. Already the peace of the desert was reaching out to her.

"You are obsessed with sand," Lucien had told her once. "Can it be you were deprived of a sandbox as a child?"

"Oceans and deserts are very much alike," she replied. "Simple, stark, unadorned. Purity and simplicity."

Halfway down the mountain was a lookout point, and she turned the small car onto the gravel and set the handbrake carefully. Like some alien planet, gaunt and mysterious, the desert stretched out to eternity. Mauve shadows etched the canyons into sharp relief, giving the illusion that hills fifty miles away were close enough to touch. The hazy sand and pale sky were bathed in soft pink light. Utter silence prevailed.

There was a small hard knot in her throat. When she breathed or swallowed, the lump threatened to burst into a torrent of tears. Perhaps it would have helped if she could have cried. At this time in her life, Simon Tanning was more than she could bear.

He had come down the stairs, morning sunlight accentuating the firm planes of his bare chest. Mercifully, he had pulled on his jeans before facing Lucien.

"Madeleine, I was going to tell you this morning," Simon said. His hair was tousled and his eyes reflected an inner pain that would have been difficult to feign, but Madeleine was staring at the floor.

"It's true I have an investigator's license. Originally I was just trailing Dean Jennings. In fact, I only became a P.I. because he involved me in something rotten. I was waiting for the right moment to tell you the whole story. But the rest—how I feel about you—that has nothing to do with Jennings. My feelings for you are real."

He reached her side and tried to touch her. She drew away, her eyes wide and staring.

"Young man," Lucien said, his voice dripping frost, "I suggest you put on your clothes and get out of this house immediately."

"Madeleine, come with me. Please," Simon said. "Tell the police everything that happened, and let them investigate Jennings."

Lucien's black brows arched. "The police? What have the police to do with us? It will be your word against Madeleine's that she ever knew Jennings. Believe me, there will be no one to confirm anything she might have told you. And Madeleine herself will deny it as soon as she begins to see reason again."

"Get out," Madeleine whispered to Simon. "Get out of my life."

The words still echoed emptily in her head as she backed the Volkswagen off the gravel and started down the mountain again. She did not want Simon Tanning out of her life. She wanted him at her side always. The angry words between Simon and Lucien were lost in her own pain and aching sense of loss. Each had accused the other of using her.

As she drove through the tamarisk trees to the sanitarium she wondered if Simon Tanning had already told the police of her part in Jennings' death.

Her mother occupied a pleasant private room, bright with chintz. The walls were covered with paintings of the desert. Sometimes when Madeleine arrived, Lola would be holding one of the paintings, and the doctors would smile and nod when Madeleine suggested that perhaps they were on the verge of breaking through the invisible wall that enclosed Lola's shattered mind.

"She knows I painted them," Madeleine would say. "Look, she's holding the one I finished on my last visit."

The doctors and nurses did not tell her that Lola would sit quietly for hours holding anything placed in her hands. The nurses tried to keep something in Lola's hands all the time, because if they did not she would absently pull her hair out by the roots.

Madeleine bent to kiss Lola's cheek. Her mother blinked once but showed no recognition. "How are you, dear one?" Madeleine asked, pulling a chair closer. Lola held a pink poodle made of curly wool that Madeleine had brought for her on a previous visit.

"Look, I brought you some oranges. Oh, I know they feed you, but I picked these on the way, and they're still warm

68

from the sun. That's the only way to eat fruit. Shall I peel one for you?"

Lola's skin was immaculately clean and her dressing gown crisp. Her thinning hair was freshly washed and combed. A flickering image of her mother in the state hospital flashed into Madeleine's thoughts. Despite the attentions of overworked nurses and orderlies, the women in the ward quickly became disheveled and grimy. The air of hopelessness saturated inmates and overburdened caretakers alike.

Madeleine stroked Lola's cheek gently. "If only I knew how to reach you."

On one of her first visits to the sanitarium Madeleine had brought her sketching materials. After an hour's silence she had taken her sketchpad and a box of pastels and begun to draw the scene framed by the window. She believed that Lola watched intently as the picture came to life. At least her faded eyes seemed less vacant. Madeleine thought of her seascapes, torn and mutilated. At least the desert paintings had been safe from her nocturnal marauding.

"Mother," she whispered sadly, her fingers tightening on Lola's limp shoulders. Lola stared back at her unseeingly.

Looking at her mother, Madeleine wondered about Lyla's death. What if my father needed more than one woman? What if he slept with Aunt Lyla as well as you, secretly, furtively? You loved him to distraction. Would you have killed your own twin sister?

There was something Aunt Cilla told me—long ago—when I pleaded with her to let you come home from the state hospital. She said the sleeping pills Lyla took had been prescribed for you, Mother. Father had persuaded the coroner that Lyla had access to them, but that only he knew that you had been walking in your sleep. It got so bad that he took you to a doctor, far away in Los Angeles. But neither of you ever told Lyla, because drugs were forbidden to you as Christian Scientists. You must have been desperate. But I know what the torments of the night are—trying to stay awake to avoid the nightmare, the shock of waking in another part of the house—the terrible things I think of in the middle of the night.

Her mother's empty eyes looked back at her. With her face devoid of expression it was difficult to imagine her being able to love or hate, or feel anything.

Don't worry, dear. No matter what, I won't send you back to the state hospital with those pathetic screaming women. But I can't go on being Penelope Marsh either. I feel as if I'm being swallowed up by a mythical creature. I'll think of something.

Madeleine's glance went to her mother's hands, catching the surreptitious movement. Lola was systematically pulling all of the pink curls of wool from the toy poodle's back.

CHAPTER 7

"One of you has to go," Simon told the cat and the pigeon. He placed a saucer of slightly turned milk on the window ledge, and the pigeon drank deeply. The cat stared implacably.

Simon raised the window to admit the morning roar of rush-hour traffic from the freeway below. At night when the long-distance trucks went by Simon imagined that the rumble of the behemoths was instead the sound of waves breaking on an unseen shore.

The corner window overlooked the freeway on one side and the parking lot on the other. He glanced at the borrowed jeep and sighed. He would probably be without wheels today.

He found it difficult to concentrate on anything but his parting from Madeleine. He had lain awake all night thinking about her. There had been no time to tell her about himself, about his hopes and fears, longings and dreams, his passion for the sea that had been the first and only abiding love he had known. And his loneliness.

Vietnam had been a shattering experience, one that he'd at first been able to live through only by closing his mind to the death and destruction around him. He dreamed of home and the life he would live. He imagined every detail of the boat he would own, how it would handle, how peaceful it would be sailing the calm seas. Then, toward the end, reality crowded in, the dream no longer sustained him. Too many of his buddies had died, too many civilians had suffered. He swung from violent anger to wracking grief. His endurance was at an end when a grenade exploded in the middle of their patrol, peppering his leg with shrapnel.

In the hospital he was at first elated that the last weeks of his tour of duty would be spent safely in bed. Then he was overcome with guilt at the relatively minor wounds he had suffered compared to the death and maiming of the rest of his patrol.

Back home, guilt turned to shame when he met the embarrassed reaction of a nation that had watched a war on television and been so sickened by it they wanted only that it end and that they never be reminded of it again. Some of the other veterans were joining student protesters, but apart from not wanting to admit all those men had died for an unpopular cause, Simon wanted no part of the head-bashing, scuffling, dragging violence of the protests. He made a vow never to inflict pain or injury on another living thing. Instead of buying his boat, he joined the Peace Corps.

Returning to the United States two years later, he had bought the *Viking,* in a sorry state of disrepair, and restored her. His peaceful existence had been shattered by Dean Jennings.

Simon pondered the irony of his becoming a private investigator, in view of his commitment to a nonviolent life. He had also allowed Jennings' trail to cool while he took time to obtain a state license. But he felt compelled to go after Jennings legally, not as some vigilante, the way he had perceived himself in Vietnam.

How many investigators on a similar case, he wondered, would have gone ahead without even owning a gun? But he had no intention of remaining in the profession.

If only he had not waited to tell Madeleine about the P.I. license. How could either of them have anticipated they would fall in love so swiftly that there would be no time for the past or even the future, in the heady living of the moment?

Love meant trust, faith, and admiration of all those qualities important in a lifetime relationship. Yet he had fallen in love with Madeleine while filled with doubt about her, wondering about chilling possibilities, suspecting the existence of a dark side of her that could destroy more than his love.

Why then was it now more important to repair their broken romance than to pursue Jennings' connections? But Madeleine had refused to answer any of Simon's calls.

"Damn," he said aloud.

Simon was grimacing at the taste of spoiled milk on stale cereal when there was a knock on his door. The studio apartment was clean but untidy. Most of his personal possessions were still aboard his boat and, therefore, inaccessible until he paid the marina fees he owed. All of his savings had gone for repairs after the disastrous charter to Mexico. He was behind in his rent, too. Perhaps it was the landlord. "Who is it?" he asked cautiously.

"Myron. Hey, let me in, man."

Unlocking the door, Simon looked down into an earnest face topped with a profusion of corkscrew curls. "Look, I'm sorry, man, but I gotta have the jeep back. We got a gig up in Pasadena tonight." Myron was guitarist in a rock group that enjoyed only spasmodic employment.

Simon fumbled in his pocket for the keys. "I tried to return the keys last night, but you weren't home. Thanks again, Myron. I owe you a favor."

"How'd it go with the bird?" Two of Myron's group were English musicians, and he had been infected with their Cockney slang.

Simon sighed. "She found out I had the P.I. license before I had a chance to tell her. And I still don't have a line on Jennings."

"She got under your skin," Myron said sagely. "The bird. I can tell."

"That she did," Simon agreed. The pigeon fluttered up to his shoulder, and he stroked bottle-green feathers encircling the bobbing neck.

"Not the pigeon, man, the bird . . . what's her name. Ma deleine."

"Good luck with the gig, Myron," Simon said pointedly.

"You said she had dark hair and blue eyes. Sort of mys terious-looking, tall and moves like a dancer or a model."

"You've got total recall."

"A short blonde with green eyes was looking for you whil you was gone."

"Did she give her name?"

"Nope. She said to tell you she'd be back this morning. Myron emptied the cereal box into a dish, drowned it in milk and wolfed it all down without blinking. When he was finishe he still looked half-starved.

Simon had showered, shaved, and placed the pigeon outsid on the window ledge when his doorbell rang. He had see Sarita at the literary luncheon. The masklike face was no disguised by outsize sunglasses. Silver-blond hair curled i two perfect arcs on either side of a swathed silk turban. H gestured for her to enter the room.

"You don't seem surprised to see me," she said. "Woul you please put that cat outside? I'm allergic to animals. I wa to hire you. You are available for hire, I take it? I mean, yo have a private investigator's license. I suppose you are boun by professional ethics to keep my identity and the nature c the investigation secret?"

Simon picked up the cat and deposited it in the bathroom "If I agree to take the job, which is by no means certain, the anything you tell me will be in strictest confidence. Woul you like some coffee or something?"

The pale-green eyes flickered disdainfully over the use dishes on the table. "No thank you. I understand Lucien threv you out of Madeleine's house yesterday."

"Madeleine threw me out, not Lucien," he corrected. Ha Madeleine, he wondered silently, sensed the gnawing doub in his mind about her? It seemed when he tried to explai about the P.I. license, about Jennings, and how it was n

74

longer important, that she had stared into his very soul and recoiled from the suspicions she saw there.

"You will take the job I'm going to offer, Mr. Tanning," Sarita said. "I know you are down to your last dollar. Your boat has been impounded. You were making a living by taking out tourists."

He was struck suddenly by the similarity between her pale-green eyes and the implacable stare of the cat. He listened as she went on. "Dean Jennings chartered your boat for what you thought was a pleasure trip down the coast of Baja. You woke up with a terrific hangover in a cantina and your boat . . . what's it called again, ah, yes, the *Viking*—and your passenger gone. You found the *Viking* badly damaged on a beach near San Diego. The police there gave you a bad time. Your boat had been beached to put illegal aliens ashore, but bandits, either Mexican or American, were waiting. The illegals were beaten and robbed. Two young girls were raped. Your boat was stripped. You were faced with a large bill for repairs and the loss of income while the boat was laid up. You decided to go after Jennings and applied for a private investigator's license. Am I correct so far?"

Simon shrugged. "It's your story. Offhand, I'd say you're already in touch with a P.I. Or, if you dug all this out for yourself, perhaps you missed your own vocation."

"Oh, there was a full report with the Customs and Immigration Department in San Diego." Her lips curved into a smile, but her eyes remained calculating. "Madeleine is a beautiful woman, isn't she? There's something about her, an air of mystery, I suppose?"

He looked away from the amused stare.

"She's very unhappy," Sarita continued. "She wants to end the masquerade as Penelope. But Lucien won't let her go. He believes he needs her to play the part. Actually, we could announce tomorrow that Lucien Cornell writes the Penelope Marsh novels and nothing would really change."

"What exactly do you want of me?"

"The same thing you want. I want you to find out what

75

happened to Dean Jennings and how they disposed of his body I'm willing to pay you to make a complete investigation."

Simon studied her for a moment. "You're not the only one who did some checking. I know you've been Lucien's mistress for years. I also know he has never laid a hand on Madeleine yet you want her out of the way enough to pay me to implicate her in Jennings' death. That's what you're really hoping, isn' it? Proof that she killed him. I might consider your proposition if you're honest with me and tell me why you feel Madeleine is a threat to you."

"I'm tired of playing second fiddle. I'm tired of running around after her, and of seeing Lucien cater to her every whim I'm tired of whiling away my evenings alone while he cooks intimate little dinners and plays father confessor, listening to her neurotic ramblings."

"Lady," Simon said quietly, "there's nothing neurotic about Madeleine. Sensitive, caring, but not neurotic. Seems to me there's been a conspiracy to convince her she's out of her mind that's come pretty damn close to succeeding. She's a talented artist who could have made it on her own if your Machiavellian employer had left her alone."

"Has she told you her mother is insane?" Sarita inquired with a nasty arch to her eyebrows. "And that no matter what the psychiatrists say, some forms of insanity *are* hereditary Did she tell you she wrecked her own studio, smashed her paintings, and doesn't even remember doing it?"

Simon swallowed. "Yes. I know all that."

Sarita changed her tactics. "I saw you watching her at the luncheon. You had the appearance of a man struck by a thunderbolt. I've seen the look on other men's faces when they first saw Madeleine. But in your case that look hasn't faded It leaps into your eyes every time you say her name."

"You've been reading too many of Cornell's novels," Simon said. "I'm not interested in your proposition. Sorry."

Women, he thought after she took her high heels out of the door. Practical, unromantic, and hardboiled. They looked like angels, felt like kittens, yelled like banshees, and clawed like tigers. Every woman he had ever known had been like that, until Madeleine.

Dared he hope that she could be different from all the others, or was he again endowing a woman with all of the wonderful attributes his father had fantasized about his dead wife?

Simon had never known his mother, and the foster mothers who cared for him after his father was swallowed up by the Korean War bore little resemblance to the mythical creature of his father's bedtime stories. As a small boy Simon had often dreamed that his mother was really the sea, and there had been no mortal woman. It seemed only natural that way, since he and his father had lived aboard a boat and the gentle rocking of the sea as they drifted off to sleep was Simon's earliest recollection. The only tangible evidence he had of those early years was an antique sextant and chronometer which had been his father's most treasured possessions, and which Simon held onto tenaciously, even through periods of financial desperation.

If I'd taken Sarita's job, I could have bailed out my boat, put a stop to one tentacle of the illegal alien traffic, and maybe cleared Madeleine, he thought. No, Madeleine would never understand.

The pigeon was pecking at the screen outside his apartment window. It cooed happily as he fumbled with the catch on the window screen.

Myron's jeep was still parked in the parking lot below. As Simon glanced down he saw Myron's curly dark hair and the guitar case slung over his shoulder as he bounded down the steps and negotiated the row of cars. Myron waved a greeting to someone at a window, then climbed into the jeep.

The window screen was open, and the pigeon fluttered into the room at the exact moment Myron threw his guitar case down on the seat beside him and turned the key in the ignition.

In the next split second Simon's shocked senses registered the flash of fire, the explosion, the cloud of debris-filled smoke engulfing the jeep. He could not see Myron's blackened and bloodstained body, nor feel his own fingers gripping the window ledge.

CHAPTER 8

Lucien was waiting for her in the dark living room. She could see his silhouette against the window as the first pale fingers of moonlight reached tentatively for the night sky.

"Don't turn on the light," he said.

She paused, her hand on the switch.

"How was your mother?"

"The same as always."

"I'm sorry about the young man. It is not like me to lose my temper. I don't want you to think I was against your romantic involvement with him. It was not that at all. His deception was what rankled—his use of you to investigate Jennings. I can't bear it when people take advantage of your vulnerability."

Madeleine sat down in the nearest chair, staring at Lucien's immobile back. As her eyes grew accustomed to the darkness, she saw that the table was set for dinner. Several covered dishes appeared untouched. Lucien must have waited all evening for her return. She felt guilty. They hadn't planned an evening together, yet she was somehow obligated to have been there for him.

"Sometimes I think you truly believe the Penelope Marsh myth you've created," she said. "Lucien, I'm not a creature of your imagination to be ruled by a stroke of your pen. I'm a flesh-and-blood woman with a mind of my own. We made a bargain, and neither of us should have any illusions about why we made the bargain. I needed the money, you needed a woman to play the part of Penelope. Any woman would have done."

He turned abruptly. "That's not true. There is a quality about you that no other woman possesses. You are untouchable, inviolate, with a sensual innocence. I have tried to protect you from the men who would spoil that aura. Simon Tanning was one of the spoilers."

"I'd rather not talk about him. I came back to pick up a few clothes. I'm leaving, Lucien. I meant it about not playing the part of Penelope any longer. I have to lead my own life. If I can't keep Mother in the private sanitarium on what I earn myself, so be it. She wouldn't want me to live in the shadow of your life. I'm certain of that. Besides, I believe I can sell my work now, thanks to you giving me the last three years and Antoine.

Lucien came toward her, moving with short imperious steps. She stood up, feeling a sense of panic, wanting to run. Yet she knew before he spoke that what he had to say would shut off her escape.

He caught her by the elbows. She could smell the musk clinging to his skin. The moonlight was silver along the top of his head, and in the darkness his features were as perfect as those on an old Greek coin. The fine wrinkles, the droop and sag of the years, and the cynicism of experience were hidden from view. She struggled for a second, but his grip tightened. His hands were ice-cold.

"You can't leave, Madeleine. Do you want to be locked away like your mother? You get claustrophic just being in a room with the door closed. Madeleine, I know what you did to your studio. Antoine told me. I also know you have engaged a psychiatrist—a Regis Vaughan, isn't it? Therefore you suspect there are unexplored areas of your consciousness."

Madeleine stopped struggling. Lucien pulled her closer, and she was aware of his bones beneath the silk shirt.

"Please let go of me, Lucien. I promise I won't run away."

He released her at once. "I didn't mean to frighten you, my dear. You know I've never pried into your affairs, but since the Dean Jennings episode I have been doing some research. I'd like to compare my theories with those of your psychiatrist. I believe I met a Dr. Vaughan several years ago, in regard to company business. Tell me, what is his diagnosis? And did he mention knowing me?"

"I've only seen him once. It's too early for a diagnosis. No, he never mentioned meeting you."

"He probably doesn't remember. It was a long time ago. Let me tell you what I've been wondering about. Is it possible that you are suffering from a dissociative type of hysterical neurosis? Everything fits, as I see it. Different personalities exist in one person, each unaware of the presence of the others. In your case I'm sure there is only one other personality, but a highly destructive and dangerous one. I should like to discuss my theories with your psychiatrist."

"I'm quite sure he would consider that not only unethical but harmful. Please stay out of this, Lucien. It has nothing to do with you."

He look pained. "I have an investment in you. The world believes you are Penelope Marsh. I have every right to protect my interests. Besides, I'm concerned that perhaps I am the cause of your problem. In persuading you to masquerade as Penelope, I may have unknowingly triggered the release of the other personality. I intended to tell you tonight that there will be no more Penelope Marsh books after the current one. Perhaps I'll resume writing under my own name later. But I promise Penelope can fade quietly into obscurity. I only ask that you play the part for me until after the release of this last book."

Madeleine felt ashamed. Cool fingers closed about her outstretched hand. "Lucien . . . you've done so much for me, and for Mother. I don't mean to seem ungrateful."

"Don't say another word. Are you hungry? I could warm this up." He gestured toward the wasted meal he had prepared.

"No, thank you. I stopped on the way back." Seeing his look of disappointment, she fought her fatigue and said, "I will ask Dr. Vaughan about what you said." A different personality . . . Madeleine wouldn't be responsible? It was a straw to clutch at.

"There is the sleepwalking also," Lucien said. "Somnambulism is a definite dissociative reaction, isolated from the conscious personality and expressed independently. And then there is your background."

"What do you mean?"

"Did you know that twins often give birth to twins? Your mother and her twin sister were one personality divided into two bodies. When Lyla died, Lola died too, but her body went on living. Somehow, instead of giving birth to twins when you were born, your mother had one child. But that child possessed two separate identities. If we discover who the other one is, then we can free you from her."

Madeleine nodded wearily. "Lucien, I'm very tired."

"I'll stay until you are asleep."

She moaned, feeling the familiar touch of the hand sliding over tense stomach muscles. Her body cringed from the encroaching fingers, yet moved toward them at the same time. There was no substance to her flesh, no feeling except where she was touched. She was floating above her body, looking down at Madeleine writhing sensuously on her bed.

Poor foolish Madeleine, wanting him so much. Flopping about with undulating hips and clutching arms, trying to grasp a ghost.

Someone was watching. She felt a prickling along the nape of her neck. Turning slowly, weightlessly, floating about the ceiling until she was in a position to find the intruder.

There were two of them, two disembodied faces. They

stared, and grinned vacantly. They were Tony Waring and Dean Jennings.

Madeleine screamed, sitting up in her sweat-drenched bed. There was a moment's pause, then footsteps running up the spiral staircase. Her door opened and the room was flooded with light.

Lucien came to her side, sympathetic and reassuring. It was only a nightmare.

She fought an overwhelming urge to run blindly into the night. Anywhere to escape the terrible suspicion that not only tormented her dreams but was becoming her constant companion during the day. The suspicion she was not yet ready to face.

The next morning, while awaiting the arrival of the psychiatrist who wore running shoes, Madeleine found the galleys of *Desire's Fury*. Lucien had no doubt been checking them the previous evening. She began to read where he had left off, halfway through.

    The rapier sliced cleanly through the flesh, so swiftly that Sir Giles had withdrawn the weapon and plunged it into his opponent's heart before the first wound began to bleed. He watched that hated face grimace in surprise and pain.

Madeleine shivered and quickly turned over several galley proofs.

    . . . and seized her by the soft coil of golden hair. Forcing her backward to the bed, he tore savagely at the fragile gown, exposing her breasts.

    "Damn you . . ." Had he said the words aloud, or was the thought so intense he merely imagined he had spoken? He wanted to punish her for her infidelities, to tear at her flesh and abuse her, as she had abused the pure and selfless

82

love he had offered. His laugh rang out again, chilling testimony to his despair.

"You made a mockery of my love for you," he said in a strangled voice. "Betrayed me with men unworthy of you. Ah, Clarissa, why could you not have been the pure sweet woman I believed you to be?"

The telephone rang shrilly, and Madeleine jumped.

Sarita's voice came over the wire the moment Madeleine picked up the receiver. "Has the psychiatrist arrived yet, or are you alone?"

"I'm still waiting for him."

"Listen, something happened. I've only a second to tell you. Somebody planted an explosive device in the jeep Simon Tanning drove. . . . Madeleine, are you still there?"

Madeleine drew several deep breaths. "Is he dead?"

"Simon? No. It wasn't his jeep. He'd borrowed it. The man who owned it is in hospital in intensive care. They don't know if he will live. Simon wants to see you, but he doesn't want to lead the police to you. He suggested you visit the sick sea lion this afternoon. I told him you'd be there. I must go."

Madeleine was still trying to digest the information, pondering the unlikely alliance of Simon and Sarita, when Regis Vaughan arrived.

"You seem very agitated this morning," Regis said, padding silently across the tiled hallway after her. "Are you still upset because of your visit to your mother yesterday?"

"Yes," Madeleine lied.

"Would you like to go up to your studio again?"

"No," Madeleine said quickly. "How about a stroll along the beach?" There was time enough to tell him of the wrecked studio later.

They went across the patio. There was no sign of Ramón working on the banks of autumn flowers, but Madeleine felt their progress was being observed. She glanced over her shoulder before she asked, "Is it possible I'm suffering from dissociative hysterical neurosis?"

Regis Vaughan smiled condescendingly. "We don't care for the word 'neurosis' nowadays. I suppose your employer came up with that particular diagnosis."

"How did you know?"

"It would appeal to his sense of the dramatic."

"But could I have a split personality?"

"Split personality and dissociative hysteria are not the same thing. And we are far from reaching any conclusions at present."

The day was overcast, and seagulls huddled together on the cold sand, fluttering aloft as they approached. They walked slowly along the smooth wet sand at water's edge.

Madeleine said, "If there was a second personality, I wouldn't be aware of it, would I? I mean, when that other personality was in control, Madeleine would be unaware of the fact. Is it possible that that other person could have committed murder?"

"Try to be patient, Madeleine. The unraveling of the mystery of the human mind has to be approached with great care. For the moment, speculation is self-defeating. Your sleepwalking and nightmares are merely manifestations of suppressed problems that affect your daylight hours. You told me you had a long history of somnambulism. When did it begin, do you remember? Was it after your aunt's death?"

Madeleine bent to pick up a shell. "We didn't go to my studio because it's wrecked. My paintings are all shredded. She went in there in the night and smashed everything."

"She?"

"Madeleine—me. Sometimes when I get upset I think of myself in the third person. Doesn't everyone? I mean, when you do something you don't like, you pretend it was really someone else who did it. I'm sorry, I'm not usually this incoherent. I've had several shocks, one right after the other. What did you just ask me?"

"Whether you remember if your sleepwalking began after your aunt's suicide."

"I believe so. I'm not sure. Be careful . . . you almost stepped on a sand crab. Didn't you see it?"

He stopped and stared at her. "You're not joking, are you?"

"About what?"

"Never mind. Are you prepared to discuss your sex life with me? I believe it's necessary. The two men who died were in bed with you, and had made love to you. Your aunt was found dead in your parents' bed. You see what I'm getting at?"

"Are you suggesting I might have killed two men because I didn't enjoy their lovemaking?"

"Did you enjoy their lovemaking?"

"No."

"Have you ever enjoyed making love with anyone?"

"Yes."

"Another woman?"

"No."

"Madeleine, I wasn't suggesting you had anything to do with the death of those two men—how could you have? Food poisoning and a virus-induced heart attack do not add up to murder. I was suggesting that we search for the source of your problem in the direction you yourself keep indicating. Your feelings of guilt about your aunt, and those two men."

"I don't want to talk anymore today. I'm getting a headache."

"Very well. But I have one other suggestion. I don't believe you should be alone at night. Will you consider having a trained nurse move in with you?"

"I'll think about it," Madeleine said cautiously. Inwardly she cringed from the vision of the white-uniformed jailors who tended her mother. "Perhaps we could talk a little longer."

They walked back along the beach, disturbing the seagulls again, although Madeleine made a wide detour. She told him all she could remember about Dean Jennings, which was very little. She told him she had recently been disappointed in a brief love affair with a new man in her life, Simon Tanning. She hesitated when he asked about Tony Waring. Her expression changed, and she fixed her eyes on the distant horizon. She began to go over the details of his death again, and Regis stopped her. "How did you feel afterward, when you found out he'd deceived you?"

Her expression was a mixture of pain and defiance. "If you want me to say I was glad he was dead, I can't. No matter what, for a little while I believed I loved him. If I'd found out that he was already married while he was still alive . . ."

"The latest man in your life, Simon Tanning, hasn't he also deceived you? About his occupation, I mean."

She looked at him, startled. She had been shocked to learn Simon was a private investigator, but not as shocked as when Sarita told her of the bombed jeep. In that awful moment Madeleine's love for Simon became a palpable force, overriding all other emotion. She realized then that her love for Simon was different from anything she had ever experienced before.

"I hate lies," she said heavily. "To be lied to is the worst kind of betrayal." Omitting to tell her he was a private investigator was not really a lie. But what if he had just been using her to further his investigation? She was tormented by the possibility. She thought of his declaration of love and his exquisite lovemaking. If it was possible for a man to pretend the emotions Simon had pretended, then there was no hope for the kind of love she had been seeking.

Yet she held back from discussing him with Regis Vaughan. She told herself silently that she was being a fool, still hoping Simon meant it when he said he loved her. She had sensed an inner turmoil in him. Perhaps it had been that feeling that drew them together in the first place. Only his inner turmoil proved to be the result of concealed motives.

"I shall see you every day for a time," Regis was saying. "When you're comfortable with me we'll make swift progress toward uncovering what is causing your sleepwalking and memory lapses. Let's concern ourselves only with this for the present. Will you think about what I suggested about a live-in nurse?"

Madeleine nodded, glancing back along the bluff where

Lucien's house stood on the headland at the other side of the bay. The house was an ugly modern structure, jutting out on concrete stilts to obtain the maximum view. It straddled the cliff like a squatting skeleton, keeping vigil on the beach below. As Lucien kept a vigil on Madeleine, she thought, a benevolent vigil, but still a vigil.

He had talked her into staying with him until the last Penelope Marsh book was successfully launched. But she didn't have to stay that long if she didn't choose to do so. Most of the time she enjoyed his company. He could be charming, sarcastically witty, and even drily humorous. Time passed swiftly in his presence. He made few demands. Yet there were moments when she felt his black stare probing her thoughts and she was drained to the point of exhaustion. On the other hand, if he went away alone on a business trip, she missed him.

Regis observed, "You feel both repelled by him and bound to him."

"How do you know that?"

"It's written on your face as you look up at his house. I've seen similar attachments. Many young women seek their lost fathers."

"Lucien is nothing like my father."

They turned to climb the cliff trail, and Madeleine felt again the eyes of the unseen observer. The feeling that her every movement was being carefully watched followed her all the way to her rendezvous with Simon.

CHAPTER 9

The sea lions were grouped about Simon. They barked noisily and scrambled for the pieces of fish. Sleek black bodies glistened as a fitful sun broke through the cloud cover.

"The local shopkeepers are up in arms," Dan told Simon sheepishly. "The sea lions have taken to wandering about the streets, begging and generally making nuisances of themselves. I tried to get rid of them, loaded them into a boat and took them halfway to Catalina, but they all made it back here before I did."

Simon smiled. "I should think they'd be a tourist attraction. You know, like the swallows returning to Capistrano."

"The local merchants are afraid they'll bite someone." Dan was a big man, burned the color of mahogany by the sun, clumsy and shambling on land but swift and graceful in the water. He often joked that the ages of all of the summer-hire lifeguards added together would not equal his years of service.

"Will they bite?"

"They might if someone hurt them."

"Yes," Simon said, his eyes moving beyond Dan as the ancient Volkswagen pulled into the beach parking lot. "We all bite when attacked." He watched Madeleine walk toward them, surprised and elated that she had come.

Dan greeted Madeleine and then left them alone with their playful audience. She glanced back over her shoulder, as though afraid she had been followed, then bent to stroke one of the sea lions.

"I'm sorry about your friend. How is he?"

"Myron? I don't know. He's still in intensive care. I spent the morning trying to reach his family in the East."

"You don't think I did this? I honestly wouldn't know how to rig an explosive device."

"Of course not. I'm more than ever convinced Dean Jennings was only one member of a gang smuggling aliens into the country. The others probably want me killed because they think I know more than I actually do about their operation. Then I'm worried about your safety, since you were the last person to see Jennings alive. I want to find out what really happened to Jennings, and who blew up Myron and his jeep. I'm hesitant about involving you, but I think you can help."

"I don't know how I can help. I've told you all I know."

"I believe there's more to it than bandits waiting to ambush the *pollos*." He was acutely aware of her nearness and afraid his comments sounded disjointed.

"*Pollos*? Chickens?"

"That's what they call the illegals along the border. What can the poor devils do to protect themselves from either the bandits or unscrupulous officials? They are literally chickens waiting to be plucked. Madeleine . . ." He reached for her, tentatively.

She took a step backward. "Why did you want to meet me here?" She looked around again nervously. *Someone followed me.*

"I called the ambulance after the explosion. The police were very interested in my connection with Myron. I was afraid they might be tailing me and didn't want you connected with it. Madeleine, I'm sorry I didn't level with you in the beginning. I was afraid to. I'm not even a real P.I. All I have is the license. I wanted to know why Jennings had used me, and I wanted to find out legally. But once I met you, nothing seemed more important than getting to know you."

"You say Dean used you. I feel used too, Simon. You

pretended interest in me when your only real goal was finding Dean. How can I believe anything you tell me now?"

He stared silently for a second, trying to hide the hurt.

"It's OK, Simon. I'll help you in any way I can. I care about people getting blown up for no reason as much as you do. There's no need for you to go on play-acting. Only I'm afraid I can't remember any more about Dean than I've already told you."

"You told me about the men you saw when you stopped in Tijuana, the street vendor and the big Mexican who looked almost Oriental. Would you go with me to Mexico to see if we can find them? We could sail down. I finished repairs on the *Viking* last night."

She considered. A mental image of a white-uniformed nurse flashed into her mind. She didn't want a nurse guarding her. Somehow that seemed to Madeleine too much like the first step down the road Lola had taken. "How long would we be gone?" she asked.

"A few days. What about Lucien?"

"I won't tell him. I'll leave a note that I need a few days to think things over."

"Come with me now," Simon suggested. "Call Sarita. Let her tell Lucien."

Madeleine agreed quickly. The overpowering sense of an unseen observer was stronger than ever.

A fresh breeze sprang up in the afternoon and the twenty-six-foot sloop skimmed the light swells gracefully. Simon had pawned his father's antique sextant and chronometer to raise the marina fees he owed. He tried not to think about redeeming them.

Madeleine opened the hatch and stood looking at the receding coastline.

"You'll get wet," Simon called to her from the stern. He was rearranging the sheets.

She looked over her shoulder. "You look more at home on a boat than on land."

90

"Once aboard the lugger and the girl is mine," he sang in a villainous baritone.

The movement of the boat was almost sensual. She could feel her hips swaying as they rode the gentle troughs. She did not dare look back at Simon again. It would have been too easy to imagine him making love to her. The awareness of his physical presence was eroding her resolve to keep her emotions tightly reined, and she studied the churning surface of the sea with dedicated concentration. Gulping in the fresh clean air, she welcomed the occasional needle-sharp spray of salt water in her face.

There was a small cockpit containing a two-burner stove and an icebox. The bunk on one side converted to a table, while the opposite bunk doubled as a couch.

"Did you know that we're in the horse latitudes?" he called to the back of her head. "That's between the westerly winds of the higher latitudes and the trade winds of the torrid zone. That means we can never know what to expect. We can be becalmed one minute and lashed by strong winds the next. There's a suspicious gray blurring of the horizon right now that could be fog creeping in. We'll stay close to the coast and hope to avoid it."

He loosened the jibsheet and brought the *Viking* about, thinking that Madeleine, like the capricious winds, was difficult to anticipate. One moment a beautiful, warm, sensitive woman and the next a mysteriously enigmatic creature, totally unapproachable. Scrambling to find his clothes that morning to go to her aid, Simon had heard her spirited attack on Lucien; yet she would not listen to explanations. Wasn't that an overreaction to finding out he was a private investigator? Did it really matter what hats they were wearing when they met? After all, she was posing as Penelope Marsh.

And then there was Lucien. Despite her resolve to leave him, she was still living in the beach house. What was her relationship with him, really? Not sexual, but more than business, Simon felt. In Lucien's presence there was a subtle change in her, as though she were aware of something that no

91

one else could see. Lucien was a magnetic individual, almost supernaturally so. Was it, Simon wondered, just the awe a young woman feels for a sophisticated older man? A father complex? No. Much more. But what? Obligation? *Was he covering for her?*

Simon climbed down into the cockpit. "How about something to drink?"

"No. Thank you."

"I meant coffee or juice. Will you please stop jumping out of your skin every time I get within six feet of you?"

Madeleine ducked her head out of the hatch, and sat down on the bunk, and regarded him gravely. She had a way of holding her head, eyes wide and searching, that reminded him of the solemn earnestness of a child trying to comprehend the intangibles of a world she sees but does not understand. That look on her face, coupled with her woman's sensual beauty, was a volatile combination. "Simon," she said, "I want you to understand that this is strictly a business trip."

"I could wear my deckhand's cap and address you as 'ma'am' if it would help." His tone was light, and he busied himself with juice can and paper cups.

"I'm sorry. I am jumpy," Madeleine admitted. "I had a feeling I was being followed from the moment I left the house. There was a car parked across the street I'd never seen before. It left when I did and stayed behind me all the way down the Coast Highway. It disappeared when I parked on Dan's beach."

"Did you see it again when we drove down to the marina?"

"No. But the traffic was so heavy by then, it could have been behind us." She took the juice, sipped it, and then said, "What if I were to join a group of *pollos* crossing the border? That seems to me the most direct way of finding out who transports them. I speak a little Spanish, enough to get by."

"That's too dangerous," he said emphatically. "Besides, there aren't many Mexicans with eyes your shade of blue. No, I believe our best bet would be to look for the man you saw talking to Jennings. The big one with the flamboyant clothes and mustache, the one you said looked like a professional wrestler."

"And if we do, what makes you think he'll tell us what we want to know? Especially if he was involved in Dean's death."

Simon looked at her curiously. "You said Jennings died of natural causes, and that you let Cornell spirit the body away to keep the Penelope Marsh name from hitting the headlines."

"That's true." She looked away. "But I wonder . . . perhaps the Mexican doctor missed something in his examination. And now there is the bombing of the jeep to consider. Perhaps there is a connection to the alien smuggling ring. If there is and they somehow killed Dean, then I . . ." She broke off.

"Madeleine," Simon said slowly, "you aren't worried that you killed Jennings, are you? You aren't afraid you're a psychopath with some sort of black widow urge to kill the men who mate with you?"

Madeleine's smile was a frozen scream, painted on her face. She tried to laugh aloud at the suggestion, but no sound came. "Of course not," she said at last. "But getting back to the wrestler, what will you do if we do find him?"

"I'm hoping a little *mordido* will grease his tongue. I didn't mention it before, but I suspect Jennings was involved with more than just running in *pollos*. Collecting from the illegals and then robbing them wouldn't bring in enough profit for the risks he took stealing my boat. And there was no reason to wreck the boat unless they were searching for something that could be easily hidden."

"Drugs?" Madeleine asked.

Simon nodded. "It could be the *pollos* were used as cover. If they were caught, Customs and Immigration might not have searched for drugs as well."

"What was that?" she asked sharply.

"What was what?"

"I heard something. Oh, Lord, you don't have rats aboard, do you?"

"It's possible. Why don't you go up on the bow while I take a look in the storage under the bunks."

As soon as she was out of the cockpit, Simon jerked up the seat cover. A pair of black eyes stared up at him defiantly.

"Get out of there slowly," Simon instructed. "And keep your hands in sight. *Comprende?*"

"Ramón!" Madeleine gasped, looking down at them. "Simon, don't hurt him. He's Lucien's gardener. Ramón, what are you doing aboard this boat?"

The Mexican uncoiled himself stiffly from his cramped hiding place, his eyes fixed on Simon. There was hatred in the stare, and Simon should have anticipated the attack. The knife gleamed suddenly in Ramón's hand. Simon slammed himself back against the bulkhead to avoid the blade as it jabbed the air in front of him.

"Ramón!" Madeleine screamed from the deck above. "Stop it! What are you doing?"

Ramón feinted, backing Simon into another corner. In the cramped space Simon's size was against him, while the slim and wiry gardener moved with the grace of a dancer. Despite the knife, Simon felt neither anger nor desire to fight back. He had promised himself never to fight again, for any reason.

"I hope you know how to sail if you're planning to kill me," Simon said, dodging another slashing motion. He blinked, seeing for one gut-wrenching second a diminutive Oriental in place of the Mexican.

Ramón refused to be distracted. His knife whistled closer to Simon's face. Simon tried to grab at his wrist, and almost succeeded. At the same instant Madeleine flung one of the seat cushions from above at the back of Ramón's head. Caught off guard, Ramón looked up at Madeleine. Simon took the advantage, finally realizing that Madeleine's life was in danger as well as his own. He seized the arm holding the knife and forced it behind Ramón's back. A moment later Ramón lay panting on the deck, Simon astride his chest.

Looking up, Ramón spat full in his face. "Kill me now, señor, for I will surely kill you the first chance I get."

Madeleine slithered down the ladder, picked up the fallen

knife, and threw it up on deck. "Ramón, why are you doing this? You followed me, didn't you?"

Simon let him up, keeping his hands imprisoned behind his back. "Great," Simon said, glancing down into the space under the seat where Ramón had been hiding. "He jettisoned the life jackets and all my spare equipment so he could get in there."

"Ramón, please tell us why," Madeleine said.

Ramón gave Simon another venomous look. "To stop him from doing what he did before."

"What are you talking about?" Simon asked.

"The *pollos*," Ramón said bitterly. "The ones you led into the trap. They were defenseless. Your boat put them on the beach for the wolves to tear to pieces."

"Ramón," Madeleine interrupted, "you're not an illegal, are you?"

The black eyes looked at her pityingly, and he ignored the question, his silence confirming the fact that he was indeed in the country illegally. "I do not accuse you, señorita. I followed you and I find this one." His head jerked in Simon's direction. "And I find the boat."

"You saw the boat before?" Madeleine asked.

"On the beach at Chula Vista. I get there too late. One man lay near death, the others beaten and robbed. The American officials already rounding them up like cattle. The two women . . . both raped. Dishonored. What hope for decent marriage for them now?"

"You went to meet them?" Simon asked. "Were they relatives?"

"*Madre de Dios*," Ramón said, the sob in his voice unashamed. "My baby sister was one of the women."

"Oh, Ramón," Madeleine breathed softly.

"This one," Ramón said, glaring at Simon. "He is guilty. They use his boat. My sister, Soledad, paid the man Jennings two hundred pesos for safe passage to California. How much was your share, señor?"

"My boat was stripped and damaged. I was left with a lump

on my skull in a cantina. Why—oh, forget it. We'll put you ashore."

"No. He can help us. Please, Simon." Madeleine caught Simon's arm, and he glanced down at her slender fingers against his suntanned flesh. For a split second he forgot the presence of the Mexican gardener, the boat drifting toward the surf, and everything else in the universe except the electric tension passing from her body to his.

"Ramón, I want to help you find the men who hurt your sister," Madeleine said, still holding Simon's arm. "I want to find out what happened to Dean Jennings. I promise you the guilty will pay, no matter who they are. Will you come to Mexico with us, and help us?"

Simon looked into eyes the color of a sunlit sea and heard his own voice distantly as he told Ramón it was all right with him.

"I will help you," Ramón said. "But if you lie about my sister I will kill you."

"There's fog between here and Catalina," Simon said as he climbed from the cockpit. "Let's hope it doesn't push close to shore." He released the jibsheet and the *Viking* heeled over and tacked away from the surfline.

"You will keep the land in sight?" Ramón inquired.

Simon did not answer. He was watching a high-speed powerboat slam through the swells. The boat had come tearing out of the marina and was headed directly toward them.

"Are we on a collision course?" Madeleine asked jokingly as the sound of the boat's engines roared across the water.

"A powerboat must yield to a boat under sail. He'll change course," Simon replied. His hand tightened on the tiller as the boat closed the distance between them. There were two men aboard, one at the wheel and the other crouched in the stern.

The *Viking* veered off as Simon jerked the tiller, but the speedboat changed course. "What the hell . . . hang on, Madeleine," Simon yelled as the boat roared by and they were caught in its wake. The *Viking* rocked violently. Madeleine was flung to the deck, and Ramón pulled her to the bunk.

There was a sharp report and something whistled overhead and tore through the mainsail.

"Stay down! They're shooting at us!" Simon shouted.

The speedboat had passed, and now the sound of the engine dropped as it made a sweeping turn. Simon could see the man in the stern held a handgun.

He waited as the boat drew alongside, calmly studying every detail of the approaching boat and the two men. From a distance he saw only business suits and ties. They reminded him of the agents who used to patrol San Clemente beaches when Nixon was President, incongruous in their setting. Finally he was close enough to see their faces.

The one at the wheel was older, a stone-faced man who looked at his companion nervously from time to time. The man crouching in the stern with the gun wore a smile like none Simon had ever seen before. Simon felt his blood chill. The gunman looked as though he were wildly amused. It was more unnerving when Simon looked into eyes of the helmsman. They were as cold as the sea and nearly as empty.

"Drop anchor," the man with the grin yelled.

"What do you want?" Simon shouted back.

"The girl."

"Who are you?"

"She won't be hurt. We're taking her home."

"With a gun?"

The speedboat nudged the *Viking*'s hull. "That was to get your attention. The gun and I are both licensed. I've been employed by Mr. Cornell to return Miss Marsh to shore." The grin widened.

"Lucien sent you?" Madeleine said indignantly, sticking her head out of the cockpit. She too stared at the man with the maniacal grin, not looking at the man at the wheel for a moment.

"Look, you guys," Simon said quickly. "You're going to damage my boat. I'll bring Miss Marsh in, but I'm damned if I'm going to turn her over to a couple of strangers in mid-ocean."

The man in the stern considered for a moment. "OK. We'll follow you. Straight back to the breakwater."

"I'll turn on my motor," Simon said, raising the hatch.

"You're not going back?" Madeleine asked.

"Look, babe, a sailboat can't outrun a speedboat. And I'm not about to argue with a gun," Simon said loudly, in a way that sounded totally unlike him. His eye was on the creeping blanket of fog. The sun had disappeared and the breeze had dropped.

The man at the wheel of the speedboat spoke suddenly. "Miss Marsh . . . it's all right. You recognize me, don't you? I've worked for Mr. Cornell for a long time."

Madeleine looked at him for the first time. "It's Mr. Sedgewick, isn't it?" she said, recognizing him.

"You know him?" Simon said.

"He works for Lucien. But Lucien has no right to do this—"

Something in Simon's eyes silenced her. She followed his gaze as it went from the horizon to the sails. There was a jagged hole in his mainsail. Still, once inside that fog bank, he could cut the engine and sail silently, tracking the speedboat by its wake. If there was enough breeze left to put them out of sight . . .

"I'm going to come about," he called to the man in the stern. "Give me some space. I'll wait until your wake passes, then head for the breakwater."

The speedboat's engines roared again, and the boat began a wide circle. The *Viking*'s motor sputtered to life. Swiftly he changed sheets: the sails snapped and the *Viking* came about, heading directly into the fog bank.

Silently the gray curtain parted to admit them. Simon killed the engine and looked into two pairs of startled eyes. "No noise," he cautioned. "I'm going to try to lose them in the fog. There's a couple of oil islands we can head for, I know the course. At least they won't risk shooting at us in front of witnesses. Just stay below and keep quiet."

They could see nothing now beyond the mist. The angry roar of the speedboat's engines blasted the silence, growing in volume as it came after them.

CHAPTER 10

Sarita clung to the massive carved bedposts. "Please, don't!" she begged. "Don't force me." Yet she longed for the very violence she cried out against.

She was wearing a transparent gown of unbleached muslin that revealed most of her voluptuous body. Lucien grabbed her hand, and she lost her balance. She fell backward on the bed, the muslin slipping to uncover a perfectly formed breast. Lucien's hands did not touch her bosom. He seized her by the throat.

"Please—" Sarita said again. Her eyes rolled and she gasped for breath.

Lucien pushed his knee between her thighs. He was dressed in black satin pajamas and a matching robe. Sarita thrashed about, longing, aching to feel him within her.

Lucien released her throat, but his manicured fingernails dug into the flesh of her arms as he held her down, watching her intently. His dark stare moved slowly downward. Her body was reed-slim, emphasizing the large breasts.

She shrieked at him, "If you rape me again, I swear I'll . . . I'll . . ."

"Go on." His voice hissed in her ear, breath cool against her cheek. "Tell me what you'll do."

Sarita trembled, yet squirmed sensuously.

"Stop that!" he said sharply, shaking her viciously. He let go of her arm and slipped his hand inside his black satin pocket, producing a length of cord. Quickly and efficiently he tied her wrists, fastening the cord to the bedpost. She tugged at her bonds, running her tongue over her lower lip as she did so, her eyes glazed slightly.

He was whispering to her, ancient words of seduction that sent white-hot flames coursing through her body. There had been a hundred other men in Sarita's life and every variation of sexual foreplay, but none had the power to bring her to this quivering state of desire.

Looking up into his hypnotic dark eyes, hearing his voice as though it were inside her head, feeling his cold fingers burn her flesh with a magic touch only he knew, Sarita spent one brief moment chasing an elusive thought on the far reaches of her consciousness. Lucien is making love to me, but he is not a part of it. He is remote, unfeeling, uncaring. As though he were a musician, playing an instrument with exquisite precision.

He was fastening a blindfold over her eyes now. When the blindfold was in place and he had satisfied himself that she could not see, he rose from the bed. She could hear his breathing, not far away. Wildfire ran through her body. She was ready and wanted him with a desperation that was driving her out of her mind, but she knew he could not be hurried.

She was panting and moaned softly. "I hate to feel your hands on me. I loathe lying here exposed to you like this, while you torment me. Please, take me and be done with it."

"Do I detect a note of invitation under all that abuse?"

"No! I hate you. Don't come near me. Ah!" The last exclamation came to her lips unbidden as she felt his hand on her thigh, cool fingers caressing.

"Oh, God," she breathed, straining at the cords on her wrists. "Untie me, Lucien, please. I want to touch you."

Behind her closed eyelids lights exploded in the darkness. She could feel the warmth of the afternoon sun seeping through the drapes, but it was black as a dungeon beneath the blindfold.

The cord on one wrist came free, and she reached for him blindly. Her fingers found smooth satin, almost as though she had seized a ghost; she could feel no flesh beneath. He was silent now, but she could smell his musk, feel all the maddening delights brought to her by his tongue and lips and hands. She was drowning in a scalding caldron of sensuality, mindless with an agonizing need for release from that most exquisite torture.

He had opened the drapes and was sitting in the window alcove, writing on a legal-size yellow pad. He wrote rapidly, neatly, the words flowing effortlessly. He did not look up.

Sarita went to him and put her arms around his neck. "Lucien, darling," she whispered huskily. She stroked the black hair back over his ears, marveling as always that everything about him was perfectly formed.

He continued to write. Looking over his shoulder she saw he was writing a rape scene for his current book.

"God, what a monster you are. Why do I love you, do you suppose?"

"That is precisely why. You are one of those women who can only care for a man who treats them badly. The psychologists claim it has something to do with a poor sense of self-worth. If I were kind to you, you would hate me. As it is, you swear you love me while flinging yourself at any man who happens by."

"Only because you leave me alone so much."

"You are well aware of my feelings toward you. If you are no longer satisfied with our arrangement . . ." His voice trailed off, and he lifted an eloquent black eyebrow.

The phone rang before she could reply, and she picked up the receiver, listened for a moment, then said, "It's Sedge. He says they lost sight of Tanning's boat in the fog. Bruno is watching the marina, but they haven't come back to shore."

Lucien snatched the phone from her, his thin lips compressed. He waited until she started toward the bathroom before speaking.

"I told you to bring her back by any means necessary . . ."

Sarita closed the bathroom door. In the steam of the shower she shivered. If Lucien found out about her visit with Simon Tanning, some of their more sadistic games could take on ominous significance. Lucien had acquired a collection of medieval instruments of torture from a now-defunct traveling sideshow. They were to be sent to the house he was building in the desert, which Sarita had never seen. He wanted it to be his own personal retreat, he claimed, and was building it in the form of one of the ancient castles that were the settings of his books.

Sarita had seen the plans for what she privately referred to as Lucien's "sand castle," and she had no desire to visit it. If Lucien wanted to go there to soak himself in the spartan atmosphere of medieval times, that was fine with her. She reveled in his domination, thrilled to the pleasure tinged with pain— so long as none of his fantasies got out of hand. She wanted no real bruises or damage on her carefully nurtured person. She had no desire to give Lucien any reason to really torture her, and she had the uneasy feeling he might, if he learned of her attempted conniving with Simon Tanning.

When Madeleine had called to say she was sailing for Mexico with Tanning, Sarita had decided to disregard the plea that Lucien not be told until absolutely necessary. Sarita knew she must cover herself. There must be no hint of complicity. She took the message to Lucien immediately. It was then Sarita learned that Lucien's longtime employee Sedgewick—who had been with him since the earliest days of his career, and was now head of Lucien's security staff—had recently been given an assistant. The man's name was Bruno. And though he worked under Sedgewick, his orders came directly from Lucien. Bruno had been detailed to follow Madeleine.

Sarita worried vaguely that Lucien had not seen fit to inform her of this earlier.

The sail to Catalina Island had been eerie. For over an hour Simon kept his boat motionless near the oil island. They could hear the powerboat searching for them, but after a time the fog became so thick they could barely see the platform above them. When the sound of the powerboat faded, Simon turned on his own auxiliary motor and began the long windless sail to Catalina.

When the fog lifted, they could see the island rising from a sparkling sea. The breeze freshened, and the sails of the *Viking* billowed. A school of flying fish broke the surface of the sea, fluttered, and then disappeared again into the depths. Madeleine sat on the bow, watching the island draw nearer.

"You know, I've never been to Catalina," she remarked.

"Twenty-six miles from California and you've never been there?" Simon asked, surprised.

"There is immigration officers, *sí?*" Ramón asked, a worried frown knitting the smooth olive brow.

"We'll drop anchor in a remote cove," Simon said. He had kept a wary eye on the Mexican, but since the man had not attempted to aid Lucien Cornell's men, it appeared he had told them the truth.

"I can't believe Lucien would send Sedgewick after us with a gun," she said for the third time. "I don't know who the other man is, but that grin of his is going to give me nightmares. I believe Sedgewick started out as a lab assistant to Lucien years ago when Lucien was a research chemist. Sedge moved onward and upward with him and became a sort of personal aide—though why he stays with Lucien, I don't know. Lucien often humiliates him, laughs at him. Perhaps Lucien has something on the man."

Simon watched her with a quizzical sidelong glance. "Or perhaps he's just loyal. There are some people who will take a great deal from a friend they love and respect. You should try to look for finer motives, Madeleine. You're acquiring

Lucien's cynicism." When she opened her mouth to protest, Simon went on quickly, "Tell me more about Lucien as a chemist."

"He started out with a company called Agri-Chem. They did some secret experiments for the government during the Vietnam War—something to do with defoliation. I don't know much about it, except every employee had to have top-secret clearance. The company was phased out some years ago during a series of mergers. I got the feeling that—like Sarita—Sedgewick is now personally employed by Lucien, rather than by one of the corporations."

The specter of napalm-burned civilians stirred in Simon's memory, and he tried to dissociate Madeleine from a man involved with chemical warfare. He said, "Cornell must want to keep you under his thumb pretty badly to send a gorilla with a gun after you."

"Lucien has a tendency to use a sledgehammer to drive home a thumb tack. I suppose it's part of his makeup as a writer of rather flamboyant fiction. Lucien likes to make dramatic gestures. I'm sure those men didn't mean any real harm."

Simon did not look convinced, but he changed the subject. "We'll stay overnight on Catalina island and get an early start for Mexico tomorrow. Let's hope the fog has lifted by then and Lucien's chums have given up looking for us."

Madeleine's glance went over her shoulder to where Ramón stood in the stern of the boat, watching the thickly wooded hills of Catalina draw closer. She was unsure whether she was glad or sorry Ramón would be chaperoning them aboard the *Viking*. It still hurt that Simon himself had not told her his real reason for seeking her out, but the flame of attraction flared ever more brightly each minute she spent with him. As soon as we clear up the Dean Jennings mess, she thought, I've got to extricate myself from Simon before he becomes a permanent part of my life. For all I know, Simon could be another Tony Waring . . .

Simon found a deserted cove and dropped anchor. Since Ramón had had to jettison supplies to make room to hide,

Simon and Madeleine decided to go ashore in the dinghy and buy something for dinner. Ramón was reluctant to accompany them, still fearful about immigration officials. He was well versed in checkpoints and borders. An island was, after all, another kind of border. Merely to look Mexican was enough to bring a demand for "papers" or a "green card."

"You'll come ashore with us," Simon insisted. "I'm not leaving you aboard to sabotage my boat."

In the dinghy gliding toward the shore, Ramón studied his two companions. He had not decided yet whether he believed the man, but Ramón liked and trusted Madeleine. From the first day he appeared in her garden, she had treated him as an equal. Her tone was never condescending, and she did not patronize him. Nor did she tease and make fun of him, as did his employer's secretary, Sarita. He also liked Madeleine's quiet air of being in tune with the sea, the sky, and the earth around her.

Still there were some things Josefa had told him about Madeleine that were disturbing, if they were true. Josefa . . . the moment that tantalizing creature came into his mind, Ramón forgot everything else.

How passionately Ramón wished he could have entered the country legally, made something of himself and courted her like a man. Even Ramón's father had not had to sneak through the border fence under cover of darkness, as Ramón had. His father had been a *bracero,* crossing from Mexico to work in the California orchards and fields with the full approval of the Department of Immigration. And then the United States ended the program because, it was felt, there were enough unemployed Americans to fill the jobs of the stoop laborers. Ramón had burned with anger at the injustices of the world even before his sister was violated.

Madeleine trailed her hand through the clear green water and then shook it vigorously. "It's freezing," she said. "So much colder than the water near the mainland."

"It always is. But look how clear it is—look, there—"

A school of fish darted by, swimming into a waving bed of kelp.

Madeleine leaned perilously close to the water. "They look like an octave of notes, and the seaweed forms the lines of the staff and a treble clef."

"You see everything as a picture, don't you?" Simon asked wonderingly. He jumped into the shallow water to pull the dinghy up onto a pebble beach. Madeleine accepted his hand as he helped her ashore. He kept her fingers imprisoned for a moment before she pulled away from him, with a glance in Ramón's direction.

Ramón discreetly followed several paces behind as they walked up the beach. "I wish we were here under different circumstances," Simon said wistfully. "This is the best time of the year to come to Catalina—it will be practically deserted."

"Simon, we have a common goal. We both want to know what happened to Dean Jennings. Let's keep it a business relationship. I *was* attracted to you, but I don't want to play romantic games with you."

"I don't like it when you use the past tense. And I for one wasn't playing games. I truly believed there was more than a fleeting romance in our future. I still think there is. We haven't had time to get to know each other. Damn, I wish Ramón hadn't decided to stow away. We could have spent a couple of days here before going to Mexico."

They reached a fork in the path between the trees. "This way," Simon said. "That's the Avalon Pavilion ahead. The main street is beyond."

Madeleine's eyes feasted on the scene before her. "It's fantastically pretty. Looks like pictures I've seen of fishing villages on the Riviera—or perhaps Portugal. The sun is so incredibly clear it's hard to realize we came through that fog bank."

"You're looking at it with artist's eyes again. Personally, I can live without the three maladies that attack places like this: quaint, cute, and whimsical. I've had it with quaint since I came to California."

Madeleine smiled. "Where did you come from, originally?"

"A fishing village on the East Coast, never mind where. It was stark and unadorned. I like simplicity."

"So do I. The unadorned landscape of the desert . . . the ocean. But I still say Avalon is pretty. A little gingerbread is nice here and there." She turned in his direction. "Why didn't you become a fisherman, instead of an investigator?"

He glanced at her, wondering how much of himself to reveal. "When I first came to California I had the idea I would live a simple fisherman's life. I'd heard about the dory fishermen of Newport, and the life-style appealed to me—one man and one small boat against the mighty sea. I didn't know their ranks were closed to outsiders. Apparently they had been squeezed into a narrow strip of beach beside the pier to sell the fish they caught. The tourists and beach-players and concessionaires and hotels simply closed in on them. Their bit of beach is now so small they feel the market can only stand a handful of them, so they quickly ran me off. Instead of living my idyllic life, I got a job with a charter fleet. I took out tourists and watched them butcher marlin. I got sick of that, quit, and tried to get by just on sailing parties."

Madeleine's eyes were filled with sympathy. "I hate it when they kill marlin too. If the fish were to be used for food, it would be one thing. But they don't even bother stuffing them anymore, do they? They just grab a couple of quick shots with a Polaroid and send the beautiful carcass to the fertilizer plant."

They reached a small market and went inside. Surreptitiously Simon pulled his wallet from his hip pocket and fingered the dollar bills inside, counting them carefully.

Madeleine was studying the small display of fruit and vegetables. She picked up a cabbage. "I'm not much of a cook, but if we get a variety of vegetables and a small amount of meat, we could stir-fry them. Tell me more about the dorymen of Newport."

"They have been compared to the fishermen of the Sea of Galilee," Simon said wistfully. "But there isn't anything to tell. They have a narrow strip of beach, and the rich have taken

107

the rest for their playground. . . . The vegetables are a good idea, but I'll catch fish for dinner, if it's OK with you."

"Perfect." She turned and smiled up at him, not realizing how close he was standing. There was a tense pause as each dealt with an overwhelming urge to embrace the other. Then they turned away, embarrassed and vulnerable, and caressed the turnips and onions instead.

That evening Simon built a fire in a circle of rocks on the beach, and the two of them prepared the vegetables and a small shark he had caught. Ramón ate with them and then moved away down the beach to find a place to sleep.

Simon and Madeleine sat beside the embers of their campfire and talked. Something new had crept into their relationship, and neither was sure exactly what it was. They were suddenly shy and hesitant with each other, treading warily, pulling back into themselves at the first sign the other might be peeling away a layer of their defenses. They tried to keep their conversation light, inconsequential.

"I had no idea shark meat was so delicious," Madeleine said. A shadow crossed her mind. Dean Jennings had told her, in Ensenada, that they could buy shark-meat tacos from the street vendors. The specter was there, hovering, above everything. Like the nightmare that would not let her be during her sleeping hours.

"It's only fair to eat them," Simon said, watching her face in the firelight. "That one wouldn't have hesitated to eat us when it grew up. Madeleine . . . what is it? Something just crossed your mind that troubled you."

"If you're going to start reading my mind, I'd better run."

His hand closed over hers on the cool sand. She did not move as his other hand went to her cheek, lightly brushing her skin. "Did something remind you of Jennings? Or were you thinking of Ramón's sister? Don't torture yourself—you couldn't have known what Jennings was up to."

"Oh, Simon . . ." She turned to him wordlessly, and his arms went around her. He kissed her, reassuringly at first, then

108

with mounting passion. She lay in his arms and let him caress her, feeling the nightmare fade in the warmth of his embrace.

After a few minutes she could not stop her body from responding, and his need had taken him further than he intended to go. He made love to her gently, tenderly, and was surprised at the fierceness of her passion.

He could not know that she was desperately clinging to the belief that she had found her one true love, hoping that it would be strong enough to blot out the ghosts of the past.

CHAPTER 11

There was the usual crowd in the cantina—young gringos swilling Tecate beer with reckless abandon, darkly pretty señoritas in the company of bold-eyed Mexican men who eyed Madeleine with open-mouthed appreciation as she, Simon, and Ramón came through the beaded hangings on the door. Simon's head collided with a gaudy piñata suspended from the ceiling.

"Quaint," he remarked with a grimace.

Madeleine smiled at him as they followed Ramón to a table. The table surface was a square of blue-and-white tiles, surrounded by exquisitely carved wood. She ran her hand over the smooth wood. "This isn't quaint, this is authentic Spanish Colonial. And it's beautiful."

"Is carved by hand in Guadalajara," Ramón said. He motioned to a waiter and spoke in rapid Spanish.

Madeleine said, "No tequila for me. I'll take white wine."

"If we are lucky," Ramón said, after the waiter departed with the amended order, "I will meet a man here who will take me to the coyote who takes the *pollos* across the border."

"Coyote," Madeleine repeated. "Whoever dubbed them that was insulting a noble animal. Do you know how you are supposed to cross the border?"

Ramón replied in an undertone, "Sometimes in a truck, sometimes by boat. Sometimes just climb through a break in the border fence. Always a different way—that's why this coyote has not been caught. Pray, señorita, that this man is the man you saw talking to Jennings. The mustached one you call the wrestler."

They had been in Tijuana and the nearby beach towns for three days. Ramón had followed several false leads, posing as a would-be illegal alien. Simon and Madeleine were passed off as an American couple interested in employing him once he was on the other side of the border, but unwilling to risk being thrown into a Mexican jail if they were caught transporting him themselves. They would pay the coyote's fee. So far this explanation had been sufficient. But Ramón secretly worried that someone might connect Simon Tanning with his boat, had the *Viking* previously put into Rosarita Beach with Dean Jennings aboard. Ramón worried even more that the coyotes might think he and Simon were border patrolmen.

The waiter returned with two glasses of tequila, a dish of lime wedges, a large container of salt, and one glass of wine. Simon and Ramón went through the ritual of licking salt, squeezing lime, and drinking tequila. Simon tried to hide his grimace. "This is not my favorite beverage," he confided.

"Drink," Ramón commanded. "You must look like a gringo who tries to be, what you call, hip."

Madeleine's gaze was fixed on something behind Ramón. "Simon," she said in a small shocked voice, "did you know

110

that on the bar there is a glass container of tequila and in the bottom of the container there is a dead rattlesnake?"

Simon nodded weakly. "I didn't think it was alive."

Ramón's teeth flashed in a wide smile. "The snake improves the flavor of the tequila."

Madeleine's eyes were jerked from the shadowed bar to the large, flamboyantly dressed man who had just entered the cantina. "I thought you said a man would take you to the coyote, Ramón. Don't turn around, but the wrestler just walked into the cantina."

"Go quickly to the restroom," Ramón said. "He may recognize you."

Madeleine kept her head down as she went through the jostling crowd toward the door marked *Damas.* She remained in the tiny ill-lit room until a blond Californian came in and said, "Are you Madeleine? Your friend said it's OK to go on out now. You hiding from the *federales,* or something?" She shrugged indifferently as Madeleine smiled vaguely and darted through the door.

Simon was alone, standing beside the table. He had already paid for their drinks. "Come on, let's get out of here. The wrestler just left with Ramón, but I'm uneasy. I think he's used to dealing with the top, not the *pollos* themselves, and Ramón might be in trouble."

Outside, they looked up and down the street. There were groups of Mexicans and Americans, a few couples, several tired-looking streetwalkers. There was no sign of either Ramón or the wrestler. Simon moved rapidly through the crowd, eyes searching each dark gap between the neon-lit cantinas and the closed but lighted souvenir stalls. Madeleine hurried along at his side, a terrible fear gnawing at her insides.

They traveled both directions, covering the extent of the main street of the small town that straggled along the beach between the highway and the sea. Simon stopped suddenly, inclining his head toward a closed and darkened souvenir stall.

Madeleine heard it then, the sound of a muffled groan.

"Get the hell out of here," Simon ordered. "Go back to the

111

motel." He plunged into the stall, knocking over several pots and a garishly painted plaster elephant.

At the rear of the stall, the wrestler let Ramón's limp body slip to the ground. The man turned to face Simon, his arms curved at his sides. The faint light illuminated a smile of anticipation on the fleshy features.

Simon charged. He tried to seize the man's arms before they could grasp him, but the next second he found himself in a bone-crushing grip, being raised from the ground. Then he was reeling backward to the accompaniment of whirling neon lights. He crashed into a display of piñatas, sending colored streamers and cardboard fragments sailing in every direction.

He struggled back to his feet, shaking his head to clear his senses. The wrestler took a step toward him, and this time Simon sidestepped and swung his fist in a wide arc. He connected with the man's bull neck. The huge body hit the ground with a thud. Simon was pleased and relieved, and completely unprepared when the wrestler's arm came up and he was again flung to the ground. Somewhere someone was screaming, and there was the clatter of breaking pottery. Simon looked up to see the wrestler casually brush aside the remains of a clay pot that Madeleine had broken over his head. Still clutching the handle of the pot, Madeleine stared, terrified, as the wrestler slowly turned his attention toward her.

On the ground, Ramón recovered his senses sufficiently to see Madeleine's peril. At the same instant that Simon climbed shakily to his feet to rush to Madeleine's aid, Ramón rolled into the path of the wrestler. The man crashed to the ground, Simon on top of him. But Simon's heart was not in it. He didn't want to fight. He just wanted Madeleine and Ramón out of there. A moment later, seeing his hesitation, Ramón crawled to them and pressed a knife to the wrestler's chin. Blood dripped from Ramón's nose, and he spoke through a broken tooth, asking questions in Spanish that were interrupted by the sound of sirens.

The wrestler grunted, flexed his pectoral muscles, and

112

ejected Simon from his chest. "Señor," he said to Ramón, brushing aside the knife as though it were a troublesome gnat, "we talk somewhere else, *sí*? Before the *policía* arrive?"

"I've got a motel room," Simon said, his voice squeezed from his throat in tight gasps. "Let's go!"

Ramón's knife remained clutched in his hand as they dashed down the street that ran along the beach. When they reached the ramshackle motel, Madeleine immediately sought a wet towel to wipe away Ramón's blood. Simon and Ramón surveyed the wrestler warily. The man lowered his bulk into the only chair in the room and surveyed them calmly. He was not breathing heavily, despite the dash down the beach. The same could not be said of Simon and Ramón, who were panting heavily.

The wrestler said, "What do you want of me, señores?" He jerked his head in Ramón's direction. "This Chicano is not the first border patrolman to try such a trick."

Madeleine dabbed carefully at Ramón's grazed forehead. He looked more than ever like a martyred saint. "I think he needs a doctor," she said.

Simon removed the knife from Ramón's limp fingers and tossed it to the table, glancing at it with distaste. "Let's level with each other. We're not border patrol. We're only interested in an American named Dean Jennings. He stole my boat, then got himself killed. We only want to know what killed him and why . . . not necessarily who. That's why we came looking for you."

"I don't know any Jennings."

"About six-one, blond hair, blue eyes. He stopped at a street vendor's taco stand in T.J. and you met him there, the same day he died."

The wrestler's small deep-set eyes blinked once, then flickered over Madeleine. "I wondered what happened to him. I thought perhaps the señorita was an undercover agent. We never saw him again. He left a party of *pollos* stranded."

Simon watched the man's expression carefully. "You didn't know he was dead?"

The wrestler shook his head. "Señor, go home, don't play tricks with me. And take that Chicano with you. If you wanted only to ask about the coyote Jennings, why did you try to pass that one off as a *pollo?* You want revenge because your boat was wrecked?"

"You knew about that?"

The man smiled patronizingly. "I know everything that happens on the chicken run. Your gringo friend did not intend your boat to be damaged. They were surprised by bandits, looking for drugs."

"And did they find any?"

The wrestler shrugged. "Enough questions. Check your gringo friend's connection on the other side of the border. No one here wanted him dead. He was too valuable to us. He got the *pollos* through the San Clemente checkpoint, found them a place to stay and jobs in Los Angeles. He collected a fee from the *pollos* and one from the sweat-shop employers—or the doctors' wives who want a live-in slave." He stood up, his bulk crowding the room. At the door he turned and glared at Ramón. "If you had not lied to me, I would not have hurt you. Even though you are a Chicano." He smiled apologetically at Madeleine. "I am a true Mexican and have much contempt for Americanized Mexicans, the Chicanos."

"Then you are in a strange business," Madeleine said, "transporting Mexicans into California illegally to turn them into Chicanos."

The wrestler shrugged again. "It's a living. Besides, when we have enough of our people on your side of border, who knows, maybe we take California back from you, eh?" He grinned widely, revealing two gold teeth, then disappeared through the door.

Madeleine stared at the closed door for a moment, then turned to Simon. "We must get Ramón to a doctor. I'm sorry we came—we've accomplished nothing."

"Not quite. We know that the alien smuggling ring didn't kill Jennings."

"You believed him?"

114

"As he pointed out, they had no reason—he was more valuable to them alive."

"Then we're back to me again, aren't we?" Madeleine asked quietly, her voice heavy with despair.

They found a doctor, who taped Ramón's cracked rib and filed smooth the jagged edge of his broken tooth. Then they returned to the motel and slept, exhausted. At first light of dawn the *Viking* headed out to sea. Madeleine made coffee and brought a cup to Simon while Ramón slept in the cockpit.

"Poor Ramón, he hoped to avenge his sister," Madeleine said.

"The wrestler and the others will be caught eventually. We can tip off the border patrol about him. Madeleine, I've been thinking. There's one man who knows for sure what happened to Jennings. He's the Mexican whom Lucien brought with him that morning. The one who drove the station wagon with Mexican plates and waited outside the motel."

"Lucien wouldn't tell me who he was, or who the doctor was. Lucien said the less I knew, the better, because . . . I sometimes talk in my sleep."

Madeleine turned to face the churning gray sea. She felt the flush creep over her cheeks and did not want Simon to see it. Lucien's voice echoed hollowly in her mind. "No, Penny, dear, you may not see the death certificate. The matter is ended. The doctor who signed it? A discreet Mexican. Penny, you know you walk in your sleep. You also talk in your sleep. It's one of the reasons I worry so about your . . . romantic interludes."

She didn't want romantic interludes. She wanted what her mother had had. A permanent relationship with a man. *Forsaking all others*. Was Simon sincere? Was he acting? If only she knew. And, being sure of him, could she then be sure of herself? Or was madness lurking around the next corner in her life too?

"What is it, Madeleine?" Simon asked.

"It keeps circling back to me. Dean wasn't the first man

115

to die in bed with me. There was Tony. And Simon, I'm afraid for you too. When Myron's jeep exploded, someone was trying to kill you. I think perhaps it was me. I was angry that you lied to me. I can't stand lies." Her hands gripped the rail, knuckles white, and there was a note of rising fear in her voice.

Simon interrupted quickly, "We've come to a dead end with Dean Jennings, but what about Tony Waring?"

"I had even more reason to kill him." Her voice was flat, expressionless, resigned.

"What do you mean?"

"He lied to me. At the time, I believed it was a revelation that came after he was dead, but now I'm not sure. Just as I'm not sure of the exact sequence of events when Aunt Lyla died."

"How did he lie to you?"

She turned to face him, eyes luminous and filled with pain. "I was so naive. I wanted so desperately for him to be the great romance of my life. But he was married, and to a society belle who had no intention of ever letting him go. She insisted on an inquest, and when it showed his death was due to acute salmonella poisoning, she saw to it there were no headlines back home."

"But you went to England with him expecting to marry him. You didn't know until after he was dead that he had been married."

Madeleine smiled wanly. "Didn't I? Oh, God, Simon, sometimes I wake up in the morning so confused I don't know who I am. Especially after a nightmare. Sometimes I lose track of time, forget things."

"Don't give up yet, Madeleine. There are too many leads we haven't explored. Maybe we should have started at the beginning, instead of the end."

"What do you mean?"

"I mean we should have started with Tony Waring's death. Could there have been any connection between him and Jennings?"

Madeleine looked away. "I hate to admit how little I really knew about either of them. After I came back from England

I thought perhaps there would be a news story about Tony, because of his wife's connections. But there wasn't. After I calmed down, I promised myself that for my own peace of mind I'd go back and see what I could find out. I suppose it's too late now."

"It's never too late. We could go together. You said there was an inquest, so there are obviously records that will tell us what we want to know."

Fear crossed her eyes, was quickly masked, and Simon stifled the thought that she didn't want to know. She was just making conversation. It suddenly became very important that they go to England and find out what had really happened there.

Finally Madeleine answered, "No. I can't go—I mean, I don't have the money. And forgive me, Simon, but I know you don't either."

Ah, but Sarita would pay, Simon thought, if I told her I believe there is a connection between the two deaths. Simon agonized for a split second what it would do to their fragile relationship if Madeleine discovered he was on Sarita's pay-roll. He would have to make it a loan instead, though he'd be in trouble either way if Madeleine found out. But going to England was too important.

"We can fly Freddie Laker's Skytrain from L.A. I can raise that much money. We can go today. And even if we can't dig up anything new on Waring, the trip will give you time away from Cornell, to be yourself. And time for us to be together."

Simon was thinking rapidly that he could leave Madeleine in his apartment while he supposedly called on Myron at the hospital and then put the *Viking* into storage. That would give him time to contact Sarita for the loan of the money.

Keeping one hand on the tiller, Simon slipped the other around Madeleine's waist and pulled her close. "I love you."

Sarita smoothed the silk shirtwaist over her hips, frowned at her reflection in the mirror, and then unbuttoned another button to reveal more skin. She dabbed gloss on her lips, then stepped backward to check the overall effect. The dress was ice blue, and her breasts were clearly in evidence through the sheer silk. She wore nothing beneath the dress but stockings, held in place by a ruffled black garter belt. She smiled at herself appreciatively and went back to her office to await Lucien.

Her office had a white-water view, being one of the rooms cantilevered over the beach. Lucien's house was constructed of mahogany, teak, and ample quantities of Italian marble and glass. There were two tennis courts, an Olympic-size pool with three Jacuzzis, and an indoor sauna. An eight-car garage housed Lucien's Rolls-Royce, his Ferrari, and a carefully restored antique Jaguar.

Guests and business acquaintances entered the house through a massive front door embossed with copper and brass, then stepped into a rotunda that was the axis for all of the other rooms of the house. Whereas Lucien had furnished Madeleine's house with carefully chosen Spanish Colonial furniture, his own was ultramodern. Since no one but Sarita was allowed to enter the master bedroom, Lucien's guests would have been surprised to find that the room resembled a medieval chamber. There was a four-poster bed, and dark tapestries covered the walls. Suits of armor and crossed broadswords adorned the room, and a glass-fronted armoire housed a rusting collection of medieval instruments of torture.

The master bedroom and adjoining bathrooms occupied the entire top floor of the house. On the floor below was a library, study, and both Lucien's and Sarita's offices. He had been in his office for most of the morning.

Sarita sat down at her typewriter, picked up the hand-written manuscript, and began to type.

He paced the darkened hall, listening to the mournful sound of the wind in the eaves. She had left him, and he knew that this was but the first of endless nights to follow.

He needed her from the very depths of his soul.

Sarita looked up, an angry set to her mouth, and her eyes glittering coldly as she surveyed the gray ocean beyond her window. Why don't you just stay on the other side of the world, and keep her with you, Simon Tanning?

The adjoining door to Lucien's office opened, and he stood there, watching her impassively. "So you decided to return to work. Have you finished yesterday's chapter yet?"

"Almost," she lied. "I took a lunch break. I didn't want to disturb you, so I just went down to the refrigerator."

"You changed your dress."

"Yes. It's new. Do you like it?" She stood up and turned around slowly, in front of the window, so he could see the outline of her naked body beneath the thin silk.

Lucien walked into the room and sat on the edge of her desk, the suggestion of a smile played about his thin lips. His eyes were fathomless. "Do you ever think about anything else?"

"Besides clothes, you mean?" she asked innocently.

"Besides sex. Sarita, you are the only genuine nymphomaniac I have ever known. Most seek the elusive orgasm and never achieve it in their sexual frenzies. But for you, my dear, life is one long uninterrupted orgasm, isn't it?"

She moved closer, smiling, and began to play with the buckle of his belt. After a moment, she shrugged off the whisper of a dress, revealing the provocative black garter belt and silk stockings beneath.

"Attractive," he agreed, "but I prefer the allure of voluminous gowns. You spoil all the mystery, Sarita. Now get dressed and get back to work. You know I don't make love in the office."

Her eyes flashed angrily, a venomous green with pinpoints of black at their centers.

At the door he turned and looked back at her. "By the way, I know where they are. They boarded a Laker Skytrain today. You see, I had Bruno watching Tanning's apartment. One of his men is now on the Skytrain with them. Bruno is coming over to give me a full report." Lucien paused, his eyes moving over Sarita with cold deliberation. "Including, no doubt, the name of the person who financed the trip."

Sarita let the dress slip from her fingers. She stared into his enigmatic dark eyes, her heart pounding.

CHAPTER 12

"I just hope," Simon said as the clouds fell away beneath the jetliner, "that we won't be overwhelmed with quaintness in England." He had changed into a business suit and wore a restrained tie. He looked so different from the casual jeans-clad fisherman that Madeleine had not been able to take her eyes off him.

"I was afraid I wouldn't get very far with the British authorities dressed like a fisherman," he had explained. Since Madeleine had not returned to the house for more clothes, she still wore the jeans, shirt, and sweater she had worn for the sail to Mexico. Her small overnight bag contained underwear and two other shirts.

She was uncomfortable with Simon's new image. He looked more strikingly handsome, but less approachable, she decided. She said, "I'll have to buy something to wear. I feel like your poor relation."

"You look like Garbo trying to travel incognito and only drawing more attention to herself because of her incredible beauty."

Madeleine smiled at the comparison, flattered and yet uneasy because she still did not know who she really was.

The plane was crowded. Foreign students returning home, footloose vagabonds with backpacks setting out on mysterious quests, retired couples taking off-season vacations. The stewardess was wheeling a cart up the aisle. Meals were paid for in advance, at the time of ticket purchase. Apart from the closely packed seats, Madeleine could see little difference between this flight and others costing twice as much. She shared her thoughts with Simon. They had been talking affluence, past and present.

"It's always been fine, if you had the money to insulate yourself," Madeleine commented.

Surmising what she was thinking, Simon said, "Even the state hospitals must have improved in the last few years. If your mother could break out of that prison of her mind, she'd tell you she doesn't want you at Lucien Cornell's beck and call just to keep her in a private sanitarium."

"Have you ever been really poor, Simon? I mean, when you didn't know where your next meal was coming from? Hungry poor?"

Simon didn't answer. At the back of his mind hovered the bleak memory of a succession of foster homes, where he was part of a family, yet not a family member, connected yet set apart. And certainly without money. He had struck out on his own the moment he graduated from high school. He had worked his way through college, served in Vietnam, done a stint with the Peace Corps, and finally, made the downpayment on the *Viking*. Had he ever been hungry poor? Hell, yes, but now was not the time to trade confidences on who had been poorer.

"No, I guess not," he said. "But doesn't it seem odd to you that Lucien's rewards are so generous for merely having you pose as Penelope Marsh? I mean, he could pay some actress to do it. The streets of Hollywood are crawling with would-be starlets. He didn't have to set you up in a fancy house, or create such an elaborate charade—unless he has ulterior motives. I think he's in love with you."

"Lucien? In love?" she said incredulously. "You're mad!"

"Maybe you're right. I suppose because I'm in love with you myself, I believe every other man is too."

Madeleine looked away from his searching glance, wanting to respond, yet fearful of the ever-present specter of the part of her over which she had no control. "Lucien has never been married, you know," she said, as though that information alone would preclude the absurd possibility which Simon had suggested. "I don't believe he could stand to share living space with another person," she continued, trying to reinforce her argument. "Sarita travels back and forth to her own apartment. It always seemed a waste of time to me, since she's at his house every day and I know she sleeps with him. But Lucien isn't capable of a grand passion. I believe for Lucien sex with her is something like having dinner with me—we're both just participants in the event. Lucien is complete unto himself."

"No man is complete unto himself," Simon remarked softly.

The aircraft shuddered slightly, and the seat-belt sign flashed on. They lapsed into silence as the captain's voice came over the intercom, assuring them in a slightly bored, fatherly tone that they would be climbing to a higher altitude to escape the turbulence.

"Maybe that's what we need to do," Simon said, reaching for her hand. "Find a place where we can escape the turbulence."

November had London in its gloomy grip. The days were short, nights filled with mist and bone-chilling dampness. Afraid that Madeleine would be upset by reliving the old nightmare, Simon left her at a modest bed-and-breakfast guest house near Gatwick Airport. The proprietor was an attractive and effervescent redhead, thirtyish and divorced, named Ginny. Ginny promised to keep an eye on Madeleine and added, with a wink, "After we get rid of you, laddie, I'll take her down to the Monk's Habit for a spot of something to cheer her up."

"A pub?" Madeleine asked.

"This one was built in the year nine hundred. You'll have to duck your head to get through the door. You'll be glad when you see the old place, so long as you don't mind walking through the churchyard to get to it. The old headstones are a bit spooky after dark. It used to be the monks' house, see, before it became an inn."

Simon grinned. "But the monks had bad habits, huh?"

Madeleine groaned. "Just try to get back to join us before dark."

After satisfying herself that there were plenty of blankets for the thin-blooded Californians, Ginny took herself off to see to her other guests.

"Where will you begin?" Madeleine asked Simon. She had insisted on separate rooms and was already regretting it. The vision of Tony kept coming back to haunt her.

"With the coroner, if he'll see me, and then with the transcripts of the inquest. Ginny tells me it will take me the best part of an hour to get into London on the train, so I might not get it all done today."

"Perhaps I should come with you."

"No. Not today, anyway. I'll work faster alone. I'll need you more later, to help interpret whatever I uncover."

"If you're not finished investigating, don't come back tonight. Stay in town and get an early start tomorrow. I'll be all right." Despite her words, an uneasy feeling had begun to develop. She felt the need to take deep breaths, and even then it seemed her lungs were starving for air. She shrugged it off, telling herself it was jet lag.

Simon considered her suggestion. "That's probably a good idea. That nine-hour time difference is catching up with me. You'll be OK with Ginny—she seems a friendly soul. Just don't let her lead you into any mischief. I imagine she's the local belle."

After he left, Madeleine bathed and lay down on her bed,

feeling more lonely than sleepy. How could he have the power to leave a vacancy in her life, when he was only going to be gone overnight? She told herself again she mustn't let herself love him. She would not be able to stand the hurt if it was all just a game to him.

A wave of dizziness overcame her, and she was glad she was lying down. She had not taken her iron pills since setting sail with Simon; that was probably the reason. She sat up and reached for her purse. Madeleine unscrewed the cap from the amber bottle marked "Ferrous Sulphate—5 grains" and took two capsules. The iron supplement was the only concession she had made to Lucien's doctor, who had given her a complete physical examination before she set off on that first autographing tour.

"You're a trifle anemic," he had told her. "No doubt due to poor diet. You could also stand a few vitamins. But it's essential you take an iron supplement." She balked at the vitamins, but recognized the need for the iron.

Lying back on her bed in the guest house after swallowing the two iron capsules, she drifted into an uneasy sleep.

The mist swirled about her as she stumbled through the gravestones. Someone was leading the way; she tried to catch up with him, but her feet sank in the oozing mud. *I'm dreaming again,* she told herself, and tried to wake up.

Suddenly the bars were there again and the hovering cloud of evil. She was cowering down, covering her face with her hands. Icy fingers were prying her hands away from her eyes. She caught frightening glimpses of the face beyond . . . Tony! Poor dead faithless Tony. She could feel the scream starting at the back of her throat as someone patted her hand reassuringly.

"You all right, ducks? Come on, love, wake up. You're just having a bad dream, that's all."

Madeleine opened her eyes and looked into a concerned but only vaguely familiar face. Of course, Ginny. She was the proprietor of the guest house near Gatwick. Simon had gone

124

to London. Madeleine sat up and pushed her hair back over her shoulder.

"I wouldn't have come into your room like this, but cor, you gave such a yell, I was afraid you were ill," Ginny was saying. "Why don't you get up and come down to the Monk's Habit with me and we'll get you a good stiff belt of brandy? That'll fix you up."

"I'm sorry—I left California in something of a hurry, and I don't have any clothes that are fit to be seen."

Ginny looked at her speculatively. "You're about my size—just a bit taller. I could lend you a dress. Come on, it will do you good to get out. They're a jolly crowd at the Monk's Habit. You can get a sandwich there too, if you're hungry."

Madeleine was only too happy to go. The room that had seemed cozy and inviting at first glance had taken on a somber oppressiveness since she had slipped into the recurring nightmare. Dressed in a flashy green wool dress and with her own sweater draped over her shoulders, she walked the short distance from the guest house to the Monk's Habit with Ginny. When Ginny turned into the churchyard and the headstones loomed out of a ground mist, Madeleine felt a frightening sense of déjà vu. She remembered the beginning of her dream.

"You should have come in the daylight," Ginny said, "and read some of the inscriptions. They had a sense of humor about death in the old days."

Madeleine thought silently that there was nothing funny about death, but then Ginny had never known the terrifying shock of being confronted by death suddenly, in bizarre circumstances.

The timbers and stone of the Monk's Habit had been worn over the centuries, giving it a shapeless air that was mellow and indestructible, yet oddly fragile. There were no sharp edges to the stone steps, and countless feet had worn indentations in the center of each step. The oak beams supporting the roof—perilously close to the heads of Englishmen who were considerably taller than the monks the house had been built for—were also rounded with age and wear.

They sat down at a tiny table, and a fresh-faced waitress brought wine for Madeleine and whisky and soda for Ginny, who was calling out greetings to the other patrons. A fire blazed in the ancient hearth.

Surrounded by the good-natured banter of a crowd of regulars, and one or two late-season tourists, Madeleine relaxed and allowed herself to think of the last time she had visited England.

She had been young, happy, and wildly in love with Tony. Would she ever be able to love like that again? Love, at that time in her life, had been the wondrous awareness of another human being, the magical way they had been able to talk and laugh and marvel at the world together. There was comfort in his touch, and breathless joy in promising herself forever, to this man, and no other.

"I'm going to England," he had told her, only days before they left. "I didn't tell you before, because I wasn't sure I'd get the assignment. There's a new rock group that's reputed to be the successors to the Beatles. I'm going to follow them around London and take pictures for a magazine article. Madeleine, come with me. Let's get away from everyone for a few days—especially old Lucien with his sinister glances. He hovers over your shoulder like a bat. I don't believe we've been truly alone since we met."

When she hesitated, he had quickly added that he loved her, wanted to be with her always. "It is forever, Tony? You're sure?"

"What do I have to do, go down on one knee and beg for your hand?" he had teased.

Looking back, Madeleine recalled with a shock that that had been as close to a proposal of marriage as he had come. Yet she had assumed he wanted to marry her, and he had not said a word to contradict the assumption.

The magic had remained until they checked into their hotel on Regent Street. Tony had flashed her one partly imploring, partly apologetic glance, then signed the register, "Mr. and Mrs. Tony Smith."

126

I'm just old-fashioned, she told herself as they followed the porter up the stairs. We're going to be married. Good lord, I'm probably the only twenty-one-year-old virgin left in the world.

They called room service and had a late supper sent up. There was cold chicken and sliced ham. Fresh fruit. And crusty English bread with creamy butter and bitter marmalade. A pot of tea and a bottle of champagne completed the meal.

Their lovemaking was a disaster. She had stiffened with fright as he tried to enter her, and he had become belligerently drunk on the champagne. He showed her a side to his nature she had not dreamed existed. She downed two glasses of champagne in quick succession, hoping it would help her relax, and he tried again. This time she gasped with pain and pushed him away.

In that instant, she realized that what she felt for Tony had nothing to do with sexual attraction. She did not want him and was embarrassed by the shared intimacies. She had fantasized some vague image of what love should be like, and because Tony had come along—handsome, witty, self-confident—she had imagined him in the role of lover when all she really felt for him was an affinity of spirit.

He was furious. "What are you playing at? What is it? You want it rough?" His hands were on her, shoving her back against the bed, numbing her arms as his grip stopped the circulation. Before she could speak his mouth covered hers again. She squirmed under him, and his knee jabbed viciously at her legs. He released her mouth long enough to say, "What the hell did you come with me for? I'm sick of your games, Madeleine. Lead me on, then stop me. It's time you learned there's a point of no return."

She started to scream, but his hand went over her mouth, and in their struggles somehow the bedside lamp toppled to the floor, breaking the bulb. In the darkness Tony grabbed her again. He was laughing drunkenly now. "It's all a game, right? You *want* me to play rough."

The fiend who thrust himself upon her, hurting and humiliating, that couldn't be dear sweet Tony . . .

Incredibly, unbelievably, the moment he rolled away from her she fell asleep—and into the grip of her nightmare.

At her side, Ginny was repeating a question. "Would you like another glass of wine, Madeleine? Think I'll have another . . . blimey!" she broke off suddenly. "I forgot to tell you why I was coming up to your room. I was so taken aback when I heard you shouting I forgot to tell you about the phone call."

"Yes?" Madeleine asked. "From Simon?"

"No, love. But the chap had an American accent. I thought it was funny when he said he was calling from Laker's Skytrain—I mean, that he was an American, working at Gatwick. He said he was checking on my address because the taxi driver said he brought a young couple who might be Madeleine Delaney and her friend. He said to tell you they'd found the bag you left on the plane and they'd send it over tomorrow."

Madeleine's heart turned over. She had only one bag, and it was in her room at the guest house.

She was aching with tension by the time she bade Ginny goodnight and closed her bedroom door. She wished Simon were not staying in London, wished they had not come to England. Trying to reassure herself, Madeleine reasoned that if the police were after her, it would not be necessary for them to use subterfuge. Who then was intent upon finding her? Lucien had sent Sedgewick after Simon's boat, but surely she was not important enough to warrant a similar pursuit all the way across the Atlantic. Unless, of course, Lucien had proof that she really had killed Tony and Dean and had incriminated himself by covering up the murders. Having gone to so much trouble, he would not want her and Simon blundering into a revelation at this late date.

Feeling weak and faintly nauseated, she poured herself a glass of water and took two more of her iron capsules. After a few minutes she lay back on her pillow and closed her eyes.

She could hear the voice faintly, drifting toward her from the black depths of the cave. She concentrated, listening, so that she could obey the commands, but her body would not lie still. She felt her limbs writhe, and she was fighting desperately to be free of the restraining arms. There was a sickly-sweet odor near her nostrils, and she choked, trying to twist her head to escape the sound of the voice, the odor of . . .

She blinked open her eyes and saw shapeless shadows. Felt herself weightless, airborne. A blast of cold air blew through her hair. Stars overhead. Then something pressing her eyelids closed again. After that there was only the suffocating feeling of indescribable evil.

CHAPTER 13

"I remember the case very well," the reporter said. "I covered it for the local press. There wasn't much national interest in it, of course—too many big stories breaking worldwide at that time. But I was struck by the story because the hotel porter insisted there had been a mysterious female with Tony Waring, while the reception clerk maintained that Waring had gone up to his room alone."

Simon leaned back against the smooth leather of the booth in the Fleet Street public house. "The judge who presided over the inquest, and the coroner, are both dead. And despite the fact that the death occurred only two years ago, I had a hell of a time finding anyone who knew anything about the inquest. It was the court steno who remembered you, Mr. Blake."

"Jack," the reporter corrected. "But tell me, what do you hope to prove by digging into it all now?"

"That it truly was a case of accidental death."

Jack Blake raised his eyebrows slightly but was too polite to question this further.

Simon went on, "I read the transcript of the inquest and saw that the clerk claimed that the hotel-register page for the day Waring arrived had been obliterated when a cup of tea spilled on it. Also that the hotel porter had been called to the stand but most of his testimony had been struck from the record. I was curious. That's when the steno suggested I contact you."

"Well, now you know why his testimony was struck. He was an old man, and forgetful—kept contradicting himself. But it seemed to me that he couldn't have imagined the woman he described. And apart from Tony Waring's society wife, there was the other American, Cornell, who discovered Tony Waring's body. I had the feeling when the porter was called to the stand that Cornell was surprised. Cornell's story was that Waring was a friend of his in the States and that since he found himself in London at the same time he'd gone to his hotel to say hello. He found Waring dead in bed and called the police. When it was discovered that salmonella killed him, the only conclusion anyone could come to was that he had gone into some Soho café to eat dinner and consumed enough of the bacteria to kill him overnight."

Simon sipped a glass of ale thoughtfully. "But no one traced Waring's movements the night before he died?"

"He'd just arrived in the country. It's not likely that anyone would have remembered him. London is a very large city, and he could have eaten anywhere. He could have been incubating the salmonella bacteria before he left home—in fact, it is probable that he was. Since he was alone, there was no suggestion of foul play. And yet . . ."

"Yes?" Simon asked eagerly.

"I don't know. It was all too simple, except for the porter's insistence that there had been a woman with him. Since Waring was married, I could understand the woman's not coming forward. But why hadn't she ingested the salmonella too?"

Simon did not trust himself to speak. *A test of your faith in her,* he kept repeating to himself.

Jack Blake continued, "Then there was Lucien Cornell, a man I'll never forget. He was a striking-looking man with absolute authority in every mannerism, every inflection of his voice. I had the feeling he knew a lot more than he was telling. I suppose my reporter's instincts wanted a better story than a simple 'death due to misadventure' verdict. I wanted to find the beautiful and mysterious woman the porter described. I kept wondering if she knew about Waring's wife and if, indeed, the missing witness had killed Waring."

"But you said it was definitely salmonella," Simon said carefully.

"Salmonella could have been administered to him. There was evidence that Waring had received an injection within hours of his death. Cornell testified that Waring probably had had an injection of vitamins before leaving the States, that he was a health fiend and always took massive doses of vitamins, especially when traveling. I couldn't help but think of that injection, and that woman who wasn't there. And why didn't Waring get medical attention? It's unusual for salmonella poisoning to be fatal nowadays—provided the victim is treated."

"Is there a chance the coroner could have been mistaken about the cause of death? What if he'd found evidence of salmonella poisoning and hadn't looked for anything else?"

Jack Blake nodded. "You're thinking of that case in the States a few years ago, in Texas, wasn't it? I remember reading about it. They dug up the body three times, and each time the medical examiner came up with a different disease that could have killed the victim. The woman's husband was a doctor, and he was accused of murdering her."

"Wouldn't it take a doctor, or someone with specialized

131

knowledge, to commit that kind of murder?" Simon asked. "I mean, a layman wouldn't have the knowledge."

"Maybe the beautiful stranger *was* a doctor? The old porter coming forward to say that Waring was with a woman didn't do the investigation any good, I can tell you that. Waring's wife just wanted the whole thing hushed up. When the porter's testimony was struck from the record my editor wouldn't let me use the story about the possible involvement of an unknown woman. So even if salmonella wasn't the cause of death, Mrs. Waring didn't want any more medical examinations, or speculation—or news stories."

"What if someone could persuade her to agree to another autopsy now? Would it be too late?"

"Far too late," Jack Blake said with a wry smile. "She had the body cremated." He leaned forward. "There *was* a woman with him?"

Simon was growing more uneasy under the man's scrutiny. But salmonella bacteria—that wouldn't be the easiest thing for Madeleine to get hold of. "Didn't you say the desk clerk denied there was a woman with Waring?" Lucien, Simon thought, had no doubt bribed the desk clerk to say Waring was alone, and to spill tea on the register. According to the transcript of the coroner's testimony, the salmonella could have been ingested within the previous forty-eight hours, but it would have taken at least eight hours to kill. And eight hours prior to his death the only person with Tony Waring was Madeleine.

Jack Blake leaned forward. "How about it, Simon? What do you Americans call it? How about coming clean? What's your real interest in this case?"

Simon's face felt like a mask; his smile was as forced as his nonchalant reply. "I'm doing a biography of Lucien Cornell. I thought, like you, there might be more to Waring's death than met the eye. But I was wrong. Lucien just happened to be here in time to discover the body."

"I didn't know that Cornell was important enough to qualify for a biography."

"He was a research chemist of some note who rose to become head of an international corporation, and then a novelist. He's quite an interesting guy."

"A novelist? Not famous though, I take it? Unless he writes under a pen name?"

Simon mumbled something unintelligible and made his excuses. "I'm really grateful, but I must be going. I spent all day yesterday tracking down the dead coroner and most of today looking for you." Simon had called the guest house the previous evening and been told that Ginny had taken Madeleine down to the Monk's Habit. Two calls during the day elicited busy signals.

All at once he was anxious to see Madeleine again. When he was with her he could look into those lovely deep-blue eyes and be totally sure of her. Away from her, the doubts crept in. There was so damn much circumstantial evidence against her. He paid for the drinks and headed for the nearest Underground station.

Ginny was surprised to see him. She was backing her Triumph out of the garage when he appeared. "Oh, hello, Mr. T. I didn't think you'd be back. I'm off to the shops. If you want a room for tonight, you can have one on the top floor. I've already let the one you had yesterday."

"Let? But I told you I'd be back."

"I know, but the gents who came for your lady friend said you'd changed your mind, and they paid the bill for both of you."

A cold feeling in the pit of his stomach began to move toward his throat. "Someone came for Madeleine? She isn't here?"

"I knew she wasn't feeling well, but she seemed all right when we went down to the Monk's Habit. Still, you might have warned me about her mental problems before you left her here," Ginny said reproachfully.

"Mental problems? Ginny, never mind, just describe the men who came for her and anything you can remember they said."

"One was a fellow with a very idiotic sort of smile, like a Cheshire cat, I thought. He did wear a nice suit and tie. Still, there was no reason for all that silly grinning."

The man with the gun in the powerboat, Simon thought, remembering the gargoyle grin very well. "And the other?"

"Oh, he did all the talking. He was Madeleine's doctor. Showed me his card and medical identification and everything. I wouldn't have let him in otherwise. But then, it was a good thing I did, because poor Madeleine was in a terrible state when we opened her bedroom door. Moaning and perspiring . . . delirious, Dr. Vaughan said she was."

"Regis Vaughan?"

"That's him. He was wearing a nice cashmere pullover under his jacket, and what looked like tennis shoes on his feet."

"Did Madeleine go with them willingly?"

"Well, she wasn't quite herself, as I said. All wild-eyed and talking funny." Ginny looked away uncomfortably. "They had to carry her out to the car. Mr. T, do you still want a room?"

"No. With luck I'll be on the Skytrain tomorrow."

"I'm sorry. I thought you knew her doctor was coming for her," Ginny said. "It's better that they get her back home for treatment. She was saying terrible things—that she'd killed two men and tried to kill another. Poor thing, she needs help."

Vague objects began to come into focus—curtains fluttering at the window, a brilliant sky beyond. The fuzziness began to clear, and Madeleine saw she was in her room at the beach house. Sitting beside the bed was Sarita. She was wearing outsize sunglasses that did not quite hide a black eye. The bruise extended down over her cheekbone.

Madeleine felt as though her body were weighted down with lead. Her mouth was dry, and she had a splitting headache. "What happened to you?" she croaked through cracked lips.

Sarita touched her sunglasses. "You blacked my eye when I tried to put you to bed."

"I'm sorry. I don't remember anything. I was in London—or rather, Horley."

Memory was coming back, and with it, anger. "Lucien had no right to do this. Sarita, this time he's gone too far." Madeleine struggled to sit up, and it was like trying to pull free of quicksand.

Sarita leaped to her feet, reaching for a hypodermic needle on the bedside table.

"If you come near me with that, I'll strangle you," Madeleine said, mustering all of her strength to get out of bed. The room was moving around her in slow, dizzying circles. Sarita had gone out of focus again.

"It's just a sedative. Regis said I should give it to you if you got wild again. I don't want my other eye blackened. If you'll calm down, I'll send for Lucien and tell him you're coherent again, so he can tell you why he sent Regis to bring you home."

Madeleine was tottering on numb feet toward her closet. "This time I'm leaving once and for all. Finally and irrevocably. Who the hell does he think he is, snatching me like some—"

Lucien's voice cracked across the room like a whip, making both women jump. "Sit down, Penny, and listen to what I have to tell you."

He came into the room and stood with his back to the window. In silhouette, with the sunlight creating a ghostly aura about his jet-black hair, his eyes gleaming, he commanded instant attention. Madeleine's protests died in her throat. She felt as though she must gather all of her strength for the confrontation. Silently she struggled with the overpowering lethargy that gripped her.

"I brought you home, my dear, because of a crisis. Your mother has run away from the sanitarium. No, wait, there is more. I persuaded your psychiatrist to bring you home on a chartered plane—at considerable expense, I might add. Dr.

Vaughan agreed that the trauma of the news might be quite devastating and precipitate any manner of reactions. As it happened, you were having one of your spells when he arrived and were quite incoherent."

Madeleine took several deep breaths and then went back to her bed and sank down. "Mother . . . ?"

"I have men out looking for her. I've asked the sanitarium not to notify the police. Don't worry, she can't get far in the desert. We'll find her. We must be more concerned about your private investigator, who seems determined to implicate you in murder."

"Simon," she began. Her head was throbbing, and Lucien seemed suddenly to be standing very far away.

"Simon Tanning," Lucien said coldly, "was being paid by Sarita. Sarita has confessed her part in the whole plot. Tell her, Sarita. And tell her also of your amorous interlude with the intrepid private investigator."

Sarita adjusted her sunglasses again. "It's true, Madeleine. I financed your trip to England. He's been on my payroll since before you went to Mexico with him. I think you're guilty as hell, Madeleine. I think you killed those two men. I also think there's a good chance you killed your mother's twin sister and put your own mother in a mental hospital."

"Sarita!" Lucien snapped. "That's enough. Tell her about your affair with Tanning."

Sarita's eyes glittered maliciously behind the sunglasses, and her hand strayed unconsciously to her breast. Her voice was slightly breathless when she said, "Pity he doesn't have a brain to match his . . . other equipment. He kisses and tells, Madeleine. He told me all about you inviting him up here and letting him make love to you on the floor in front of the fire. About the nonsense you babbled about love being like the clashing of two trains on a track, though actually he said it was like making love to a corpse—"

"That will do, Sarita," Lucien interrupted. "I believe Madeleine gets the general idea."

Madeleine put her hands to her throbbing temples. Simon,

she thought weakly. Oh, no, Simon. With everything crumbling into a dark hole around her, his betrayal was hardest of all to bear.

Lucien was beside her, stroking her hair. "I'm sorry, princess. I know you aren't feeling well, and I hated to hit you with all of this at once. But I had to tell you why I brought you home, and to make you understand why you can't leave. You need Regis, my dear. You're on the verge of a complete breakdown. You must let us take care of you."

"Regis . . ." Madeleine repeated, with dawning realization. "You got to him, didn't you, Lucien? He's your man now too. How did you do it?"

Lucien smiled. "You exaggerate my power. Regis was concerned about you, and, perhaps, about his lucrative practice, which might have been damaged if news leaked out that he had been treating the famous Penelope Marsh who was possibly implicated in the death of two men. Regis was naturally anxious to bring you home so that nothing else would happen while you were still undergoing treatment."

Across the room, Sarita turned away to hide a malicious smile. Regis Vaughan had been more anxious to keep buried a certain incident in his past involving an extremely young girl.

Madeleine said, "What a friend you are, Lucien. You don't really give a damn about the fact that I might have killed them, you're only concerned with covering it up."

"I've never claimed anything else," Lucien answered frankly. "Haven't I told you in the past that there are a select few of us who are above the laws of the common herd? You and I belong to that elite group. We can't let the peasants destroy us. It has always been so, down through history."

Madeleine wanted to get up and run, but her body refused to move. She was so tired. If she could just sleep for a while. . . .

Lucien's hands were lightly touching her face, turning her head so that she looked into his eyes. His hypnotic black stare made her feel dizzy again, despite the cold imprint of his

137

fingers. "I've shielded you, princess, even from yourself. I tried to tell you, remember? There are times when Madeleine is not in control of her body, when some other personality takes over. The wrecking of your studio was one of the times. The other personality is jealous of Madeleine's painting, so she smashed the studio. You know it's true. No one could have done all that damage while you slept in the house. The noise of the breaking glass alone would have awakened you—unless it was your own hand smashing the glass. Just as the other personality went wild when we brought you home and you attacked Sarita. Hush . . . no, listen to me, Madeleine. Don't fight me. Sarita is partly right. You did kill Dean and Tony, and very probably your aunt. But it was not Madeleine's doing, it was the other personality. Regis believes if we can discover what triggered the creation of that other personality, then you can be cured. We have given her a name. We are going to call her Madge until you can tell us more about her. Madge is a very violent individual, with almost superhuman strength. You can see what she did to Sarita's eye in just a minor scuffle getting her into bed.

"Princess, I've never told you of the nights I've held you while you screamed obscenities and struggled to be free. Fortunately we always knew when such an occurrence was imminent, because you would become very withdrawn for a day or two, then the evening before Madge manifested herself you would not speak at all and your eyes would be glazed, as though your body had become an empty shell. That signified a transition period—one personality had departed and the other was not yet in possession."

Madeleine lay back on her pillow, feeling oddly at peace. She thought of the swift passages of time, when hours had slipped away without her realizing they were gone. Of course, it all made sense. She felt a curious detachment. Now that her own worst fears had been confirmed there was nothing to do but accept Lucien's offer of help.

She had drawn back from the brink of revelation so many times. How could she have been so blind? She thought of a dozen hints and clues she had chosen to ignore. The unguarded moments when she thought of Madeleine as a separate person. The rage she had suppressed when some heavy-breathing male colleague had put his hands on her. *The certain knowledge of why Aunt Lyla had died* . . .

A warm sense of well-being was creeping slowly along her veins as she stared, transfixed, into Lucien's eyes. How very kind he had been. He had never touched her in lust. He had been like a father, more of a father than Kevin Delaney had ever been. Kevin was like Simon, rugged and virile and carelessly sexual. All of their feelings in their genitalia . . . who had told her that? She murmured something, feeling too sleepy to care who it was.

The bedroom door opened silently, and Regis Vaughan stood on the threshold. Madeleine was vaguely aware of him moving into the room, followed by someone else she could not see.

Just before she slipped into a trancelike sleep, she realized the second visitor was wearing a white dress, and white shoes and stockings. She was a nurse, just like the nurse who had guarded her mother, so long ago, before she became an empty shell. An empty shell . . . had someone else just said that? Her eyelids were like lead. Sleep . . .

CHAPTER 14

They finally let me speak to Madeleine on the phone. She terms she never wants to see me again. Got a cut off of abusive care. He lost his right leg and both his hands. I guess I told you that yesterday." Simon sat stiffly.

Dan was feeding the circle of noisy sea lions when Simon strolled down the beach toward him. Dan straightened up, recognizing the only other adult on the beach that hot November morning.

A Santa Ana wind had come roaring down the canyons, bringing dry heat and the pungent scent of sagebrush. The blinding brilliance of the sun in a bright clear sky made it a perfect day, but Dan knew that as the wind continued to blow it would bring smog from the inland valleys. Then a brown smudge would mar the horizon and his chest would ache with every breath he took.

Simon bent to pat the head of the smallest sea lion. "This is the one Madeleine brought to you, isn't it? He looks like a boss I had once, named Alphonse."

Dan nodded, grinning. He recognized in Simon a fellow sea rover and was sympathetic about all of the problems plaguing the younger man. Simon was one of the few adults who had never asked Dan what a man his age was doing still "playing on the beach" as a lifeguard. Nor had Simon been reticent about admitting his own claustrophobic horror of being confined to city office or suburban domesticity. Simon had waved his hands, embracing sky and sea, and admitted, "Guess I was born too late, Dan. I need the physical challenge of dealing with a mighty adversary."

"There's none mightier than the sea," Dan had agreed. "No man is ever going to program the tides with a push of the button."

Simon's eyes had feasted on the panorama of the sea. "Nor tame her rage with a tranquilizer."

"How's Madeleine? And your friend Myron?" Dan said now. It was the third day in a row that Simon had strolled down to the beach, and Dan knew a great deal about his affairs.

"They finally let me speak to Madeleine on the phone. She told me in no uncertain terms she never wants to see me again. Myron is out of intensive care. He lost his right leg and both of his hands. I guess I told you that yesterday." Simon sat down wearily.

"Did you get in touch with the Australian Consulate?" Dan asked.

"Yes. They suggested I cable the police in all of the major ports of entry. I don't know, Dan. It's a long shot. But if Madeleine's father is still alive, and I can find him . . ."

Maybe he could clear up the loose ends of Madeleine's childhood. Perhaps he could find out what had caused Madeleine to suddenly hate Simon. There had been moments of despair in the last days, when Simon had been on the point of giving up, yet some stubborn need to know the truth still prodded him forward. He told himself it was for Myron's sake, for the sake of Ramón's sister, brutalized on a lonely beach. But he knew the real reason. He loved Madeleine. He would always love her, no matter what the truth about her. His love did not demand that she be flawless. To ask himself if he could love her if she admitted to murder was so hypothetical a question he had no answer. He simply could not consider the possibility.

Simon wondered if he had told Dan more than he should have. Yet there was something about Dan that reminded him of his father and inspired trust. He had a quiet strength, and a love of the sea and all its creatures. His life might be solitary, but he was singularly at peace with the world.

Dan said, "I caught a mess of mackerel and bonita. Want to stay for breakfast?"

"Do I!"

They walked back to the fire pit, where Dan had already piled driftwood. The cleaned fish were waiting in a bucket of seawater.

"I hope her father is still alive, and that he'll come back to see her," Dan said. "But I wouldn't make too much of a nuisance of myself up at the Cornell house if I were you, Simon. Lucien Cornell is a very rich and influential man. I'd hate to see you in trouble with the law."

"I'll be careful. I'm hoping I'll be able to catch Ramón coming or going. Maybe he can tell me what's going on there. At least he'll be able to find out something from Josefa, the maid."

Dan struck a match, and the rolled newspapers under the wood burst into flame. "Simon, there's someone else you might talk to. He stopped by here this morning with a donation for the sea lions from Madeleine. His name is Antoine, and he's Madeleine's art teacher. Apparently she is taking lessons again."

Antoine owned a small gallery in Laguna Beach. In addition to his private lessons, he gave group lessons in a room behind the gallery where several students worked. Simon had to wait until the class broke up. Antoine then informed him icily that he had no intention of discussing any of his students, for any reason.

Simon's attention was riveted on a seascape that stood out from the other paintings on the walls like a rare gem in a gaudy display of rhinestones. He moved closer, almost expecting to feel the salt spray in his face. The painting was unsigned, but it was a twin to the one he had admired in Madeleine's living room. Perhaps the light was subtly different in this one, as though it had been painted at a different time of year. But it was undoubtedly the same stretch of ocean and the rocks uncovered at low tide along the beach in front of Madeleine's house.

"Where did you get this painting?" Simon asked slowly. Both Sarita and Madeleine had told him of the destruction of all of the paintings in the studio. "And don't tell me it's the one that was hanging in Madeleine's living room, because that one was signed by her—this isn't. This is the same picture only darker, more somber." He spun around, a sudden possibility flashing into his mind. "Are you passing this off as one of your own pictures, Antoine old buddy?" And the silent question, *And, if so, are you also involved in trying to drive her out of her mind?*

"Of course not. It is Madeleine's work. It is not for sale. It is perhaps the best thing she has done." Antoine's eyes did not meet his.

Simon kicked the shop door closed and flipped the "Open" sign over to "Closed." "You'd better start answering questions. Is Madeleine being held against her will?"

Antoine stared incredulously. "Are you mad? Of course she isn't. I gave her a lesson today, as I always do. She hasn't been well. She's had a nervous strain and is for the moment in the care of a nurse." The swarthy Frenchman gestured angrily with his hands. "Who are you? How dare you burst in here like this? How dare you imply I have stolen my student's work? It is here merely for safekeeping."

"Safekeeping?" Simon repeated.

Antoine's eyes darted toward the door. "There was . . . an accident at her studio. Some paintings were destroyed. Lucien did not want this one to be destroyed. It was her best."

Simon digested this information and felt the first glimmer of hope.

Regis Vaughan padded silently out onto the deck, where Madeleine lay on a chaise longue reading the newly printed *Desire's Fury.* She had read it both in manuscript form and in galleys, but there was still a freshness about the book. There was no doubt that Lucien could put his readers into the middle of the action, making them feel what his characters felt.

"I finished it last night," Regis said as she looked up. "It's good, but the ending left me dissatisfied." He pulled up a chair and sat beside her.

Madeleine resisted the urge to swing her legs down to the deck. After all, wasn't this the traditional pose of psychiatrist and patient? "That's because there's a sequel," she said. "Lucien's working on it now. He's promised it will be the last novel under the Penelope Marsh name."

"Tell me how you feel when you're dressed in the Penny Marsh clothes, facing the world as the author of her books."

"Like a cheat."

"Always?"

"In the beginning it was like a game, like the little girl dressing up in her mother's clothes."

"Did you dress up in your mother's clothes when you were a little girl?"

A flush spread up over her cheeks. "Yes."

"Why does that embarrass you?"

Madeleine thought of her father, big, black-haired, handsome Kevin Delaney. Home for short visits, fussed over by everyone. Lola and Lyla dressed in their very best, the house spotless and filled with the essence of violets. Two fluffy golden heads on dainty, diminutive bodies always formed a barrier between Madeleine and her father. They chattered, laughed at his jokes, and fed him the delicacies they had prepared.

After he had greeted Madeleine and given her the small gift he always brought, there was little time left for his daughter, because Lola and Lyla did not want to share him. Madeleine forced herself to look back into her memory and see herself as she draped the pink feather-trimmed negligee around her thin child's shoulders, slipped her feet into pink high-heeled mules, and clumped down the stairs. Her father had been sitting on the couch, a sister on either side of him. The three of them looked up in astonishment.

For a second Madeleine, smiling shyly, waited, expecting her father to open his arms so that she might fling herself into his embrace. She would kiss his cheek and leave a bright-pink lipstick imprint behind. The essence of violets was tickling her nose. She was afraid she would sneeze and dislodge the false eyelashes which had been so difficult to apply, and which had come to rest slightly askew. Her dark hair was hidden under a flower-bedecked straw hat.

Then Kevin Delaney threw back his head and roared with

laughter. Lola and Lyla covered their bright-pink lips with their lace handkerchiefs and giggled.

It hadn't helped that her father followed her when she raced back up the stairs to her room, leaving the pink mules behind. He had taken her in his arms and tried to comfort her as she sobbed against his chest. He smelled of tobacco and whiskey.

"Baby, honey, don't cry. In a few years you'll be able to wear negligees and heels and lipstick and, honey, no one will laugh. We weren't laughing *at* you, baby, honest."

If they were not laughing at her, then what were they laughing at?

"The memory is painful," Regis Vaughan said. "But talk about it, it will help." He was losing her, he knew. She was becoming more withdrawn. She had not been able to relax with Regis, despite his daily visits, since her return from England. The stern and morose Nurse Williams was less of a threat to Madeleine's peace of mind than Regis' sympathetic presence.

Madeleine swung her legs over the side of the chaise and stood up. She walked to the rail and leaned on it, eyes fixed on the horizon. There was no wind today, and the sea was empty of sails. "You haven't succeeded, have you, Regis?" She had started using his first name, because Lucien did. "You haven't been able to get the elusive Madge—or whoever my phantom twin is—to reveal herself to you."

"We have not determined there *is* another personality," he corrected, moving to her side. "We're only sure that there was a trauma in your childhood that we haven't been able to bring into the open yet. That trauma caused your recurring nightmares and your sleepwalking—as well as the brief memory lapses. We have to take things a step at a time, and uncovering that childhood trauma must come first."

"But a second personality is possible, isn't it? There could be a Madge as well as a Madeleine."

She wants to believe there is another personality, Regis Vaughan thought, making several rapid mental notes. Madeleine is blameless . . . if Madge committed a crime.

145

"Very well," he said aloud. "Let us assume there is a Madge and she is responsible for the wrecking of your studio. She also struck Sarita, blacking her eye. This is all we can say for certain she has done. It is much more important to discover what happened when you were a child to cause her to manifest herself. I know that since I went to England to bring you home you've been having difficulty trusting me. Please believe I am not collaborating with your employer in any way. Anything you tell me will not be revealed to Lucien, or anyone else."

His hand slid along the rail until it came to rest on hers. She stared at his hand but barely felt his touch. He wore a heavy gold wristwatch and two expensive-looking rings. His nails were perfectly manicured, reminding her of Lucien's, except Regis' hands were smaller, with short blunt fingers. Lucien's hands had long graceful fingers and the suggestion of strength, despite the languid and indifferent gestures he made. If Lucien's hand had been lying on hers, she would have felt the icy chill of his touch all the way to her toes. Regis Vaughan's touch was comforting.

"Nurse Williams tells me you slept like a baby again last night," Regis said. "You haven't walked in your sleep since she's been watching over you."

"I'm not asleep all the time she watches me. Sometimes pretend."

"You didn't tell me you were having trouble sleeping. could give you something."

"No!"

"All right. But tell me, is it possible you've been having the nightmares without Nurse Williams knowing?"

Madeleine turned haunted eyes in his direction, and he brittle composure cracked. "Worse than ever. But that's no all. When I wake up I'm filled with a terrible violence—as i I'm about to do something ghastly." She was shaking now her fingers and toes were numb. She could not tell him of the erotic nature of the violence she felt on waking. It had been difficult enough to keep it from the watchful Nurse Williams Regis was watching her, waiting, and all at once she coul

146

not stand it. "For God's sake, you're supposed to be the doctor." Her voice rose hysterically. "Why can't you do something? What the hell good are you anyway?" Her knees buckled.

Seeing her sway unsteadily, Regis quickly put his arms around her, and she clung to him. The trembling gradually subsided. He patted her head gently, not speaking, fulfilling her momentary need for her missing father.

Josefa's voice, from within the house, announced, "*Sí, señor*, she is on the deck." Madeleine did not appear to have heard, but a moment later when Lucien stepped through the French door Madeleine looked up at Regis in a startled and guilty way. She disentangled his arms and pushed him away.

Lucien's glance took in the scene but showed neither surprise nor interest. He was accompanied by Ramón, who was carrying a large basket of flowers. Lucien motioned for Ramón to place the flower basket on the wrought-iron table beside the chaise. "Good morning, princess. Regis. Have you noticed the remarkable clarity of the air? Nothing like a Santa Ana wind to sweep away the fog, smog, and sundry other gloomy pollutants that plague us. Of course, there are some who insist the devil wind also changes the personalities of susceptible mortals. Which author wrote that when the Santa Ana blows, timid little housewives finger butcher knives and eye their husband's necks?"

"Raymond Chandler?" Regis suggested. "There is some physical distress, due to the extreme dryness of the air, that causes mood changes."

"And perhaps blatant disregard of ethics?" Lucien asked pleasantly. Before Regis could reply, Lucien went on, "Of course, the wind isn't blowing now, so we merely have what the meteorologists call a 'Santa Ana condition,' do we not? If you have finished your—treatment, Regis?" There was only the slightest hesitation before Lucien used the word, but the mocking twist of his mouth and the slightly raised eyebrow expressed clearly his unspoken censure of the psychiatrist's conduct with his patient.

Madeleine shivered, despite the heat of the day. Catching Ramón's tortured glance, she said, "Lucien, you promised to find out what happened to Ramón's sister."

"She is being held as a material witness against the man who, along with your friend Jennings, transported her into this country."

"Held? Where?"

"Why, in prison, of course."

"But she hasn't done anything—not really. She isn't a criminal."

"What do you propose be done with her while the man who brought her here is awaiting trial? She is, as the Department of Immigration now likes to call them, an undocumented alien. It is common practice to hold them in prison until the trial. After that she will be deported."

"Can't you do anything?"

"What?"

"Have her released into your custody. Break her out of prison and send her home. Anything. For God's sake, Lucien, she was beaten and raped and thrown in jail. Hasn't she suffered enough for the crime of trying to join her brother here?"

Lucien's expression was disinterested. "Our friend Ramón is also an undocumented alien. Did you know?"

"Oh, Lord," Madeleine breathed. "What's to become of them?"

Lucien smiled indulgently. "To please you, princess, I will do what I can for them."

The temporary burst of energy appeared to leave Madeleine exhausted. She sat down limply, her eyes glazed. "Lucien, did you call the sanitarium? Is there news of Mother?"

Regis Vaughan was startled. He knew that when he had arrived Madeleine had been on the phone with Sarita, who had given her the good news that Lola Delaney had been found unhurt, wandering aimlessly in the desert.

Lucien's expression did not change. "Your mother has been found, my dear. She's all right. I'm sorry, I instructed Sarita to call you. That's why I brought the flowers, by way of celebration."

There was a blankness to Madeleine's face and eyes that was of deep concern to Regis. After a moment she said, "Oh . . . yes." She looked bewildered. "But did you personally call the sanitarium . . . that's what I meant."

"I did. The staff assured me she suffered no ill effects. You can go and see her as soon as you're feeling stronger." Lucien was absently pulling petals from the flowers in the basket, and contemplating Regis Vaughan in a speculative manner.

Regis knew from that look on Lucien's face that there was going to be another uncomfortable confrontation with Madeleine's employer. Regis had already regretted taking the case of Penelope Marsh.

CHAPTER 15

Built into the hillside on the west side of Lucien's sprawling house was a greenhouse. Divided into segments to provide the different temperature, humidity, and soil conditions necessary for the various plants, the greenhouse had been installed in the days when Lucien was a research chemist. Certain plants had been used in his experiments. Later he began to collect orchids and other exotic specimens.

Ramón liked the moist heat of the greenhouse and the privacy afforded by plants and vines. Mainly he liked it because it was here Josefa had first brought him a message from their employer and had lingered for a stolen kiss. Since that happy moment the two of them met there whenever they could get away from their chores.

On this particular day the mood was spoiled by Josefa's anger. "You are a fool to trust any of them," she declared. "Do you really believe the señor will get your sister out of jail? Pah, you crazy wetback, they don't care about you or your sister. There are a hundred more like us to take our places."

"The señorita—she cares," Ramón said obstinately.

Josefa's eyes flashed as she disentangled his fingers, which had been playing with the buttons of her blouse. "You are like the stupid gringos who hover around her like moths to the fire. She is good-looking, so she must be good—*sí?* You fool, she is a crazy woman. Why else do they have a nurse watch her at night? And the mind doctor who comes every day?"

"You're jealous of her," Ramón said triumphantly, reaching for her again. "No need, *chiquita,* it's you I love."

Josefa tossed a luxurious mass of dark curls over her shoulder and glared at him. "And I was attracted to a man who vowed vengeance for the wrong done his sister. What became of that man, Ramón? He disappeared on a boat with the madwoman. She cast a spell on you too. Can you not see—it all circles back to her. *She* went to Mexico with Jennings. *She* led you back there to the coyote who nearly killed you. Maybe he was supposed to kill the man Tanning too, eh? You ever think of that?"

"But he let us go. And didn't the señorita save my job here when we got back? The señor was angry that I was gone, and she pleaded that I had a sick relative."

"Maybe she is afraid you know more than you do," Josefa said ominously. "And wants to keep an eye on you."

"The man Tanning was waiting for me when I came to work this morning," Ramón said, hoping to change the subject.

Fear crossed Josefa's face. "Don't talk to him," she urged, glancing about as though expecting him to materialize. "Don't

150

trust anybody. What if the señor sees you talking to him? That new man, the one with the crazy grin, he stays at the house all the time now. And Sedgewick, he is there too. I don't like those men. They watch the señorita's house and the beach. What if they see you with Tanning?"

Ramón squared his shoulders with a slight swagger. "I am not afraid of them. No matter what I do, they can't give me to the *policía, sí?* They are—what they call it?—harboring an illegal alien. Besides, Tanning thinks he gets information from me, but really I watch him. I will find out if he is responsible for hurting Soledad. Josefa, tell me something about the señorita I can give to Tanning."

Josefa shivered in his arms. "No! I am afraid of her. Did you not see the black eye she gave the señor's secretary?"

Ramón pondered this revelation uneasily. It was not the kind of incident Simon Tanning would want to hear about his beloved.

"I must go," Josefa said. "He will miss me." She kissed his mouth quickly, then sped away through the beautiful, indifferent orchids.

After she was out of sight, Ramón picked up the shears and snipped an orchid blossom. Ten minutes later, orchid in hand, he was approaching the deck where Madeleine lay on her chaise longue staring moodily out to sea.

"Señorita . . . Señorita Madeleine," he called to her softly.

She looked around slowly, then saw him standing just below the deck. He smiled and tossed the orchid up to her.

"I am sorry you are ill. I hope you will soon feel well again and go swimming in your ice-cold ocean."

Madeleine smiled and held the delicate blossom to her face.

Neither of them could see the figure on the beach below, watching the house through his binoculars. The glasses swept the house again and came to rest on the Mexican gardener. Bruno grinned. First the Mexican had a rendezvous in the greenhouse with the maid, now he was with the lady of the house. Bruno's demented expression split his face in an ever-widening chasm.

Regis Vaughan was in the office of the nursing home he owned jointly with another doctor. The last patient of the day had gone, and Regis was clearing his desk. He sighed when the phone rang.

Lucien's voice had an excited urgency. "I believe Madeleine's other personality is going to reveal herself. Can you come over right away?"

Regis sighed again. Lucien Cornell was taking up more of his time than his patient. This was the third false alarm within days. "What makes you think so?"

"That vacant, glazed look persisted all day. This evening she was completely withdrawn and didn't speak at all during dinner. She's acting strangely now."

"May I speak to Nurse Williams?"

There was a pause, then the nurse came on and confirmed Lucien's belief that he was needed.

"I'm on my way," Regis snapped and gave the nurse instructions on how to handle things until his arrival.

Madeleine was sitting near the window overlooking the sea. The room was in semidarkness, lit only by a fire in the hearth and the dim glow of the Mexican *triángulo* on one wall. Nurse Williams discreetly withdrew as Josefa led Regis into the house.

"Madeleine . . . " Regis said softly. "It's Regis Vaughan."

She inclined her head slightly toward the sound of his voice. Her eyes were wide, unseeing. She did not answer. Nor was there any response when he touched her, or repeated her name. He pulled a chair in front of her, sat down, and grasped her limp fingers.

"Madeleine," he said sharply. "Come back. Don't withdraw. Listen to me."

She stared straight ahead, as though he hadn't spoken.

"Madeleine, everything in your early life taught you to abandon problems," Regis said, his voice raised, authoritative. "Your aunt's suicide, your father's departure for Australia, your mother's withdrawal into herself were all forms of running

152

away. You ran away too, when you began the masquerade as Penelope Marsh. But part of you wanted to rebel, to stand and fight. You sought my help. Now you are trying to run away again. Madeleine, do you hear me?"

Her eyelids descended in a slow-motion blink, as though her lids were too heavy to control. He could see her pupils were dilated. Her lips moved soundlessly.

"Madeleine . . . are you Madeleine? Or are you someone else?"

She shook his hands free of hers with a violent motion, stood up, and clutched the back of the chair for support. She moved away, walking with the careful precision of someone afraid she was about to collapse. At the door she looked back, as though about to speak. Then she disappeared into the hall, slamming the door behind her.

He almost collided with Nurse Williams in the hall. "She went upstairs," the nurse said.

Regis ran up the spiral staircase. Madeleine's bedroom door was locked, and no amount of knocking and begging would persuade her to open it. After a while he went back down the stairs.

"You'd better go to her," he told the nurse. "There's no point in unlocking the door for me if she won't talk to me."

They both jumped as the French door to the deck opened suddenly. Instead of an expected gust of wind, a man stepped into the room. Regis swore softly under his breath as he recognized the silhouette.

"Well?" Lucien asked.

"I don't discuss my patients with *anyone*," Regis said shortly. He nodded for Nurse Williams to go upstairs.

After she was out of sight Regis said guardedly, "It appears you may have made an inspired guess in regard to dissociative hysteria. It would be totally improper for me to tell you more than that."

Lucien nodded, frowning. "Madge exists. I knew it. Now we have to find out why. The trauma of her aunt's suicide and

153

mother's mental collapse, of course. But why does Madeleine feel guilty?"

"Please leave the treatment to me, if you will. I can't tell you how much damage amateur psychologists do."

Lucien reached out and flipped on a lamp. He studied Regis' expression in the white light. "Ah, but, doctor, I am not amateurish in any of my undertakings. As you no doubt remember from our interview before you went to England for me."

Regis flushed. "I agreed to go because of my concern for my patient. Not because of your threats."

"Of course, doctor," Lucien said smoothly. "And I'm quite sure you have overcome your proclivity for extremely young girls by now."

"That incident was unsubstantiated . . . and years ago—"

"In Canada. Yes, I know."

"I see no reason to continue this conversation."

"Nor do I. I'm sure you get the point." Lucien switched off the light and added softly, "Tread warily, doctor. Don't do anything foolish. I'm sure we both only want to help Madeleine."

The days went by in whirling confusion. Madeleine felt she was being tossed on a flotsam-filled sea and was unsure which piece of floating debris she should clutch in order to stay afloat. Lucien treated her as though nothing unusual had occurred, and for this she was grateful.

"If you were to contract a minor illness, such as a cold or stomach ailment," Lucien said, "you would simply do all you could to help your body recover and then wait for it to pass. Just think of Madge in the same light. A slight illness of the mind, my dear, that will surely pass."

"But, Lucien, what about Dean Jennings? In Tony's case, I think I believe it was an accident. He could have ingested the salmonella before we ever left California. But in Dean's case it's different. And there is his connection with the alien smuggling ring to be considered. Lucien, it would really help me to know for sure what caused Dean's death. Would it be too late for an autopsy?"

"What would be the point? The Mexican doctor said Jennings died of a heart attack, possibly virus-induced. If we demand an autopsy now, how do I explain that Sedgewick posed as Jennings' next of kin and spirited the body away? We would be crucified by the press more for the cover-up than for the deception. You should have thought of this earlier, princess, when you asked for my help. It's too late now to change what was done. And the reasons for secrecy haven't changed, either. Can you imagine what the press would have done with the story of Penelope Marsh being in Mexico with an alien-smuggling drug runner who turns up mysteriously dead in her bed?"

Josefa came through the atrium, followed by the silently padding Regis Vaughan, and Lucien stood up to leave.

"Lucien, before you go," Madeleine said, "there's something I want to mention. I need time alone. Someone is always with me, and I'm beginning to feel trapped. I want to start painting again. I feel empty without it. But I won't be able to paint with someone breathing over my shoulder. You can lock me in the studio if you wish, but I must paint."

Lucien and Regis exchanged glances. "I don't see why not," Regis said.

"I'm not sure it's a good idea," Lucien said. "Remember the fury with which Madge wrecked the studio. Madeleine's painting is evidently the cause of great animosity."

"I'm not convinced yet there is a Madge," Regis said. "And even if there is, she apparently takes over while Madeleine sleeps."

"Lucien, I must paint," Madeleine said. "It isn't a matter of wanting to, or liking to, or even needing to. I *must*. Sometimes I feel that Josefa might scoop up a couple of pairs of paint-smeared shorts and Ramón drive my old VW to the junkyard and then there would be nothing left of me. I have this sense of my whole life being an illusion—it never happened, therefore I do not exist."

Regis nodded gravely. "This feeling certainly adds credence to the possibility of a second personality. It's possible that even during the nights she is not actually in your body, she is present nevertheless, planting these thoughts and feelings while you sleep. I've noticed that first thing in the morning you are distant, disoriented—unnaturally so."

"Something like posthypnotic suggestions?" Lucien asked, his tone still slightly mocking, as though Regis had just revealed himself to be incompetent.

Regis shifted his feet uncomfortably, wondering how Lucien always managed to get a step ahead of him. Regis had been considering suggesting hypnotherapy to Madeleine.

"If I could start painting again," Madeleine said, "I'm sure it would help suppress these feelings." And perhaps help the aching sense of loss since Simon had gone from her life. But she knew better than to give voice to this thought.

"Very well," Lucien said. "Tell me what you need."

Within the week her studio had been restored and restocked with paint and canvas. Several seascapes were in progress, but after a time Madeleine devoted all of her time to one picture, which she carefully hid behind blank canvases when she was not in the studio.

She was working on a portrait of a woman, and she felt compelled to finish it, to the exclusion of everything else. It was almost as though the brush were held by someone else. She had begun to paint in a way she had never painted before. Swift, sure strokes captured the image of her mother, as she had been years ago. Soft, fluffy golden curls framed the delicate features. The long braid at the back of her head had been unpinned and draped over one shoulder, in a cluster of ringlets that went with the eighteenth-century style of dress. The clothes were as Lucien described them for Clarissa, in *Desire's Fury*. Now, into the background of the picture, Madeleine was weaving the other elements of the story, all in somber hues and blurred outlines.

156

CHAPTER 16

Madeleine lay in bed, her head turned away from the silent white-uniformed figure who sat nearby. Everything had been too ordinary. No nightmares, no sleepwalking. *As long as I do as I'm told, nothing bad will happen to me.* The thought seemed to have been planted there by someone else.

She wanted desperately to go to see her mother, but Regis felt it unwise. Lucien agreed. "After all, princess, she won't know you. Your mother is as she was before, no better, no worse. Have I ever lied to you, my dear? You know I have not. Don't be tiresome and insist on visiting her just now, there's a pet. Regis says he's on the verge of a breakthrough."

Regis would tell Lucien anything he wanted to hear, Madeleine thought. Lucien had been hounding him so.

Cautiously Madeleine turned her head. Nurse Williams was motionless, her head back against the chair, one arm dangling over the side in an attitude of complete relaxation. Was she asleep yet? Time was fleeting. It would take four and a half hours of hard driving to reach the sanitarium. Even if she merely looked in on her sleeping mother and left immediately, it was by no means certain she could make it back before dawn.

Madeleine worried about the sleeping pills. Still, two Seconals should not harm a healthy woman like the nurse. Regis had supplied the Seconals without question when Madeleine asked him. She told him she had been unable to sleep, and it was true, the nurse confirmed it, as did Madeleine's own smudged eyes and obvious fatigue. The capsules had been dissolved in the bedtime pot of tea Madeleine had invited the nurse to share with her, her own cup poured in advance.

She could hear the woman's deep, even breathing now. One foot found the floor, then the other. There was no need to stop and dress. Her clothes and purse had been placed under the Volkswagen seat earlier. Madeleine sped silently down the stairs.

There was an unexpected exhilaration to being out of the house in the middle of a deep still night. She floored the accelerator. The wind, still blowing from the desert, whipped her hair. As the lights of the town were left behind, the sky was filled with a blazing host of stars, dancing and beckoning.

"I'm me! I'm Madeleine Delaney and I'm real," she sang to the star-filled night. "There is no Madge. Dean died of a heart attack and Tony ate spoiled food in some restaurant before we ever left the country." Hadn't the medical book assured her that Tony could have ingested the salmonella at any time within three days? And as for the exploding jeep, that was an accident, and not an attempt on Simon's life. *Simon . . . oh, God, Simon, how I miss you.*

The exhilaration of escape faded as she thought of Simon. Everything else she could have accepted, rationalized, except, of course, Simon's telling Sarita her most private thoughts and the details of their lovemaking.

And yet, perhaps there was an explanation, even for that. No, the real reason she could never see Simon again had to be faced. Madge would kill him. Momentary flights of fancy when she rationalized everything away had to be followed by grim reality. There was a twisted part of her mind where sex and death intermingled and released the murderous Madge.

At the desert sanitarium the sleepy night nurse tried to persuade Madeleine to wait until morning to visit her mother.

"She's in her room? She *is* here?" Madeleine said. She was breathless from dashing in from the parking lot, and her hair was wildly windblown. She was aware of the nurse's professional scrutiny and tried to sound as calm and normal as possible.

"Of course she's here." The nurse was looking at her oddly. "She's been here since you and Mr. Cornell brought her . . . how long ago? Two years? Three?"

"But . . ." Madeleine stopped short. "You mean, she didn't run away from you? She hasn't been missing?"

"Our patients don't run away," the nurse answered frostily.

"I want to see her. Now."

The nurse backed down before a determined stare and the urgency in Madeleine's voice. "I'll get an orderly," she said, picking up the phone. "We aren't used to visitors arriving in the middle of the night."

Lola lay serenely in her bed, her wasted features in repose. The dim light was kind, it restored her former beauty and hid the vacant stare and slack mouth. Looking through the glass panel in the door, Madeleine thought of the portrait she had painted. The woman was her mother, dressed as Clarissa in *Desire's Fury*. Why? Some far cavern off Madeleine's mind had conceived the idea and compelled her hands to execute the picture. Madeleine shivered and turned away from the spy window. For the moment, it was more imperative to get back before she was missed than it was to answer the why of that strange compulsion.

Lucien had lied to her about her mother's disappearance. But Lucien never lied to her. Madeleine's head began to ache.

The return drive along the tortuous mountain road was an agony of holding the small car against the onslaught of the wind. The Santa Ana was blowing up again, and the first silver knife thrust of the sunrise sliced the horizon. Time was growing short. They would discover she was gone. Trees were down along the route, and Madeleine was forced to detour.

Madeleine was exhausted when she stumbled into the house and fell against Nurse Williams. The white-clad arms shook her free. "Upstairs, Miss Delaney. And into bed before he gets here, or we're both in trouble."

Madeleine was happy to comply. She fell asleep immediately and, despite the morning sunlight flooding the room, plunged at once into the nightmare. She was shaking the bars of the cage, arms like lead. Her silent scream filled the space all around her as the hovering black cloud appeared. She could feel the icy touch of the vapors—sticky, evil, suffocating. The more she struggled, the more the cloud enveloped her. She could not breathe. She gasped and trembled with terror, until at last the scream burst from her throat, awakening her.

She was lying on the kitchen floor. She could feel the cold tile under her body, the warm air blowing across her face from the open window. She jumped as a pungent odor assailed her nostrils. Opening her eyes, she saw Nurse Williams replacing the cap on a small bottle. "She's coming out of it," she said to someone unseen.

A cool hand came down on Madeleine's forehead. "Princess? Are you feeling better?"

"Lucien? What happened? How did I get downstairs?" Her mouth was dry and her head pounded. Her words sounded blurred.

"It was Madge, princess. She took over again. I'm sorry, my dear. You were doing so well. Regis will be here shortly. We're going to take you back to bed. All right, nurse, you may go and see how Josefa is progressing."

"Josefa?" Madeleine climbed unsteadily to her feet, assisted by Lucien. "Has something happened to Josefa?"

"We're afraid it might be a fractured jaw. Regis will take care of her. He has a medical degree, you know."

"How did it happen?" Madeleine asked. She knew before he spoke what the answer would be.

"You mustn't blame yourself. It was Madge."

Madeleine could not speak. Her throat was constricted and

a large bubble of terror was lodged somewhere near her heart. It was true. There was another personality that invaded her body. That other woman who lashed out violently at anyone who was in her path.

Simon stood on the dock and surveyed the wreckage of the *Viking*. His mouth was set in a grim line, and his gray eyes were hard. He barely heard the chorus of hypothetical explanations for the explosion that had shattered the cockpit and torn a large hole in the hull of his boat.

"You must have left something flammable aboard," the owner of the boat in the next slip accused. "Dammit, you could have blown up every boat on the dock. Sheer carelessness."

"No warning," another voice put in gleefully. "Poof—just like that. It's a good thing there were plenty of people about. Everyone rushed over with fire extinguishers."

Simon turned his back and strode away. He caught the bus back to his apartment. The sky to the east was heavy with a billowing cloud of smoke. The Santa Ana wind and accompanying tinder-dry air had brought about the usual rash of brushfires in the hills. But there was no way a fire could have started accidentally on the *Viking*. He had not even had any gasoline aboard for the small engine. Someone had deliberately sabotaged his boat.

When Simon reached home, the cat jumped down from the window ledge and the pigeon scolded him shrilly for being absent. Funny, the door wasn't locked. He was sure he had locked it before leaving. But the phone call about the explosion on his boat had awakened him from a deep sleep, perhaps in his rush he had forgotten.

Cat and pigeon glared at him. Neither of them had been fed.

"OK, you guys, take it easy. I haven't forgotten you." Simon peered into his nearly empty refrigerator. There was half a can of processed meat and a container of delicatessen potato salad. He dumped both into the cat's dish and mashed everything together. Placing the dish on the floor, he watched as the pigeon waded into the food. The cat stared at him malevolently.

Simon picked up the phone and dialed a number. "Dan? Yeah, it's Simon." After explaining what had happened, Simon said, "Remember you offered to loan me your Hobie-Cat if I ever wanted to try it? Can I use it today? What? Hey, that'll be great. When can you get here?"

He sat down to await the arrival of Dan and his car. The yellow Western Union cablegram that had arrived the previous night lay on the kitchen table. Simon frowned. He had to be back here tonight, at six o'clock, California time. The exchange of cables had set up the phone call, and he mustn't miss it. Kevin Delaney had finally been found, wandering the sheep stations of the Australian outback.

The cat began to stalk the pigeon, circling, with tail twitching and eyes narrowed. Oblivious, the pigeon gobbled the food. The cat pounced, shrieking like a banshee. Reeling under the attack, the pigeon fluttered aloft, clutching at the light fixture. The cat settled down to eat, daintily separating the meat from the potato salad. Then, when the meat was finished, she devoured every scrap of the salad. When Simon left with Dan, the cat was going through its ritual cleansing while the pigeon hurled insults from above.

Dan drove Simon down the Coast Highway. The hot weather had brought the usual throngs to the beaches, but Dan said he had called in a replacement lifeguard to take his place. "Can your boat be repaired?" he asked.

"I don't know. I couldn't stand to look at it."

"I've got a few friends in the business. I'll get someone to look at it for you. Meantime, you use my Hobie any time you want. I'm taking a couple of weeks off and heading down the Baja for some fishing. You can use my car while I'm gone, too—I'll leave the keys."

"Thanks, Dan. I'll try not to get either blown up," Simon said gruffly.

"Just one thing about the Hobie," Dan added. "Those blasted sea lions think it's their personal transportation—probably because I've used it so many times to try to haul them back out to sea."

Simon grinned, the tension broken.

"Tonight's the night for the phone call from Australia, right? Do you think Madeleine's father will come back?"

"I'm going to tell him Madeleine is ill. It seems to be true, from what Ramón told me."

There was a brisk breeze and the craft flew across the sea, despite the weight of two plump sea lions who accompanied him.

The day grew hotter. After his nerves stopped jumping and he had exhausted the possibilities of the Hobie, Simon returned to Dan's beach and swam for a while. The rest of the sea lions were frolicking in the surf, to the delight of the youngsters playing hooky from school.

It was nearly five o'clock when he returned to his apartment. An hour from now he would know if Madeleine's father planned to return from Australia, or at least help unravel part of the mystery surrounding her. At the back of Simon's mind was the nagging fear that Kevin Delaney would tell him of a long thread of madness in the women of his family—Lola, Lyla, Madeleine. Why else had Kevin run away?

The apartment was strangely silent. Simon paused on the threshold, not understanding what was wrong. Then he saw them, lying side by side in a grim parody of the combat they feigned in life. The two small bodies were stiff, the eyes wide and staring. The cat's paw was curved toward the pigeon's head as though in the act of cuffing the bottle-green neck, but cat and pigeon had been dead for some time. Staring at the two small corpses, Simon thought of the processed meat and potato salad that had been destined for his own lunch.

Something fluttered on the periphery of his vision. Turning back toward the door, he saw a scrap of material was caught on the torn screen. A small piece of denim that was smeared with oil paint. Madeleine. She wore denim shorts, usually paint-smeared.

CHAPTER 17

Lucien studied the portrait of Lola. He walked away from the easel, stopped, and looked back at it. "You have created a compelling picture of Clarissa," he said, his voice strangely hollow. He turned and smiled at Madeleine, his dark eyes vibrantly alive. "I had no idea you were so gifted, since I've seen only your bleak seascapes. I believe I will suggest to my publishers that you do the next cover."

Madeleine stood at the window of her studio, staring out at the iridescent sea. The wind had freshened and sailboats moved briskly across the horizon, their spinnakers bright splashes of color in the sunlight. There had been a time such praise from Lucien would have sent her spirits soaring, but today it fell flat. She seemed unable to concentrate on anything said or done around her. He had not recognized that the portrait was of her mother. Of course, Madeleine had painted a much younger woman, Lola as she was long ago, not as Lucien knew her.

"You know, princess, looking at that picture, I believe I have at last decided what the title of the final Penelope Marsh book is going to be. You have captured so perfectly the deadly allure of a woman merciless and wanton as Clarissa. She married Sir Giles Cameron at the end of *Desire's Fury,* as you know. She will be Lady Cameron in the new book."

"You promised this would be the last." Madeleine struggled to put herself into the conversation. Each day that passed seemed to bring a deepening sense of detachment that, had she had the strength, she would have worried about. It was so unlike her to be lethargic, listless to the brink of stupor.

"I am going to call it *Deadly Lady.*"

Madeleine digested this information silently. The title seemed to conjure up more than a piece of fiction. She wondered if she herself had inspired it, rather than Clarissa. Madeleine murmured something about it being a good title. Then she said, "Lucien, why did you lie about my mother running away from the sanitarium? The night nurse said Mother never left." There, she had asked the question she had been trying to get out all day.

"I didn't lie. Your mother ran away and was found wandering in the desert. The staff at the sanitarium were understandably anxious to cover their laxness. The nurse who told you it did not happen lied, not I."

Lucien seemed to glide across the room toward her. She blinked. He placed his cool hands on her shoulders, massaging with icy precision. "You've been working too hard, princess. Why don't you give it up for today? Go and take a nice warm bubble bath and have a nap. Then put on a pretty dress. I'll concoct an elegant dinner for us. Something cold, perhaps. And ice-cold champagne. I'm serious about your doing a painting for the cover of my book. Doesn't that please you? Perhaps a new career is beginning for you. Just think, you'll be free of my clutches forever."

Madeleine wanted to move out of range of his cold fingers, but she did not. Perhaps it was a trick of the light, but when she glanced over her shoulder at him his skin seemed to have taken on a waxy sheen. "I can't leave right now. I'm expecting Regis. He couldn't make it this morning."

Lucien's brows descended threateningly over his eyes, and his mouth twisted into the expression of impatience which he had begun to assume the past few days at the mention of Regis' name. "I'll call him and cancel. He knows he's supposed to be here in the mornings. Go on, princess. Rest before dinner. You can drift off to sleep thinking about your picture for the cover of *Deadly Lady.*"

Madeleine went up the spiral staircase, and like a white shadow, Nurse Williams emerged from the kitchen and followed. *Deadly Lady*, Madeleine thought, as she lowered herself into a steaming tub. Ah, yes, but *who* is the deadly lady? Is it Lola, or Lyla . . . Clarissa . . . or perhaps the mythical Penelope Marsh? But no, the deadly lady was, of course, Madeleine's alter ego, the elusive Madge, who showed herself to everyone but Madeleine.

"Please, señorita . . ." Ramón begged. His haunted eyes were fixed on Sarita as she slowly unfastened her blouse. She was sitting on the edge of her desk with the light behind her, and even before the buttons were undone it was obvious she wore nothing under the thin garment.

She smiled and licked her lower lip. "What are you afraid of, Ramón? The señor has gone to Los Angeles and won't be back before dark. And didn't I have good news for you? Your sister will be released and you are going down to San Diego to see her. Surely you could be a little more grateful?" Sarita pouted, enjoying the man's discomfort as he squirmed under her coy glance.

"Please, señorita. Do not play with me." Ramón had been caught alone by Sarita in the past. She would tease him until he made the inevitable pass, and then order him from her sight, leaving him to worry about the sort of retribution that might befall him. There never had been any, but Ramón knew only too well how docile an illegal alien must be in order to keep a job this side of the border.

Sarita laughed softly and tugged open her blouse. "Did you ever see anything more beautiful, Ramón?"

166

Ramón hung his head. Damn her, damn all of them. Most of the street names in the neighborhood were Spanish and had been so long before the advent of the gringo. It was not he who was the interloper. He took a step backward, seeking escape.

She pounced like a playful kitten. Before he could gather his wits, she was pressing herself close to him, grabbing at him with greedy fingers. Her caresses were brazen, intimate.

He responded, certain she would then push him away and order him to leave. Instead, she guided his hands to her body.

In a single motion, she unfastened the wrap-skirt she wore and let it fall to the ground. She shrugged off the blouse. Her body writhed beneath his touch.

Ramón forgot everything but the temptation of that voluptuous form. He was excited and fearful at the same time. Suddenly she exploded into quivering spasms, sinking her teeth into his shoulder, gasping and clawing wildly at his back. She raked his face with her fingernails. "Get off me! Let me go or I'll yell for help," she screamed, her face livid.

Startled, Ramón obeyed. He pulled away from her, blinded by desire and terror. Blinking, he saw Sarita calmly pick up her blouse. He fingered the long oozing scratch on his cheek. There would be similar marks on his back, he was sure.

"Señorita," he said quietly, "you are a bitch."

She smiled. "And you, Ramón, are fired. You've got thirty minutes to pack your things and get out of here. Lucien said to tell you if you ever show your face on this side of the border again, he'll have you prosecuted."

She buttoned her blouse and patted at her hair.

"You did this thing . . . knowing all the while the señor was dismissing me," Ramón said.

"Of course. I never get my butter where I get my bread, Ramón. I wouldn't have let you do it to me if you were going to stay."

Ramón turned on his heel, wanting to be gone before he struck her. "It was not *I* who did it to *you*, señorita," he flung over his shoulder.

Sarita merely smiled and picked up Lucien's handwritten draft for the latest chapter. She sat down at her typewriter, humming softly as she began to type.

Clarissa melted with need of him. She wanted to feel her husband's strong arms about her, his weight crushing her to the bed, his manhood deep inside her. Yet the memory of their quarrel at dinner kept her at her embroidery hoop even as he tarried over his brandy at the dining table. Had there ever been a time in their turbulent marriage when they were not hacking at one another, one way or another? Clarissa picked up her hairbrush and ran it through her long dark hair—

Sarita stopped abruptly, swearing in annoyance. Long *dark* hair? Clarissa had pale-gold hair. It was unlike Lucien to make such an error. Sarita picked up the correction fluid with an exclamation of exasperation.

Regis Vaughan said sharply, "There's no need for you to be here, Nurse Williams. You should be sleeping now if you expect to remain alert tonight."

Nurse Williams looked at Madeleine, who nodded. The white orthopedic shoes clumped up the spiral staircase.

"How are you feeling, Madeleine?" Regis asked. The cool professionalism of his tone did little to calm Madeleine's panic. Her fingers dug into the arms of her chair. "What shall we discuss, doctor? How about Josefa with her jaw all wired? Josefa, who never did me any harm."

"She probably tried to stop Madge from leaving the house."

"It wasn't Madge who left. It was me. I planned it and I did it and I was aware of everything I did that night. What I did to Josefa I did during a short morning nap."

"And that established for you the fact that Madge takes over while you sleep? Madeleine, although Madge has not revealed herself to me, I must consider the possibility of an alter personality. You see, everyone has different sides to their peronalities, the patterns being part of a normal whole. Someone with a multiple personality has one or more alter personalities who are hate-filled and violent, who lash out at family and strangers alike. Those personalities are also self-destructive."

"And if there is another personality in me," Madeleine asked cautiously, "what would the treatment be?"

"You'll have to explore your past and come to grips with it—especially the events you have buried in your subconscious. First, I would have you keep a notebook of information as you remember it, along with current feelings, and fears, and beliefs. Write down anything you find too painful to express orally. I would also like to observe the progress of your paintings on a daily basis. You may express more through your painting than you can put into words."

"I'll try to do what you ask, but I may forget. You can look at my paintings anytime."

"I have another suggestion, but first I want you to tell me more about your dreams. In particular, if you can remember dreaming before the attack on Josefa."

Madeleine put her hand to her brow, pressing with her fingers. "I can't remember."

"Then tell me again about your recurring nightmare. Is it erotic in any way?"

"Well . . ." Madeleine said, embarrassed to talk about it. "No doubt you psychiatrists could find it full of erotic symbolism. I suppose the bars I see might be considered phallic symbols. Isn't that what you'd call them, doctor?"

"If that's what you want to call them."

She leaned back in her chair and closed her eyes in resignation. "The black cloud in the dream changes shape. It moves, hovers, sometimes it's like a cloud of insects, sometimes a giant bat. I am terrified of it, and it's coming closer all the time. I hear it whispering to me—"

"Hear it? Are you sure? It's unusual to hear anything in a dream, but my research into other documented cases of multiple personality has turned up the fact that patients do indeed hear 'voices' inside their heads."

"I do hear *something*. I'm so afraid the black cloud is goin to touch me. I don't know what will happen if it touches me.

She looked down at her lap, regarding her fingers twistin and restlessly plucking at her thighs. Sometimes there are othe elements, she thought, but I'm not going to tell you abou them. Things that happened during the day or evening take o distorted forms. At other times the dream begins innocentl enough and then changes, becomes overwhelming. Once dreamed I was reading one of Lucien's books, and as I watche all the words crawled off the page and flew up into the air an became that hovering black cloud. And then, instead of fearin it, I was at once moist and ready and wanting . . . oh, God . . . don't dare think of what I was wanting. . . ."

"And shortly after dreaming this dream, you often fin yourself out of bed and in another part of the house. You eve went outside once or twice?"

"Yes. But not always. I mean, sometimes I wake up sti in bed."

"I believe the dark cloud approaching is Madge. Your othe personality moving in to take over your body. The bars perhap represent the barrier you have erected to keep her out."

"Josefa is the only person still alive who has seen Madge, Madeleine said. "Will she be able to help us when she ca talk again?"

"Possibly. She's in a private nursing home I own. Di Lucien tell you that she is also an undocumented alien? Ther won't be a problem of her bringing charges for assault."

"Oh, God, I'm not worried about that. I'm worried abou what Madge will do next. Perhaps the bars in the dream rep resent the cage I should be locked in, so I can't hurt anyon again. Regis, is insanity hereditary? My mother—"

"We believe in some cases the tendency to mental break downs can be inherited, as well as some forms of ment illness. But only the tendency. We're still groping in the dar with the human mind, no matter how knowledgeable we tr to appear."

"That tendency was always there in my mother, and in Au

170

Lyla. I see it now. They were both so fragile, so easily hurt, like very old paper that crumbles when you try to bend it. I remember they used to weep for days when my father went away. Everyone in town would bring their cares to mother and Aunt Lyla. They would sit up all night trying to think what could be done, then end up more devastated in mind and body than the person whose problem it was in the first place. They were so terribly sensitive to everyone around them. They just couldn't bear unhappiness in others, so how could they stand their own?"

"You have inherited their sensitivity, Madeleine, but that doesn't mean you will be destroyed by it. In fact, it is your sensitive nature that leads me to suspect the presence of another, very different, personality. The woman who cannot bear to step on a sand crab is not the woman who brutally attacked Josefa."

"A sand crab?" Madeleine repeated, not understanding.

"You don't remember, do you? It happened the first time we walked on the beach. It's not important. Madeleine, I must ask you again, have you ever, at any time, taken drugs?"

"No! Why won't you believe me?"

"Could someone have administered a drug without your knowledge?"

"You looked for needle marks and didn't find any. You think I took LSD, don't you? I told you before, I have never taken any drugs."

"When I found you in England, you appeared to be hallucinating. It was more than a nightmare. Perhaps I was within minutes of confronting Madge."

"Regis, I'm beginning to panic. I don't know how much more I can take. Keeping a journal seems too slow a process. Can't we do anything else?"

"There is one other approach we could try, if you're willing. Hypnotherapy. It's been used successfully in similar cases."

Madeleine hesitated, unsure.

"Lucien has never tried to hypnotize you, has he?" Regis asked sharply.

"No. I didn't know he knew how."

"I should have mentioned this before, but I met Lucie
once, years ago. It isn't surprising, really—we live and wor
in a small community. I only met him once, and I had no wa
of connecting Penelope Marsh to him when you called. Hi
company was researching mind-control drugs, and I was ana
lyzing some of their scientists, to be sure the chemicals the
were handling had no ill effects. Lucien thought it was amusin
to hypnotize one of them before sending him in to me, to prov
mind control was possible without drugs. Like all amateurs
Lucien was fascinated by the immediate effects without bein
concerned by the possible side effects. But he assured me h
regarded his power as merely a parlor-game pastime."

"I've never seen him hypnotize anyone."

"Good. And I'm aware of his concern for you. It's mor
than a mere token concern for a valued associate. I believe yo
may be the daughter he never had. But while we're on th
subject of Lucien, I must tell you that I feel strongly that yo
should take control of your own life."

"Meaning?"

"Have you considered giving up the Penelope Marsh rol
and devoting all of your time to your painting, and to wha
you want to do?"

"Yes. But playing the part of Penelope isn't like a job whe
I can just give a couple of weeks' notice and quit. There ar
commitments. And there's my mother."

"And you feel trapped by your commitments?"

"No! I didn't mean that."

"Yet something is causing your nightmares and somnam
bulism."

Two dead men, Madeleine thought. "You mentioned hyp
notherapy?"

"I would attempt to regress you back to the trauma yo
have buried in your subconscious. When we know what it is
I'm confident you will be able to deal with it."

At last there was a glimmer of hope. Madeleine felt tear
spring to her eyes. In her gratitude she flung her arms aroun

172

him impulsively. "Yes, Regis. Hypnotize me, regress me . . . anything to end the nightmares. When shall we begin?"

"Perhaps tomorrow. There are one or two simple exercises to do to find out if you will be a good subject." He looked over her shoulder and saw Lucien coming across the slate-flagged entry hall. Regis did not move from Madeleine's trusting embrace, for fear of shattering their tenuous rapport. Lucien raked him with a single eloquent glance.

Lucien brought over one of his gourmet dinners that evening. He dismissed everyone, including Nurse Williams, while he and Madeleine dined.

"Just like old times, princess." he said, placing a chilled dish containing artichoke hearts, marinated and suspended in aspic, in front of her.

To please him, Madeleine had dressed for dinner in a white evening dress. Her hair was piled on top of her head and fastened with a spray of fresh flowers. Candlelight illuminated the gold cutlery and table centerpiece of red roses. The fragrance of the flowers was lost in the drifting cloud of incense.

Madeleine had long suspected that Lucien's sense of smell was not as keen as his other senses. She was overpowered by the jasmine-scented incense that she was sure burned because Lucien thought she liked it. Lucien had considered her a hippie when he found her on the beach. Occasionally he still made little gestures like lighting the incense candle, and Madeleine was unsure if this was a concession to what he believed she enjoyed, or a subtle reminder of her life before he took her under his wing.

Lucien was busy with the crepes that were to be the next course. His graceful hands moved quickly and efficiently.

"How is the book coming?" Madeleine asked, picking at the artichoke hearts.

"Very well. I'm past the doldrums of the middle and approaching the excitement of the end. It's always easy in the beginning and the end. Like life itself, I suppose. I shall have more time to devote to you, my pet. Has it been terribly boring for you, spending so much time with that white-uniformed wardress and Regis?"

Madeleine murmured noncommittally.

"Odd sort of fellow, isn't he? I'm no longer convinced he is quite as brilliant in his field as I was led to believe. I'd hoped he would make faster progress exorcising Madge."

Lucien placed in front of her the crepes, with a delicately flavored filling of crabmeat and a rich sauce. He picked up his wineglass and surveyed her over the rim. He was dressed in a white dinner jacket, and Madeleine reflected silently that they were like two white-clad ghosts, going through the motions of dining when food was no longer a needed sustenance.

Madeleine said, "Regis is helping me."

"You wouldn't care to have another doctor come in to give us a second opinion?"

"No. I'd rather stay with Regis. I'm getting used to him."

Lucien's lips curved slightly, and he ran his index finger along the thin line of his mustache thoughtfully. "You're not attracted to him, are you, princess? Beware, it's a common pitfall for a patient to fall in love with her doctor."

"Of course not," Madeleine said. Then, because Lucien continued to smile suggestively, she tried to change the subject. "Regis is going to try to hypnotize me, to regress me back to whatever may have caused my sickness.

"Good. I want this whole episode ended and Regis on his way before the last Penelope Marsh book goes to print. I shall need you to play the part to perfection, my dear, so we can gracefully retire dear old Penelope."

"We'll have months, won't we? You haven't finished writing it yet."

Lucien rose and went to the serving cart containing chafing dishes. He began to carve the roast duckling with the precision of a surgeon. "Knowing it is to be the last Penelope Marsh romance, I am giving it my all."

"But it doesn't have to be *your* last book. Why not just write under your own name? Sarita says you could announce

174

that you are Penelope Marsh tomorrow and nothing would really change."

"Sarita talks too much."

"She's in love with you, Lucien."

"Sarita is incapable of loving anyone but herself. She tolerates me for the comfortable job, the exorbitant salary I pay, and the opportunity to spend most of her time in luxurious surroundings. Madeleine, my dear, you are still so very young in many ways. Your definition of love is childlike in the extreme. Someday you will realize what real love is and know all of the imitations and infatuations for what they really are."

"Have you ever known real love, Lucien? Was there ever a woman who was able to make you drop that forbidding facade?"

Lucien contemplated the sliver of roast duckling on his fork for a second, then placed it carefully in his mouth. The expression on his chiseled features was almost sensual as he chewed slowly, savoring the hint of herbs and the bouquet of the wine marinade. His eyes closed, whether in consideration of the depth of her question or in appreciation of his own culinary arts Madeleine did not know.

She looked away, concentrating on her own plate. She had never been able to give herself to the pleasure of eating in the way Lucien did. She strongly suspected he enjoyed it more than his sex life, if indeed he really had one. Sarita threw out not-so-subtle hints about their relationship, but it was difficult to imagine Lucien assuming that expression of rapture while savoring Sarita's body.

"Yes, Madeleine," Lucien said softly. "I have known real love. As you will one day. Be patient. There is a soulmate for everyone."

The bars formed a solid barrier. She turned and saw they were behind her too . . . to the left, to the right. Something—some monstrous unseen presence—whispered obscenities in her ear.

She was crying, she could taste her tears. The black cloud

of evil moved closer, flapping and flitting. She was down on the ground now, her hands over her eyes, trying to blot out the horror about to engulf her. The sound of its voice throbbed in her ear. She could feel the icy touch of fetid breath. The cloying scent. There was something sticky on the ground beneath her knees. She was shivering with cold, but the stickiness was warm, flowing. . . .

Madeleine opened her eyes. Her heart pounded as though it would burst. Darkness was all around her. She was not in her bed. She was kneeling on the ground. No, she felt the cold touch of tile, and something warm trickling about her bare knees. Groping with her hands to feel the floor in front of her, she grasped bare flesh, then wetness. Before her fingers touched the cold hilt of the knife, she knew it was blood that was soaking her.

Madeleine screamed, then scrambled to her feet, slipping on the blood. She collided with a wall and used it to feel her way along to a light switch. In the bright glare that flooded the studio, Madeleine saw the butchered body of Regi Vaughan. On the easel, the faintly smiling portrait of Lola dressed as Clarissa, looked down at the slaughter.

CHAPTER 18

The jet screamed low overhead and touched down with a grinding squeal. Simon watched the plane taxiing along the runway for a moment and then moved away from the terminal window and toward the passenger disembarkation exit.

He recognized Kevin Delaney the moment he appeared. Battered bush hat, khaki safari jacket, ink-black hair sprinkled with gray, and Madeleine's deep-blue eyes. A handsome man, growing a trifle florid with age, but with youthful high spirits and bravado still evident in a cheeky grin.

"Kevin Delaney? I'm Simon Tanning." His hand was taken in a bone-crushing grip.

"Ho, mate. Where's Madeleine? Isn't she with you?" The grin faded. "She's that ill, is she?" Over the years an Australian inflection had crept into his speech. He had worked as a traveling salesman, often flying with bush pilots to remote stations in the great Australian outback.

"I'll explain on the way," Simon said. "Have you been through customs?"

"In New York. Just got to pick up my gear when it's unloaded. Where is my little girl?"

They made their way down the escalator to the luggage carousel and stood waiting.

"She lives in Laguna Beach, in a fancy beach house. There's a nurse and a . . . doctor taking care of her. Kevin, she is ill, but her illness isn't physical."

"Oh, sweet Jesus, not mental? Simon, me boy, I can't stand the helplessness of not being able to do something for a woman whose mind is gone." His rugged features crumpled.

"She isn't insane, but I'm convinced someone is trying to drive her out of her mind. I can't get near her, and I'm afraid she's in terrible danger. But they'll have to let *you* in."

Kevin reached for a canvas bag on the carousel. "Why won't she see you, mate? You told me on the phone you loved each other."

"I'll tell you the whole story on the way home, then you can decide what you want to do. You've come a hell of a long way to get here, Kevin. That alone tells me you care about your daughter. I don't want to know why you've neglected her all these years. What counts is that you're here now when she really needs you."

They walked to the parking lot. Kevin was quick to notice the eyes of every passing woman moved in Simon's direction. Kevin wondered silently if his daughter had been overwhelmed with jealousy, as poor demented Lyla was, so many years ago. Yes, he'd done right to leave for Australia, hard though his life there had been. There'd never been another woman after Lola, not for any length of time anyway. He'd had his mates and his weekend binges and, as the years passed, he'd given up telling himself he'd return to see his only child one day. After all, she'd be a woman by now and probably wouldn't want a drunken old swagman—as he was pleased to call himself, despite its Australian meaning—to cast a blot on her nice suburban life. Probably married, with children . . . she'd be well into her twenties by now.

"A friend loaned me a car," Simon said. "Now I can tell you everything in private."

They were caught in rush-hour traffic on the freeway. As objectively as he could, Simon told Madeleine's father all he knew, not sparing himself in the narrative, nor Madeleine.

"Cor, mate," Kevin breathed. "I don't know what to think. You believe there's some connection with smuggling aliens? Maybe that Mexican, Ramón, blamed my Madeleine for his sister getting hurt. Or maybe some other friend of Dean Jennings' is after her."

"No, I don't think so. Ramón has been deported, and so has Josefa, the maid. And though Dean Jennings took Madeleine to Mexico as cover for his activities, he was killed, or died, before he involved her in any way."

"What about the other fella, Tony Waring, in London? Maybe its someone connected to him."

"Waring's death was definitely an accident. I'm sure Madeleine had nothing to do with it."

"You say your jeep was blown up, your boat sabotaged, and your cat and pigeon poisoned. Boyo, you've got a lot of faith not to believe Madeleine is responsible. If she isn't trying to kill you, and the illegal-alien smugglers aren't, then who is?"

Simon swerved as a motorcycle cut in front of him. "I've a hunch, but I'd rather keep it to myself for the moment. I don't want to cloud your vision with anything but facts."

Kevin frowned, concentrating. He brought up Antoine, and then Sarita, as possible suspects, and when Simon destroyed those arguments he threw up his hands. "Mate, me brain is starting to ache. They won't let you in to see Madeleine. You see a nurse and a doctor going in and out. And yet it's Madeleine you're afraid for, not yourself. If they let me in, what shall I tell her?"

"That I love her," Simon answered softly. "Kevin . . . what about Lola? Will you go and see her? It's none of my business, but I think it would be a good idea. Madeleine will be more kindly disposed toward you if you do."

Kevin sighed. "She's still a vegetable, you say? I'll go. I don't want to, but I will. You say Madeleine has visited her all these years? Mate, that's devotion."

"She is her mother, after all," Simon pointed out.

Kevin turned to stare at him. The flight had been endless, the time difference disorienting. He wasn't sure what day it was, and fatigue was taking its toll. "What are you talking about?" He whistled disbelievingly. "Cor, don't tell me Cilla

Dougall never told her? I asked the old biddy to break it to her gently when things quieted down after Lyla's death."

"I don't understand," Simon said. "What do you mean?"

"Lola ain't Madeleine's mother, mate, that's what I'm telling you."

Madeleine's mother had been the daughter of a successful commercial artist who had married Kevin against her parents' wishes and moved west with him. Their marriage had been brief and stormy. They tore each other to pieces and loved each other to distraction.

Kevin was unfaithful during one drunken period of estrangement. His wife found out and left him. She left the infant Madeleine, only two months old, behind. Kevin believed she'd left the baby because she intended to return as soon as he'd been punished enough. She went home to her parents, called them from the airport, and was tearfully reunited with them.

On the drive from the airport to their home, her father was distracted for a moment and their car plowed into an oncoming truck. All three were killed instantly.

There had been women in all of the small towns scattered throughout the West where Kevin traveled. None of them meant anything more than an overnight diversion when he was on the road. He told Simon that he was wild with grief at the death of Madeleine's mother, and he freely admitted he chose her successor by the simple means of flipping a coin.

"It could just as well have been Lyla as Lola," he confessed. "I needed somebody to take care of the baby while I was on the road. Neither my wife nor I had any relatives."

"What about Cilla Dougall, the woman in Santa Barbara you told Madeleine was your sister?" Simon asked.

"She was married to my brother, but he'd left her before he was killed at Pearl Harbor. Cilla wouldn't take the baby then. She'd just married Dougall, see."

"But why Lola and Lyla? Wouldn't it have been simpler to marry a woman without a sister? I mean, it sounds like you were romantically involved with both of them."

Kevin looked sheepish. "I was. But a baby is a lot of work. I'd resented all the time my wife gave Madeleine. I figured twin sisters was ideal. They were gentle souls—they were already mothering everybody in that little town. I figured the two of them could help with the baby, as well as keep each other company when I was on the road. That was the trouble with Madeleine's mother, see. I left her alone too much. A woman can't take all that loneliness."

"But why didn't any of you tell Madeleine her mother was dead?"

"Lola asked me not to. She wanted Madeleine to believe she was hers. I should have realized things were coming to a head with Lyla, should have known they were both balanced on the edge."

"You didn't sleep with Lyla after you married Lola? Did they know about each other before?"

Kevin shrugged his broad shoulders. There was still a boyish guilelessness about his blue eyes. The clefts in his cheeks and chin gave him a roguish grin that Simon was sure had probably saved him from female wrath on many occasions. "The ladies always were me downfall, boyo. I never could resist the little darlin's. Honest, though, I tried to play it straight with Lola. I had a heart-to-heart with Lyla and explained to her that it was one thing me sneaking around with her when I was just sneaking around with Lola . . ."

Simon blinked and shook his head. "Delaney, I've got to hand it to you for your sheer gall."

"I don't know if Lola ever knew in those early days. She never said anything to me. I'll tell you, it was a bit eerie, making love to Lola, knowing her sister was in the same house. See, before I married Lola, I used to breeze into town and stay a couple of nights at a motel. I'd call the house and whichever sister answered the phone, I'd invite to my room."

Simon shook his head again, at a loss for words.

They reached Simon's apartment. Then ate some sandwiches, and Kevin put away a formidable quantity of beer. Simon had already decided that Kevin would not present himself at Madeleine's house until after he'd had a night's rest. Besides, there was much to be learned and time needed to digest the information before Kevin faced Madeleine.

Although Kevin rambled in the telling of his story, it was fairly easy to piece together what had happened. Kevin had not fooled either sister for a moment, but they had accepted his choice and tried to live with it because they both loved him. For Lyla, the years became an agony of seeing the man she loved retire at night into her sister's embrace. And, because she loved her sister too, pain and guilt, combined with her own need, slowly eroded her fragile hold on sanity. Lyla began to think that she and Lola were one woman and that woman was Kevin's wife.

One night she entered their bedroom and climbed into bed with her sister and brother-in-law. Kevin left the next day and swore to Lola he would not come back unless Lyla moved out of the house. At length Lola begged him to return, telling him that Lyla was herself again. When Kevin returned to them, it did seem that Lyla had forgotten her previous lapse. Lola, however, was troubled by insomnia, brought about by forcing herself to remain awake in case Lyla again tried to force her way into their bedroom. Lola's nerves were ragged from lack of sleep. When she fell into brief periods of exhausted oblivion, she walked in her sleep. Concerned, Kevin drove her into Los Angeles to see a doctor. Sleeping pills were all the doctor could suggest. Lola begged Kevin not to tell Lyla about the pills, because their Christian Science upbringing forbade the use of drugs.

"I was glad to get out of the house, I don't mind telling you, mate," Kevin confided, giving Simon a look of bleary melancholy. "Between one woman pacing the floor at night and the other watching me all day with those hurt eyes. The worst of it was that I was beginning to mix them up. They were identical twins, but I'd always known one from the other. Only now Lola was wild-eyed from lack of sleep, and Lyla was wild-eyed from whatever was ailing her. Lord, I never meant to do it, but I came home one afternoon and Lyla was in our bedroom and I thought she was Lola."

Lyla had not disillusioned him when he took off his clothes, dived into the bed, and smothered her with kisses. He had stopped for several drinks before he arrived home, and in the warm blur of his whiskey-laden passion all he was sure of was the essence of violets and the negligee he had given his wife for her birthday. He had mounted Lyla and was plunging happily into her when Lola returned from the market. At her side was Madeleine. Lola turned and left without a word.

Kevin stumbled from the bed, cursing Lyla, cursing the day he had met the two of them. He swore he would never come back. He'd go to his sister-in-law in Santa Barbara, who had again been widowed, and make arrangements to take Madeleine to her. They were loonies, both of them, and he wanted no part of them. He bade them a last goodbye and left the house.

The police caught up with him a few days later and broke the news. Lyla had taken an overdose of sleeping pills and was dead.

" 'Lyla?' I asked them, over and over again. 'Are you sure it was Lyla?' The pills were prescribed for Lola. Lyla didn't even know about them. You know, Simon, the thing was, when I got home, I wasn't even sure myself which sister was dead. Madeleine was just a little girl, and she said her Aunt Lyla was wearing her mother's negligee and perfume and was dead in her mother's bed. But I kept thinking, she'd been found dead a couple of days *after* that day I found her in our bed and thought she was Lola. Now surely she hadn't stayed there for days, still wearing Lola's negligee. And what about my little girl? God, Simon, I couldn't hardly face her. She'd come in and seen me in bed with her aunt, naked as a jaybird and in the act, large as life."

Simon silently refilled Kevin's glass. Madeleine had not mentioned being present when Lola found Kevin in bed with her twin sister. What if . . . he tried not to form the thought, but everything both Kevin and Madeleine had told him pointed to a certain nagging suspicion. What if everything that Madeleine feared was true? The childhood trauma could have been a little girl administering to her aunt an overdose of sleeping pills because she had hurt her mother. And, at that moment, the other violent personality could have emerged from the dark recesses of Madeleine's mind. What followed from that was almost too painful for Simon to deal with. Wasn't it possible that the other personality also killed Dean and Tony and attempted to kill Simon? All, in a twisted mind, could have been as guilty as Lyla.

CHAPTER 19

With characteristic California abruptness, the weather changed the following morning. Dense white fog swirled in from the sea to join the low cloud cover. The temperature had dropped twenty-five degrees overnight.

Simon closed the window against the seeping chill, and thought how empty the window ledge was without cat and pigeon. Their death had left a hole in his life. He must find time to look in on Dan's sea lions. The mental picture of Madeleine diving into the cold sea to rescue the sea lion pup came into his mind, dispelling the doubts of the previous night. She couldn't be a psychopath; she was too compassionate. His spirits lifted as he remembered that today he might get to see her again.

Kevin Delaney was still snoring in Simon's bed. Simon folded the blanket on the couch where he had spent the night, showered, shaved, and made coffee before Kevin opened an eye and groaned. "Seems to me American beer didn't used to be that strong—not compared to Aussie." He struggled out of bed. "Or maybe I'm just getting old."

"Have some coffee," Simon advised. "I've been thinking about our strategy. Let's just go unannounced. If we phone Sarita ahead of time . . . well, let's just say I trust her as much as I believe in her virginity. Though I did borrow money for our fare to England from her, so I guess I should be more charitable." Simon frowned, remembering that the debt was still outstanding. Sarita had been delighted to put up the money when she heard Madeleine was going to accompany him. Simon insisted it was just a loan and would be repaid. Sarita craftily suggested he consider it expense money in his investigation, and in the haste of departure, the issue had not been resolved.

"You make a living as a P.I.?" Kevin asked.

Simon shook his head vehemently. "I'm new to the game. I doubt I'll pursue the occupation once I find out if Dean Jennings had any connections on this side of the border. I'll leave the coyotes, the wrestler and the others, to the border patrol."

"Then what do you do for a living?" Kevin was demolishing a plate of bacon and eggs, his hangover apparently forgotten.

"I own a boat, or what's left of one. I used to take out vacationers, tours of the local waters, that sort of thing. I tried working indoors once and felt like I'd been sent to jail. Though I still feel like a kid playing hooky sometimes when I'm on my way to the marina and I see the traffic backed up on the freeway headed in the other direction, toward the high-rise offices. Almost everything I want and need in life is out there on the sea."

"Almost?"

"I get lonely. I gave up looking for a woman who'd be willing to share my kind of life long ago. Then I met Madeleine, and I could see how it could work with the two of us. Only I blew it. I wasn't honest with her. It wasn't that I lied to her, exactly. I just didn't tell her everything. You had enough to eat? We should get going."

As they drove down the Coast Highway, Kevin expressed his amazement at the changes that had taken place during his absence. "Where the hell did all the people and buildings come from?" he asked repeatedly. "And the tall buildings! Have they decided there won't be any more earthquakes?"

"They're designed to withstand them. Expect there'll be a few seasick people when the really tall ones sway in a strong tremor. Kevin, have I prepared you for Lucien Cornell? He can be intimidating."

"Madeleine's boss? Oh, sure, mate."

"Apart from everything else—his money and power and position—there's something mesmerizing about him. You find yourself staring into those black eyes of his and forgetting what you were going to say. He has what theater people call a commanding presence. I've been doing some extensive checking on him the last few days. He retired from actively running the company a year or two before the first Penelope Marsh book was published. There had been so many mergers and buy-outs of smaller companies, so much diversification, that it was hard to even find the first company that hired Cornell as a chemist. Apparently he was quite brilliant. He discovered several space-age bonding compounds, among other things."

"His father left him a tidy sum of money, and Lucien bought stock in the company. Eventually he became chairman of the board. They did secret government work in the early days of the Vietnam War. He also published several chemistry textbooks. Then he tried his hand at a mystery novel. I found a copy. It was good, hellishly scary, but it needed editing badly.

After it was published he acquired an agent, who steered him to the historical romances. His agent sold the first of them to a different publisher, under the Penelope Marsh name, since historicals by women writers were more popular."

Kevin nodded. "And Penelope got so popular the press wanted interviews and talk shows were after her. So Cornell hired my daughter to play the part. Simon, did you ever think that could be Madeleine's trouble? When Madeleine was a little girl I remember once she dressed up in Lola's clothes and plastered makeup all over her face. Came clumping down the stairs in high-heeled slippers, false eyelashes stuck on her forehead. We couldn't help but laugh. God, I wish I hadn't. When I pulled myself together and went after the kid, she was sobbing like her heart would break. But she looked up at me with such a look in her eyes, I've never forgotten it. There was a sort of dignity about her when she said to me, 'Daddy, I won't do it again. I won't ever be someone else again. I'm me, aren't I, Daddy? I'm just me.' Simon, I didn't know what to say. She was like a miniature woman speaking to me, instead of a little girl."

Simon swallowed the lump in his throat. "That's her house up ahead. Behind the blank stucco wall."

In response to their summons on the intercom, the wrought-iron gate was opened by a strange Mexican maid. She led them silently through the atrium, along the hall, and into the living room. The fog was still hanging thickly over the ocean, blotting out the view and filling the room with ghostly gray light.

Madeleine was sitting in the window, staring into the fog. Lucien occupied a chair near the sputtering log fire. He had a yellow legal-size notepad on his lap, which he placed on a table before rising to greet them. Both Simon and Kevin stared at the back of Madeleine's head, but she did not turn around.

"So, Mr. Tanning," Lucien said, his eyes raking the two men. "You turned up the long-lost father. I'm afraid Madeleine isn't terribly interested, but I had you admitted because I was curious about a man who would abandon his daughter. Princess, aren't you even a little interested in what he looks like after all these years?"

Madeleine's head turned slowly, a jerky, puppetlike movement. Simon was shocked at the blank expression on her face. He caught his breath, taking a step toward her before Lucien raised his hand.

"Keep your distance, young man." Lucien's pale fingers pressed a button on the side of his chair. Instantly the door opened and a stone-faced man entered the room. Simon recognized him as the one Madeleine called Sedgewick.

Glancing from Lucien to his bodyguard, Simon fought a wild urge to smash their heads together. He wanted to drag Lucien around the room by his throat, and to hell with the gun bulging significantly in Sedgewick's pocket. Simon had a strong feeling the gun was for show and the man would not use it. He would not have felt the same had Lucien's other guard been there, Bruno of the maniacal grin. Simon did not pause to reflect that the pacifism he had practiced since returning from Vietnam was being severely challenged.

Kevin Delaney brushed a tear clumsily from his cheek as he stared at his daughter. "Lord, Madeleine, you look just like your mother," he began, but Lucien interrupted.

"I assume you want money. How much?"

"Money!" Kevin gasped indignantly. "I came to see my little girl, dammit, not to be insulted by you, mate." He clenched his fists and glared defiantly at Sedgewick.

Madeleine stood up unsteadily, gripping her chair for support. Simon could see she was deathly pale, and there were dark circles under her eyes. "Please, Lucien, it's all right. How are you, Father? Have you seen Mother?" Her voice was a whisper.

Simon shot Kevin a warning glance. This was not the time to break the news that Lola was not Madeleine's mother. Madeleine was weak, disoriented, but trying valiantly to get hold of herself. If Simon had not heard her say so vehemently that she was afraid of drugs, he would have sworn she was under the influence of a powerful tranquilizer.

"I came to see you first, daughter. Are you all right? Simon tells me you haven't been well."

"I'm fine, thank you. You'll need directions to the sanitarium. Lucien, would you mind?"

"Not at all," Lucien said smoothly. "Sarita will give you a map. I'll send for her. She wishes to speak to you, Mr. Tanning, about your agreement with her." He nodded toward Sedgewick, who disappeared. Lucien turned to Kevin and said amiably, "It will be pleasant this time of the year in the desert. No doubt you remember, Mr. Delaney, that our climate is such that we can be cold and damp along the coast while the sun blazes on the deserts on the other side of the mountains."

Sarita appeared, subdued in a severely tailored suit. Simon noted the outsize sunglasses, and the reason for them. Her silvery-blond hair was badly in need of washing and reminded him vaguely of unkempt cotton candy.

It's all a charade, Simon thought, as Sarita said in a flat, rehearsed voice, "I wish to terminate your employment as an investigator on my behalf, Mr. Tanning. You can keep the money I paid you."

"I wasn't working for you, Sarita, and you know it," Simon said. "What are you trying to do?"

Lucien's voice cut in. "Mr. Tanning, did you or did you not accept a sum of money from my secretary?"

"Yes, but—"

"Then there's no more to be said. It's irrelevant anyway. I thought we might as well tidy up loose ends. The matter is of complete indifference to Madeleine."

Simon felt a rising sense of panic. Any moment he and Kevin would be out on the street, and nothing had been accomplished. "Mr. Delaney would like to speak with the doctor who is treating Madeleine." He appealed to her directly. "Madeleine, your father has come all the way from Australia. You can surely spend a little time alone with him."

Madeleine's expression remained uninterested, but when she raised her eyes to his he could see reflected there the hurt accusation. The pain in her eyes was more than his deceiving

her about Sarita hiring him. Someone had told her something
else, something about him that wasn't true. I've got to see her
alone, he thought.

"The doctor is out of town at the moment," Lucien put in
"Where are you staying, Mr. Delaney? I'll have him contac
you."

"Good God," Kevin said suddenly. He was staring at
picture hanging over the fireplace, seeing it for the first tim
since he had entered the room. Simon's attention had bee
riveted on the window where Madeleine stood, but now h
turned and saw that the seascape that had hung there formerl
had been removed. In its place was a portrait of a woma
dressed in eighteenth-century costume. She was a lovel
woman with a sensual but vacant smile. There was a forbiddin
background of crenellated castle walls and gun embrasures
gloomy chambers and sinister faces were superimposed ove
dungeon walls.

"Lola or Lyla?" Kevin muttered under his breath. He turne
to Madeleine for an answer, but she had sunk wearily into he
chair again and was staring at the fogbound sea.

"I see you are admiring your daughter's rendition of m
deadly lady," Lucien said, turning to follow their gaze. "She'
lovely, is she not? Lovely, but heartless and cruel. Her nam
is Clarissa." A small smile of pleasure plucked at his thin lip
as he looked up at the portrait. "She is exactly as I describ
her in *Desire's Fury*. How could anyone resist a book wit
Clarissa tempting them from the cover? So you see, even whe
Penelope retires, there is still a plan in the cosmos for M
deleine and me. She is the gifted artist who will render pain
ings of my fictional characters. There is always a reason f
meetings and partings. Although we mortals sometimes co
fuse the reasons. Do you not agree?"

"Madeleine was always clever at drawing, a throwback
her grandfather, I reckon. When she was a little girl I used
save my old advertising brochures for her."

"I'm afraid we're tiring Madeleine," Lucien said. "Sari
will take care of you gentlemen and show you out."

Simon glanced at Madeleine, who did not turn around, and then at Sedge, who shifted his weight and let his hand stray to his pocket. Simon said, "We'd better go, Kevin. The phone number and address are the same, Sarita."

The fog was thicker than ever. Simon inched Dan's car up the highway.

Kevin grumbled, "I still think we should have hung round."

"I'm going to get in there and see Madeleine alone." Simon leaned closer to the windshield, peering through the empty mist, reminded of Madeleine's empty expression. "I'll see her tonight, after dark. But first we're going to see if Regis Vaughan really is out of town. Whatever else he is, he is a qualified M.D. and psychiatrist. I can't believe he'd go away and leave Madeleine in that state. I hardly recognized her."

"You think Lola still looks like that portrait? God, Simon, that was the thing about the twin sisters—they looked like sensuous angels if you can say such a thing and it not be blasphemy. They were ladies—gentle, well bred—but by God, in the sack they were something else. You could see it in their smiles. Couldn't you see the promise in that smile, Simon?"

"Kevin, do you think either of them was fooling around with another man while you were on the road?"

Kevin squirmed in the passenger seat. "Christ, I hope not. Or do I? I've been taking the blame for what happened all these years. But what if there was another man? God knows they weren't spring chickens when I first met them, nor virgins either. And neither of them had been married before."

"It's just a thought. It occurred to me that Lucien never mentioned that Madeleine had painted a portrait of Lola. I wondered if he was aware of it, or if he had ever met Lola as a young woman."

"If Cornell had ever met Lola and Lyla, I'd have known. They lived in a small town. Besides, Madeleine would have remembered him."

"There was something about the way he looked at the picture," Simon said, groping in his memory for what had seemed odd at the time. "It was eerie, almost as if he were putting himself into the picture, or knew the woman personally."

Simon wiped the steam from inside the windshield. "Something is nagging at me, something I heard or saw that should give me a clue about what's going on. Perhaps it was the way he looked at the picture, the way he said 'Clarissa.' I don't know. . . ."

The fog was beginning to dissipate by the time they reached the freeway. An hour later they were parking in front of a small brick building hidden behind a screen of tropical plants. "We've got to find out what Vaughan's prognosis is, and he's sedating her," Simon said as they walked into the reception area. "She told me she'd never agree to drug therapy, yet she looked stoned out of her mind."

Simon told the receptionist, "We must see Dr. Vaughan right away. It's an emergency."

The receptionist looked him over carefully, checking his left hand, then gave him a dazzling smile. "I'm sorry, Dr. Vaughan was called out of town a few days ago."

Simon leaned on the counter and smiled back engagingly. "But you have an emergency number where you can reach him."

"No. I'm sorry. Dr. Whitaker is taking all his calls. He's our staff doctor here. Are you a patient of Dr. Vaughan's?"

"The patient is Madeleine Delaney. Get Dr. Whitaker out here, would you? It's urgent."

She hesitated, then picked up the phone in front of her and said, "A gentleman to see Dr. Whitaker urgently. It's about Madeleine Delaney, one of Dr. Vaughan's patients." She smiled again at Simon. "If you'll have a seat in the waiting room."

They waited fifteen minutes and then a portly, balding man in a wrinkled green surgical gown appeared. "I'm Dr. Whitaker. I'm afraid you must have the wrong Dr. Vaughan. We've checked our Dr. Vaughan's records carefully, and he had no patient named Madeleine Delaney."

Simon flashed his wallet, containing his investigator's license. "Regis Vaughan. He's about five-eleven—fortyish, white hair, hazel eyes, wears expensive clothes with running shoes. Drives a Mercedes. Recently made a fast trip to England."

Whitaker blinked. "I'm sorry. The truth is, we don't know where Dr. Vaughan is. Several days ago we received a rather cryptic note from him, saying he was taking a short vacation because he'd been under a personal strain. He said he had to get away for a time and he'd be in touch. We haven't seen him since he left here last Friday in response to a call from one of his nurses. The note was delivered the following day."

"Was it a handwritten note?"

"No, it was typed, but signed by him, I'm sure. If the patient is in distress, we would be happy to help her, Mr. . . . ?"

"Tanning. I suggest you file a missing-persons report on Vaughan without further delay. Come on, Kevin, let's go. I've got a suspicion that time is running out."

CHAPTER 20

Nurse Williams had been dismissed. Madeleine wished she were still in the house. But there were only Lucien, Sarita, and Sedge. And tonight there would be only Lucien. Sarita would go home to her apartment, and Sedge would discreetly disappear while Lucien joined her for dinner.

Madeleine struggled with the lethargy that had overcome her. Not even seeing Simon again—and her father, after all these years—had penetrated the fog that enclosed her mind. Dragging limbs that were like lead, she moved from the bathroom to the bedroom.

A dress box lay on her bed, and beside it the new gown Lucien had brought for her. It was identical in every detail to the dress Madeleine had painted for Lola in the portrait. The pale icy-blue gauze was gossamer-fine and would, when worn by a flesh-and-blood woman, reveal every inch of her body.

Madeleine had taken the sedative willingly at first. Anything to blot out the horror of Regis' body lying in a pool of blood, the butcher knife protruding from his chest. Staggering down the spiral staircase, she had called in vain for Nurse Williams. When Madeleine was certain she was alone in the house she telephoned Lucien and, after what seemed an eternity, he appeared at her door.

He asked no questions but made her bathe, change her nightgown, and then take a strong sedative. She lay in her bed, all of the lights blazing, listening to the sounds of Lucien dragging the body down the stairs, cleaning the bloody trail.

At length, in spite of herself, she slept. Opening her eyes next morning, she looked into Lucien's concerned smile. He sat beside her bed, immaculate and unruffled.

"Did I kill Regis? Was he dead? Oh, God, let me have dreamed it."

"Madge killed him," Lucien said. "You are not responsible for what Madge does. Princess, drink this and take this pill."

She protested feebly, but obeyed. She was shaking violently. After a few minutes everything Lucien was saying made perfect sense. There was really no need for her to be concerned. After all, Madeleine was not a murderer. Madge was solely responsible.

No, Regis was no longer in the house. No, there would be

194

no police or questions. Nurse Williams was gone too. She had received a sudden summons to the bedside of her sister in the East and had left immediately. That was why Regis had come over. He had volunteered to take the nurse's place overnight. "Hush, princess, sleep, dear. You are so very tired. . . ."

Madeleine was not sure how many days had passed. Somewhere deep in her numbed senses a small voice kept trying to be heard. Call the police—call someone. Do something. Later, perhaps. Later I won't be so tired.

She had no energy to paint, so spent her days lying on the chaise or sitting in the window, either staring out to sea or reading all of the Penelope Marsh books again. She skimmed through *Devil's Desire* and *Temples of Love*, lingered over *Sweet Fulfillment* and *Promise of Love*, but read every word of *Desire's Fury*, and then immediately started to read it again.

Lucien was pleased with her. He cooked delicacies to tempt her appetite, brought her soothing drinks, massaged her shoulders, neck, and temples, brushed her hair gently.

"How idyllic it is," he said, smiling benevolently at her. "Just the two of us, like this. Although I must have Sarita come in and type the final draft of *Deadly Lady*. After that I shall dispense with Sarita's services. I gave my princess my word, did I not? No more Penelope Marsh. And I have never broken my word."

Sarita finished typing the manuscript that afternoon. The dinner was to be a celebration. The appearance that morning of Simon and her father had been a surprise to all of them. Madeleine was still amazed that she had taken it all so calmly. Nothing seemed to matter to her anymore.

The manuscript for *Deadly Lady* was neatly stacked in a box on the hallstand, ready to go to the post office for mailing to Lucien's New York agent. Madeleine had glanced at it longingly as she went upstairs for her shower. She had read all of the novel except for the last chapter. Sarita brought a portable typewriter over and typed the final chapter with Lucien at her side, making last-minute changes. They used Madeleine's living room, as Lucien did not want to leave Madeleine alone, but she had been in her bedroom and did not hear how the story ended.

Madeleine slipped the filmy gauze over her head. She surveyed her reflection in the mirror and said, "You're Lucien's deadly lady."

The title reverberated in her head. There would be a carbon copy of the manuscript somewhere downstairs; Sarita always made one. It was probably still in the living room, ready for Lucien to take home with him later. Madeleine steadied herself by placing her hand on the banister at the top of the stairs. The spiral staircase writhed before her blurred vision. *Got to get hold of myself. No more pills. Musn't take any more of Lucien's pills.* She slid one foot tentatively forward and found the first step.

She did not know why she felt compelled to read that last chapter, considering the effort it took merely to walk, but she was driven by some undefined force. There would never be a better opportunity. Sarita was gone. Lucien was busy in the kitchen with some culinary delight. She could see Sedge patrolling the beach below the house.

Reaching the living room door, she stood for a moment, taking deep breaths until a wave of dizziness passed. There was a manila folder on the table. She moved toward it groggily, picked up the folder and collapsed into the nearest chair. Beads of perspiration dotted her brow and upper lip, her hands were cold and shaking. She read every word, slowly, painstakingly, fighting to concentrate:

Marsh/DEADLY LADY CHAPTER 24 PAGE 303
 The gale shrieked along the edge of the cliff as though trying to tear the castle from its foundations. Rain pelted the windows and hissed down the chimneys. Pacing the great hall, Sir Giles slammed his fist into the palm of his hand impotently.
 "Sir," the elderly steward said nervously, "shall I go

upstairs and fetch her ladyship? She was not expecting you, sir."

Raindrops dripped from Sir Giles' cloak, and his boots were spattered with mud. His leanly handsome features were contorted with pain and rage, but his voice, when he spoke, was coolly objective. "The carriage, steward, which bears the coat of arms of my rival, and which presently awaits his pleasure in my stable—you will instruct one of the stable boys to drive it back to Trelane Hall. A horse for the boy's return can be harnessed to the carriage."

"But sir—" The steward broke off before he said what would surely have cost him a beating. After all, the steward reasoned, perhaps Sir Giles was unaware that Sir Stephen Trelane was at this moment in Lady Clarissa's boudoir. Oh, lord in heaven, the steward prayed, his knees shaking, let them hear the master's voice and let Sir Stephen be gone before he goes upstairs to her.

The steward, in common with the rest of the servants and, indeed, with everyone who knew Clarissa, felt a compelling loyalty toward the lady. They had no way of knowing that her beauty and gentle manner were but a cunning mask that hid not only her infidelities but the wanton destruction of the men who loved her.

Sir Giles stared into the leaping flames of the fire. Hellfire, he thought, could it be worse than the hell Clarissa had created for him here on earth? "Are you still there, steward?" he asked, without looking around.

"I be on my way to the stable, sir," the steward said, although he had not moved.

"Go, then. And upon your return, bring me brandy. Bring me a great deal of brandy, steward. Then you will take more wine up to my wife and her guest. You will take my very special brew to them."

The storm that raged within him made that puny effort of nature outside pale by comparison. Yet he was in complete and absolute control. Sir Giles picked up the brass poker and nudged the blazing log.

He knew this was Clarissa's last night in her mortal body. There could be no further duels for her honor, no more forgiving and starting anew. Sir Giles had suffered more torment at her fair hands than any human could be expected to withstand. This was her last wanton act of cruelty.

That he must die with her Sir Giles knew and accepted. Their love would endure only when their spirits were freed from their mortal coil. But first, Stephen Trelane would die . . . slowly, horribly.

Clarissa sighed and lowered her eyelids so that her gold-tipped lashes brushed the tenderly curved cheekbones. Her heart was beating audibly as his hand closed over her breast. She made no move to stop him, knowing she could not. Her flesh was too weak; she had never been able to resist a hot-blooded young man with broad shoulders and firmly muscled thighs. She was insatiable and hated herself for her affliction. If only she could have been worthy of her husband. He was worth a score of such men as Stephen Trelane. While Sir Giles occupied himself with noble quests that of necessity took him from her side, the faithless Clarissa melted into the arms of the nearest oaf wearing breeches.

Clarissa gasped and Stephen cursed with annoyance when there was a timid knock on the door. They barely had time to cover themselves when a serving wench entered the room. She carried a fresh bottle of wine. "I'm sorry, milady, I brought the wrong wine with dinner. Please, milady, the butler will whip me if he finds I did not follow his instructions. This is the one I was supposed to bring. Please let me pour you a glass now."

Stephen laughed at the girl's discomfort. "Pour away, wench. We would not want to see your fair skin marked by your master's whip. I daresay we can find room for another glass of Sir Giles' finest brew, can we not, Clarissa?"

Clarissa merely nodded, the white heat of her passion

*scalding her. The pause in their lovemaking fueled her
desire to fever pitch. Mercifully, the cork had already been
removed from the wine bottle, and the girl filled their goblets and withdrew. Stephen surveyed her over the rim of his
glass, then raised it in a silent toast and drained the wine.
"Drink, my love," he said, licking the ruby liquid from his
lips.*

Madeleine started as she heard Lucien's voice in the kitchen.
He was on the phone, telling his agent the manuscript would
be on its way in the morning. She skimmed rapidly through
the rest of the chapter. Sir Giles had put a powerful but slow-
acting poison in the wine which caused brief periods of
oblivion, and hallucinations lasting many hours. The horror of
the periods of consciousness was heightened by the gruesome
tortures inflicted upon Stephen Trelane as he hung, manacled,
from the dungeon wall. Clarissa was forced to watch.

Madeleine looked away, the words fading out of focus.
Lucien had so graphically brought the scene to life that Madeleine could almost hear sizzling flesh and feel the agonizing
pain of branding irons and thumbscrews.

What is Lucien doing? she thought, horrified. How can
readers accept a hero such as Sir Giles? She skimmed rapidly
through the remaining pages.

The novel ended with Sir Giles strangling Clarissa as he
made love to her. He then leaped with her body in his arms
from a parapet on the castle to the storm-tossed sea below.
Stephen Trelane was taking his last breath at the same instant.

Madeleine closed the manila folder. She was shaking, and
her legs were numb. Black despair swept over her.

Remembering Lucien's previous Penelope Marsh books,
Madeleine realized with a jolt that *Deadly Lady* was a radical
departure from the earlier successful historical romances. Nor
was Clarissa, in this second book of her adventures, his usual
heroine. Although she had started out in the earlier book as
a pure spirited young woman whose sensual appetites had not
yet been awakened, in *Deadly Lady* Clarissa had become a

faithless wanton with whom no reader would be able to identify.

The violent ending to *Deadly Lady* would surely never be approved by Lucien's editor and publisher. Why had he written such a book? The entire manuscript seemed almost to have been written by a deranged imitator of Lucien's earlier style.

Madeleine looked down at the dress she was wearing. The dress described as Clarissa's gown in her death scene. Her skin crawling, Madeleine wanted to tear the dress from her body. But at that moment Lucien came into the room.

He looked at her in surprise. "I thought you were still upstairs, dressing. Oh, princess, you wore the dress. Magnificent, magnificent. Stand up and let me admire you."

As unobtrusively as she could, Madeleine slipped the manila folder to the seat of her chair as she stood up. She turned around, pirouetting grotesquely, acutely aware that Lucien was carrying a bottle of wine. The wine . . . he's been giving me sedatives in the wine. And the iron pills are probably sedated as well. I took some in London, and Regis found me babbling incoherently. Got to . . . get hold of myself. Must think. Why? Why? To keep me here, dependent on him . . . to keep me from going to the police, or committing myself. He means well, but this isn't the answer.

She jumped as Lucien moved silently behind her and placed his hands on her waist. He turned her to face him. She was aware again of the bony angles of his body beneath the dinner jacket, the gaunt hollows of his cheeks, the shadows of his eyesockets. His fingers felt cold through the thin material of her dress.

"We will drink to your loveliness, princess, as well as a toast to launch the last Penelope Marsh novel." His cool fingers drifted to her hair, brushing back an errant strand. "In the novel I gave you fair hair, so they wouldn't recognize you, my love. But your own dark hair is more beautiful than any golden locks. Your hair is rich, lustrous—it feels like silk to my touch."

"You're forgetting, Lucien," Madeleine said lightly. "I am

Penelope—the author—not Clarissa, the heroine. You've been working too hard, you know. And you've been worrying about me. I love you for it, but you've got to send me to a hospital, and then you must rest."

His hands fell from her waist, and he moved to the Spanish-style bar in the corner of the room, where the wineglasses stood. Madeleine stared at the red liquid, glowing in the light from the fire. She could not dispel the images from the book. It was little wonder that Lucien was troubled by the same problem. He had lived with his characters through two hefty volumes, thinking of them day and night even when he was not actively writing. She remembered hearing a conversation about writers when she was at college. Someone had pointed out the number of authors who descended into madness and the statistics about alcoholism among writers. Someone else had asked if possibly it was not so much that the profession caused the afflictions, but that it attracted those already afflicted.

Lucien was watching her, and she had the uneasy feeling he could read her thoughts. Aloud, she said, "It must be quite a letdown, when you finish a book." She was thinking about what many Penelope Marsh fans had told her— "You know, I *dream* about your characters, they are so real."

"A sense of relief, nothing more," Lucien said, bringing the glass of wine to her. He raised his own glass. "To my deadly lady, and to the death of *your* deadly lady."

Madeleine brought the glass to her lips, but did not drink. "I'm not sure I want to drink to Madge's death, Lucien. Isn't that my own death too?"

"Not at all. Madge will disappear and you will be whole. Her death is a figure of speech only. Now drink up and I'll serve you a meal fit for a queen."

"Lucien, could I have an ice cube for it?"

He frowned. "Ice is death to wine, Madeleine. You know that."

"Please?" Somewhere on the edge of her thoughts a small

voice ridiculed: So you switch wine glasses, as in the old movies; *his* glass is empty—what now?

"Very well. How can I deny you anything tonight?" He went back to the kitchen, and she walked unsteadily to the dining alcove overlooking the sea.

When he returned she was seated at the table, watching the white sails of a boat out on the bay. The night was clear, and moonlight shimmered on the surface of the water. The sail was barely visible. Madeleine thought idly that the harbor patrol should be more alert to boats without running lights.

The tiny ice cube in her glass was not enough to dilute the wine, and whatever else the glass contained. "To your book, Lucien," she said. She picked up her water glass and drank.

"You toast my book in water? Come now, princess." There was an edge to his voice.

"Tonight I don't want to dull my palate with wine," she said. "No, don't tell me that my appetite will be enhanced. I'm honestly sick to death of wine."

"How very perverse of you, Clarissa," Lucien murmured.

Madeleine caught her breath. "Clarissa?" she repeated. Her hands felt clammy as she kneaded them under the table.

Lucien laughed. "A slip of the tongue, princess. Perhaps you're right. Perhaps I have been working too hard on the book. This one did seem to drain me more than the others." He placed a covered dish in front of her. "Tonight we are having a meal as authentically eighteenth-century as I have been able to make it. I couldn't find any swallow's tongues, nor could I bring myself to singe a live goose. Did you know our ancestors used to tie a live goose in the center of a circle of fires, and it ran frantically around singeing its flesh—"

"Please, Lucien, spare me!"

"They were so marvelously cruel. It was an art with them. As I was saying, the best I could do for our dinner is beef cooked over a wood fire on a spit, and only those vegetables that are in season, with specially selected herbs, of course."

She barely tasted the food, but ate with dogged determination. She had the vague idea that the effect of the last sedatives she had taken would be diminished by the intake of a large amount of food. Lucien was in an expansive frame of mind; he talked endlessly and appeared not to notice how much trouble she had merely staying awake. In the candlelight he appeared to her like some splendidly sinister demon. Shadows played across his sculptured features and deepened the blackness of his hair and brows. His eyes seemed to have taken on the reflective quality of dark mirrors, in which it seemed the fires of hell itself danced and flickered.

"A writer's world is the total realm of experience and thought," he was saying. "My writing has plunged me into areas of consciousness I never would have dared imagine existed. There is a satisfying harmony to fiction not present in life."

"Do you see all of us as an assortment of character traits, Lucien? Do you say, 'Let me see, I need a streak of blind loyalty, so I'll lift that trait from Sedgewick, a total lack of subtlety, so I'll describe Sarita.'"

Lucien smiled secretively. His eyes glowed with appreciation as she spoke, as though contemplating something for which he could take the entire credit.

"What about that man you hired with the demon grin—Bruno? If ever there was a sadistic small-time hood type, it is he. Is that why you hired him, to describe him in a book?"

Lucien laughed delightedly. "Isn't he marvelous? I found him in Las Vegas, working for the criminal element there. Yes, good old Bruno comes as close to being perfectly cast as it's possible for a real person to be. But don't let that demented smile deceive you. He's no idiot. In fact he has a superior, if slightly distorted, intelligence. Sedgewick doesn't like him, but Sedgewick is getting old and soft. I intend to retire him from the security division. If Bruno works out, I shall give him Sedgewick's job."

So that was why Sedgewick had been looking somewhat thoughtful lately, Madeleine thought. She squirmed uncomfortably as Lucien's stare seemed to pierce her brain.

Lucien was sitting with his back to the undraped window,

and every time Madeleine looked beyond his face she saw the same small boat circling the bay, the one without lights. When the boat passed through a broad beam of moonlight she could see that it was a catamaran; the twin pontoons were clearly visible. It was not, therefore, Simon Tanning's boat. Why should it be? *Because I need him desperately. I'm suddenly afraid of Lucien.*

CHAPTER 21

Simon had seen Sedgewick patrolling the beach late that afternoon. Waiting until dusk, Simon eased Dan's Hobie-Cat over the light swells, eyes searching for offshore rocks as he tacked in close to the beach. There was a moderate surf running, and while he had no wish to smash Dan's boat, there was no other way to get into the house except from the private beach.

In the moonlight it was difficult to judge the size of the approaching waves. He moved in closer to the white rim of surf, then held his breath as he felt the boat picked up on the crest of a rolling breaker. The ride to the beach was fast and nerve-wracking, but the Hobie slid down the front of the wave like a surfboard and glided smoothly toward the beach.

Simon jumped into the shallow water and pulled the boat up to the dry sand. The beach was dark and deserted. On the clifftop Madeleine's house showed dim lights. Picking his way carefully up the shifting trail, Simon thought about the pieces of information that had dropped into place during the crowded hours since they had visited Madeleine. Was it only yesterday morning?

It had been Kevin's idea to look for the nurse who had cared for Madeleine. They called Regis Vaughan's partner, Dr. Whitaker, and asked if there was a special nurse or nurses they used for in-home treatment. An agency, he was told, supplied temporary help. The agency was most helpful. Yes, Dr. Vaughan had called for a nurse to live in at a house in Laguna Beach. A Miss Williams had been sent there. Yes, they would be happy to have Nurse Williams return the call. She usually checked in each evening to see if there were any messages.

Nurse Williams was indignant when she called. "Look, if you're a friend of Miss Delaney's, I suggest you tell Dr. Vaughan she shouldn't be left alone. Quit? I didn't quit. I was dismissed. Mr. Cornell came over to the house and told me my services wouldn't be needed any longer and I was to pack and leave there and then. Miss Delaney was sleeping. What could I do? It was Mr. Cornell who was paying me. I phoned Dr. Vaughan, and he was as surprised as I was. He said to do as I was told, and he'd be right over to talk to Mr. Cornell."

"When was that?" Simon asked.

"Let me see . . . Friday night."

"Friday. The day Vaughan disappeared. And you're sure he was going over there?"

"He was there before I left. I wasn't about to leave my patient, sleeping or not, until someone took over."

"Did you hear anything of his conversation with Cornell?"

"No. I just picked up my paycheck and left."

Simon paused just below the top of the cliff. From the beach below came the unmistakable bark of a sea lion. Damn. One of them had followed the Hobie. He waited a moment, but the bark was not repeated, and the sound did not appear to have alerted anyone to his presence. He was just below the retaining wall that marked the beginning of the terraced gardens of Madeleine's house.

First Ramón, then Josefa, now Vaughan. All had disappeared after being involved with Madeleine—to say nothing of Tony Waring and Dean Jennings. And then there were the attempts on his own life to consider—Myron's jeep, the poisoned cat and pigeon, the explosion on his boat. All of this, he was sure, had been the work of one person. Simon cursed the time he had lost chasing the red herring of the illegal-alien smugglers. Dean Jennings' ugly profession had nothing to do with his death. Dean Jennings had died for the same reason Tony Waring died—and probably Ramón and Regis Vaughan. The two women, Josefa and Nurse Williams, had been spared because they were not a threat. Simon was sure Josefa would be found in Tijuana somewhere, waiting for another coyote to bring her back across the border. But the men had all loved Madeleine or lusted after her—or someone thought they did. That was the common denominator.

Simon had not told Kevin of his fears. The two men had gone over every possibility. Every shred of information had been pooled and dissected. Pacing the apartment, long into the night, Simon drew a thread of suspicion from the maze of bits and pieces and half-formed ideas. But was there any real basis for his theories? That was the nagging doubt.

He reasoned that Madeleine's other personality emerged when Tony Waring made love to her. The murderous Madge had then hibernated until Dean Jennings made love to Madeleine, almost as though the alter personality was jealous of Madeleine's lovers. The emergence of the other personality also coincided with another change in her life. She had become "Penelope Marsh" and moved into Lucien Cornell's world.

Had Lucien been the trigger to release the darker side of Madeleine's personality?

He had taken under his wing a sensitive and unsophisticated girl who was afraid of physical love because she had seen what it did to her family, despite the fact that Madeleine had blotted out the memory of being with her mother when they found

206

Kevin in bed with Lyla. Lucien had molded the artistic free spirit that was Madeleine, creating a sophisticated woman who wore the right clothes, dined elegantly, rode in a Rolls-Royce, and moved in expensive and insulated surroundings. He had shut her away from the world except to take her out occasionally and show her off as "Penelope Marsh," a creature of his imagination as surely as any of the fictional characters he created.

Simon stopped pacing and slapped his forehead as suddenly his speculation showed him another possibility. And a motive for it.

Lucien had indeed been Madeleine's mentor for three years. What if, like Svengali, he had created a woman and then fallen in love with her?

For Lucien, the woman's image, like everything else in his life, must be perfect. She could not be allowed to give herself to another man.

The other man must be destroyed and Madeleine taught a lesson. She would awaken to find her lover dead at her side. Lucien must have been hard on their heels when she and Tony Waring arrived in London. Madeleine was given a strong sedative while Tony was injected with salmonella.

Dean Jennings presented a problem, since no one knew where his body was or what exactly had killed him. Then Simon remembered something he had turned up while checking on Lucien's background. Agri-Chem, the first company Lucien had worked for as a chemist, was engaged in chemical-warfare research for the government during the Vietnam War. There was one particularly gruesome chemical Agri-Chem was studying, a chemical which, when placed on the human skin, could penetrate the epidermis and take with it into the bloodstream the bacteria normally found there. Once the bacteria were in the bloodstream, however, they would swiftly kill the victim. Even if a postmortem were performed, the process of death would be almost undetectable. Especially, Simon reasoned, to a small-town Mexican doctor.

Simon had no way of knowing whether or not Dean Jennings

had died from the application of that chemical nor whether Lucien had administered it. But he wanted to believe that Madeleine was not a killer despite the doubts that assailed him.

The lights in the house were dim. Simon approached the window cautiously, inching along the wooden deck. He could not hear anything from inside. Lucien and Madeleine had just finished dinner.

Madeleine was dressed in pale blue, a floating creation that looked vaguely familiar. She still moved in that listless way that was totally unlike the vibrant woman he had first met. She was saying something, her lips moving slowly as she supported her head on her hand. Lucien nodded, turning his head slightly to show his profile. Simon thought grudgingly that it was a splendidly decadent and Satanic profile. Lucien rose and moved to Madeleine's side of the table, helping her to her feet. His eyes glowed in the darkness, in the manner of a nocturnal hunter stalking his prey. Simon considered risking Sedgewick and his gun to plunge to the rescue, but at that moment Madeleine made her way toward the spiral staircase. Lucien did not follow her.

You're reading all sorts of danger into an ordinary situation, Simon told himself. Lucien had suddenly become an almost supernatural menace, with little to go on but his association with a company that had experimented with, and eventually discarded, chemicals dangerous to human life—plus the man's known power to hypnotize. That, Simon thought, and the fact that I'm afraid he's in love with Madeleine. Am I just afraid to compete with him? What can I offer her compared to all of this?

Inside the living room, Sedgewick had appeared. Lucien spoke to him and then disappeared into the hall. Simon barely had time to plunge into the tangle of bougainvillea vines before Sedgewick stepped out on deck. He walked the length of the structure and then went back into the house, moving through the living-room door and out of sight.

Simon opened the sliding glass door and stepped inside. A

fire in the grate illuminated the room, but all of the lights had been turned out. He went through the hall and up the stairs. He could hear Sedgewick in the kitchen, clattering dishes. No doubt finishing up Lucien's gourmet meal.

Madeleine was not in her bedroom. The bed was undisturbed and the room in darkness. Simon went up the short flight of stairs leading to the studio and pushed open the door.

She was sitting in front of her easel, staring up at a canvas in progress. The room was flooded with moonlight but was damp and cold. The pale light touched the painting and revealed a series of scenes, each blending into the next. Several women were in various poses, one peering with frightened eyes from the window of a carriage, another tied to a four-poster bed. He caught his breath as he recognized the face staring with mute appeal from behind the barred dungeon door. Madeleine herself. She heard him then and turned her head. "Lucien?"

"He's gone, Madeleine. I had to see you alone." He dropped down beside her, taking her limp hand into his. He kneaded her fingers, trying to bring her back to life.

"You've been drugged, Madeleine—or hypnotized, or both. Lucien is using some means to keep you docile and subservient. Madeleine, try to think. Can you tell me what happened to Regis Vaughan?"

Even in the moonlight, which created shifting patterns as errant clouds drifted across the sky, Simon could see the fear in her eyes at the mention of Vaughan's name.

"I killed him."

Simon took a deep breath. "Do you remember killing him? Madeleine, you're weak as a kitten. How did you do it?"

"Madge did it. She stabbed him in the chest with a butcher knife. It's no use, Simon, I can't pretend any longer. I'm a psychopathic killer, and I believe my mother is too. I think she killed her sister. You know the old saying—madness runs in the family. In our case, it's true."

"Lola isn't your mother, Madeleine. You aren't even blood relations. I'm sorry to break this to you so abruptly, but we haven't much time. Your father had expected Cilla Dougall to tell you. Your real mother was killed in a car accident when you were a few weeks old."

Madeleine was silent, reflective, for a moment. Then she said, "It doesn't really change anything— especially not between you and me. I hate you, Simon Tanning. I hate you because you made me love you and then betrayed me with Sarita."

He wrapped his arms about her chillingly remote body. "Tell me about Vaughan. We'll talk about us later. Was Lucien here that night? Did Vaughan make a pass at you?"

He felt her try to pull away from him, but kept his arms around her. "No, Simon," she said. "You tell me about Sarita. Was she better in bed than I was? I suppose she must have been—I haven't had her experience. But I thought perhaps what I lacked in technique I made up for in sincerity. . . . I thought loving you made it . . . different."

So that was it. Simon felt a surge of anger. "You thought I made love to Sarita? I wouldn't touch her with . . . Madeleine, I swear I didn't. She offered to pay me to find out what really happened to Jennings, but I turned her down. I borrowed about eight hundred dollars from her to get us to England. I intend to repay her as soon as I can get back to my boat charters. I didn't know where else to raise that much money that fast. It was stupid of me not to tell you, and I apologize."

"You were never honest with me."

"Madeleine, sweetheart, I know I came to you flying false colors in the beginning, but I do love you. I'll never keep anything from you again."

"It doesn't matter anymore," Madeleine said dully. "Simon, don't pin your hopes on any kind of a relationship with me. I killed three men. And if you would like some more proof, take a look over there on the shelves with my sketchpads. Look at the book with the red cover."

The book was titled *Explosives: Brief History and Manual.* Simon turned the volume over in his hand and looked across the room at her. "Are you telling me you rigged the device that blew up Myron's jeep?"

"I must have, Simon, when Madge took possession of my body."

Simon dropped the book and went to her, drawing her to her feet. "You're getting out of here and into a hospital for treatment. You're so weak you can hardly move. He's been poisoning your body with drugs and your mind with hypnotic suggestions."

She stared at him, seeing love and a fierce protectiveness blaze from his eyes. She wanted to weep. She did love him— so much that she feared for his safety more than she feared the nameless terror that stalked her.

"Is Lucien still in the house?" she asked. She shuddered, remembering dinner. Was it her imagination, or had Lucien made love to her with his eyes as he slowly consumed the food? She had squirmed under his relentless stare, feeling naked in the gauze dress.

"He went home, but Sedgewick is down there. You go and get dressed. I've got Dan's Hobie-Cat on the beach, so just gather up a few things in an overnight bag and we'll be off. I'm going to have to take care of Sedgewick, though, before we leave."

"He has a gun."

"We'll try to get out without being seen. He's in the kitchen finishing up your dinner. I'll stand by the kitchen door while you go out the French door in the living room. If he hears anything I'll be in a good position to clobber him as he comes out."

She put up her hand and touched his cheek. "Oh, Simon! Can this be the gentle person I know? Oh, God, how I wish I could be the woman you want me to be."

His finger went to her lips. "You are." Then he kissed her lightly, reassuringly, and opened the door. They descended silently to the floor below. Madeleine went into her room while Simon studied the spiral staircase and hall. The fire in the living room was dying down, and there was only a red glow

211

across the parquet floor. There was a band of light under the kitchen door. Simon's deck shoes fell silently on the stairs.

Madeleine came slowly down the staircase carrying a canvas beach bag. Simon watched as she went across the living room and disappeared through the French door, then he followed.

Outside they sucked into their lungs the cold clean air. Madeleine felt alive again for the first time in days. Simon's hand was warm on hers as they made their way down the cliff.

"I bet old Sedgewick won't miss you until morning," Simon whispered.

"Where shall we go?" Madeleine whispered back. The sound of small rocks shifting on the trail was the only accompaniment to their voices. The tide was low, and slow-breaking waves lapped languorously at the beach.

"We'll stay at my apartment for tonight. We're lucky it's low tide. We shouldn't have much trouble launching the Hobie through the surf."

They were down on the beach, approaching the dark silhouette of the boat, when the raucous barking began. Alphonse and two of his companions had crawled up on the canvas sling between the pontoons of the boat. The three sea lions bellowed excitedly as they drew near.

Madeleine cried out, startled, and Simon tripped over one of the sea lions and fell heavily to the cold sand. There was a moment of confusion, noisy protests, and the sting of flying sand in the darkness.

Almost instantly the thin beam of a flashlight appeared on the deck of the house above. It began to move rapidly down the cliff toward them.

"Sedgewick," Simon muttered. "Grab the other pontoon and shove."

Madeleine stood frozen, staring over his shoulder. Simon felt the hairs on the back of his neck stand up at the expression on her face. He spun around and looked into the evil grin of Bruno.

In the darkness Simon could not see whether there was a

gun in the man's hand. Unarmed, Simon had nothing to protect himself or Madeleine from the vicious thug before them.

But Simon was violently angry. He had gone to great lengths to avoid violent confrontations since Vietnam, trying constantly to atone for what he'd done there. But he had had enough shoving around. He didn't stop to consider the odds before he hurled himself at Bruno's grinning face.

Simon was bellowing with rage, oblivious to everything but his determination to get Madeleine on the boat and away from that madhouse. He pummeled Bruno with fists, warded off return blows. The flashlight shone into their eyes as Sedgewick circled, trying to get a clear shot at him. Simon had his hands around Bruno's throat, and the grin slid from the man's face.

Shoving with all his might, Simon sent Bruno crashing into Sedgewick. Then he moved in, holding his body sideways, hand ready to slice, foot poised to deliver the *coup de grace*, the way they had taught him in the army. The way he swore he would never fight again.

They were both down on the cold sand. Bruno was not moving. Sedgewick groaned and buried his face in his arm. Simon stood looking down at them, the red haze fading from his eyes. Two guns lay beside the figures on the sand.

Simon was about to turn to Madeleine when something struck him on the back of the head.

CHAPTER 22

Simon opened his eyes and groaned as a hundred demons with hammers pounded his skull. His head throbbed. Images blurred, came into focus, blurred again. Someone was holding a wet cloth to his head, and his clothes were soaking wet. He was shivering, and the clicking sound he heard was the chattering of his teeth.

A woman's voice said, "Come *on*. You're too heavy for me to lift, and if you don't move the tide will pull you out to sea."

"Madeleine?" He blinked in a cold gray dawn. Sarita was bending over him.

Sarita's green eyes and cool expression registered more annoyance than concern. "Madeleine isn't here. And neither is Lucien. When I came to work this morning I found a note from him telling me he's terminating my services. Oh, he left a handsome check, but I really deserve a little more than money from Lucien Cornell. And you should be grateful to me, too, Simon Tanning. If I hadn't arrived you would have drowned any second now. You're lucky I saw you from Madeleine's window."

She did not add that she had gone to Madeleine's house bent on the destruction of Lucien's manuscript, the last act of

214

a woman scorned. Lucien's note had instructed her to mail the script to his agent and then take a well-earned vacation. His check had been extremely generous, and he promised to call her when he returned to town. But Sarita knew he would not.

Simon got up on his hands and knees. The beach swam dizzily. The water was lapping at him insistently. Fighting to stay conscious, he struggled to his feet. She was right—a few more minutes and the strong tide would have pulled him out to sea. Was that what Madeleine had been hoping when she hit him? There had been no one else on the beach. Unless—was there really a Madge? Dan's Hobie was still on the beach. There was no sign of the sea lions that had given away their presence. Simon followed Sarita up the cliff trail to the house.

"I'll get you some coffee," Sarita said. "And see if I can find you some dry clothes."

He dropped to the chaise, and it seemed only seconds passed before she returned with a cup of steaming coffee. The scalding liquid brought his circulation back and a measure of coherence to his thoughts and speech.

"You're sure that Madeleine and Lucien went away together?"

"Yes. I know where. Do you want to go after them?" Her eyes narrowed, seeing possibilities.

"You know I do. But how do I know you aren't setting me up?"

"Lucien is obsessed with Madeleine. The only way to get her out of his mind is for her to go away—preferably with another man. With Madeleine out of the way, I'd have a chance with Lucien. It's always been as simple as that."

"So he *is* in love with her. Simon was pleased to know he'd been right about Lucien's feelings toward Madeleine. But he was puzzled. "Why has he never told her so, never tried to make love to her?"

Sarita paced up and down the deck. She was wearing a green suit with a silk shirt and looked the picture of elegance. The tailored jacket did not hide the flamboyant breasts, but their statement was less provocative than usual. Her makeup was slightly more obvious in the morning light, and the downward slant of her mouth and nervously plucking fingers told their own story. "She was like a goddess to him," she said bitterly. "To be placed on a pedestal above all other women."

"Was? Why do you use the past tense?"

"I suppose because I want it to be past tense. I want him to see she's just a woman, like me or any other woman."

"You really care for him, don't you?" Simon said wonderingly.

Her lips compressed tightly. "I don't intend to lightly toss aside the ten years of my life I've given him. I intend to be Mrs. Lucien Cornell."

"Where did they go?"

"Lucien's sand castle." Sarita grimaced, then explained. "Lucien's been building a house in the desert. I know where it is, approximately, although I haven't seen it. There's no road—you reach it either by plane or with a four-wheel-drive vehicle over rough terrain. He wanted it to be as remote as one of the castles he writes about in his novels. Few people know about it, but I had to know because I took care of the business aspects during construction. Lucien started to build the place shortly after Madeleine came to work for him. Yesterday morning he told me to be sure the Cessna was washed, gassed up, and cleared for takeoff last night."

The sun came up, sending a cruel beam of light across Sarita's cheekbone, where the ugly bruise was not completely concealed by makeup. Her eyelid was still puffy.

"Who gave you the black eye?" Simon asked.

"Lucien. Although Madeleine thinks she did. Oh, I don't blame him. He found out I loaned you the money to take her to England. He lost his temper. Simon, don't you see? That's why he belongs to me. With me he could always be himself. He always maintains that tightly controlled, urbane manner in public, but he's not like that at all. He's a very volatile man. His imagination and emotions are so much more vivid and violent than other people's. He can't bear to be thwarted or

216

lose out in any way. But he never lets anyone but me see that side of him. He really should have lived in the time he writes about, so that he could have brutally taken anything he wanted and eliminated anyone who stood in his way."

Simon's fists were clenched at his sides. He felt almost as much revulsion for Sarita as he did for Lucien. Simon's instincts told him he would regret it if he cooperated with Sarita, yet there was no one else who could help him find Madeleine. He shook his head, trying to clear his senses. "Kevin Delaney will be showing up soon. I told him to come looking for me this morning if I didn't return."

"He won't bring the police, will he?" Sarita asked in alarm. "Look, I'll help you if you keep the police out of it."

"I just want Madeleine. Besides, I haven't anything to give to the police. Lucien's been too clever—there's no evidence to implicate him in anything. I promise I'll get Madeleine away from him if you level with me. Who blew up Myron's jeep and poisoned my food? Was it Sedgewick?"

"No. Sedgewick is in charge of the security division of the various companies Lucien controls and acts as a sort of bodyguard for Lucien. Sedge wouldn't go beyond bending the law a bit. Lucien has the connections to hire just about anyone for anything he wants done. One man rigged the jeep, and another broke into your apartment to poison the food. Bruno provided the men."

Sarita looked away, wondering if Simon had seen the fragment of paint-smeared denim attached to the screen door of his apartment. That had been Sarita's own idea. When Lucien had instructed her to drive Bruno's man to Simon's apartment she had decided it might be her chance to get rid of Madeleine too. It was rather a pity Simon hadn't died. She'd have had Lucien by now if Madeleine had been arrested for murder.

"OK. I'm ready for a hot shower and some dry clothes."

She led him to the nearest bathroom and looked him over with a practiced eye. "You're too big for Lucien's clothes. Maybe one of his sweaters would stretch over those shoulders and I can toss your jeans in the dryer for a few minutes. Well, don't just stand there. Take them off."

Self-consciously, Simon peeled off the wet jeans. Sarita smiled, ran her tongue over her lips, and stared at his damp shorts. "Those too. You don't want to catch pneumonia, do you?"

Simon reached for a towel from the heated rail, wrapped it about his middle, and then yanked off his undershorts.

Sarita pouted. "Spoilsport."

"What happened to Regis Vaughan?" Simon asked with calculated suddenness.

Her surprise was not feigned. "He went away on vacation, didn't he? That's what Lucien told me."

"Madeleine told me Vaughan is dead."

"She killed him?" Sarita asked eagerly.

"She thinks she did. I wonder if he's really dead, or if it's all part of a plot to convince her she's insane. I'm even beginning to wonder if Dean Jennings is really dead. After all, all we know is that Madeleine *believes* they are dead. There are no bodies."

"Tony Waring is dead. His body was returned to this country in an urn. His wife had him cremated."

There was something in her expression, a mixture of her own feelings of self-importance and the nearest thing to guilt it was possible for her to feel. Simon caught her wrist, jerking her toward him. "What do you know about the Tony Waring episode?"

"I hired him. I could see how it was going between Lucien and Madeleine, and I wanted to remove the competition. I thought if Tony could get her into bed with him, Lucien would see that the goddess had feet of clay. I paid Tony to fake an elopement with her, then told Lucien so he would arrive only a few hours after they did. I wanted to be sure they were in bed together when he arrived. I didn't think Tony would die from it. His death *was* accidental in the end, wasn't it?"

Simon dropped her wrist in distaste. "Nice people you know, Sarita."

218

"Oh, Tony wasn't that diabolical. I was just too clever for him. He had a society wife who made him feel inferior because of her money and old family name. Tony was a photographer, quite a good one, but he felt like a nonentity. I coaxed him into bed when he came to photograph Penelope Marsh, then blackmailed him into my little plan. He was so afraid his wife would find out about me he was ready to do anything, including telling Madeleine he loved her and wanted to elope with her. He was going to England and figured his wife wouldn't find out about Madeleine if they went there."

She moved closer, looking up at him with a smile of invitation. She put her hand on the bare skin of his chest and caressed him. "You've no idea how persuasive I can be." Her hand slid downward before he could stop her. Angrily he shoved her hand away, wishing again he did not need her knowledge of Lucien's whereabouts.

"Get out of here while I shower. And start making me a map of the location of Lucien's sand castle. Then get Kevin on the phone. He's at my apartment. And where's Sedgewick? Is he likely to show up here?"

"He's with Lucien. He pilots the plane. Simon, honey, you've really turned me on. I love the rough stuff. You wouldn't like a little comforting before you go to rescue the damsel in distress, would you?"

"Get out of here," Simon growled.

Madeleine was crouched behind the black bars of the cage. The batlike figure hovered, withdrew, returned. She did not cry out, but extended her arms, opening herself to that cloud of evil. There was no point in fighting any longer. She was a part of it and it was a part of her. The fear that had kept it at bay was gone, and in its place sensual longings tantalized her body, bringing to each nerve ending delicious, unbearable tension. She moaned, tried to move, but could not. The black cloud had enveloped her, and she could neither see nor feel anything else.

Something cool touched her skin. Moist, icy, hot, it traveled

219

from her throat to her bare breast, circling, stopping at the hard little point of her nipple. She writhed as she felt her nipple drawn up into the cool moist mouth. When the tension in her breast became unbearable, the sucking mouth released her.

There was a faint hint of musk. Fingertips outlined her body, tracing planes and hollows, soft swellings and long curves. The chill touch moved in and out of fingers and toes. She was tumbling headlong into a boiling caldron of desire, mindless and lost in the fever of passion, of an animal need for fulfillment. Someone was screaming. Was that Madeleine screaming? Or was it Madge—screaming, demented, crazy with sensual desire?

Cool breath in her ear. Whispers. Her body throbbed and pulsed. All of her feelings were between her legs. She parted her thighs willingly as the unseen fingers touched the soft mound.

Laughter, low and triumphant. Deep, resonant, reverberating laughter. Guttural murmurs. Lip-smacking, tongue-clicking. Delicious. A gourmet delight for the senses. Her back arched and she thrust her pelvis upward, blindly seeking his mouth and tongue. Taste me. Take me.

Colored lights exploding in the darkness. Inky darkness. Black velvet. Blindness. Blindfold?

Never like this before, princess? Never with those oafs who took you before. Patience! not yet. Lips, kisses, caresses, tongue darting, fingers everywhere. Hips wildly undulating. Hands tugging at bonds, wanting to be free, wanting to touch in return.

Tell me!

Yes. Please.

What?

Inside me. Please—come inside me.

Later, perhaps.

Not real. A dream. Someone was screaming again. The torture of the cool caress, the lips and tongue that promised and then withdrew.

Pain. Turbulence. Bruised. Flailed. Tossed through a black

hole in space to where all the demons of the senses waited. Flashing, piercing lights. Impaled. Probed and violated. The tension was agony. She was limp, drained, empty; yet on fire. Helpless. Too intense. Numb. Tissues, every nerve invaded, tortured mercilessly. Take me, for God's sake!

No release, just a sudden stillness. How long did she lie shaking and burning? After a time, a quivering, tentative approach to the merciful sleep of exhaustion.

Head throbbing, body aching, Madeleine awakened. She was tied by her wrists to a four-poster bed, the curtains and canopy smothering the light. She was naked, shivering. She cried out, and the bed curtains parted.

Lucien smiled at her. He was wearing a black cloak, lined with red satin. "Good morning, Clarissa. As you will see, it is your husband, Sir Giles, who awaits your pleasure. But never fear—Sir Stephen is at this moment racing to your rescue." He laughed and sat down beside her, his dark eyes feasting on her naked body.

The light from an oil lantern standing atop a brass-bound chest beside the bed illuminated a medieval chamber and sent yellow light flickering on the dull gleam of the knife he slipped from a scabbard attached to his belt.

Madeleine screamed. His hand closed over her mouth. She gagged, choked. "Stop it," Lucien commanded. She nodded, weakly, and his hand was withdrawn. He flicked the knife under the silken cords binding her wrists, freeing her.

"Lucien. . . ."

"Sir Giles. Do try to enter into the spirit of the charade."

"Lucien, please. . . ."

"It's just a little game, princess. We've both been working too hard. Now it's time to relax, enjoy ourselves. Here we can indulge all of our whims and fancies. I have a hip bath ready, filled with warm water scented with sandalwood. When you are bathed and fed you will enter into the spirit of things, I'm sure. Your dress is over there."

Madeleine's glance found the pale-blue muslin dress, dangling from a hook attached to a rough wooden ceiling beam.

"Lucien, where are we? I don't recognize this place. She sa
up, swinging her legs over the edge of the bed, fighting a wav
of nausea. Her head was pounding. Everything seemed to b
swathed in a misty veil. The unfamiliar room, the unfamilia
Lucien. "Am I still dreaming? Is this all part of the nightmare?

His hand went under her elbow, steadying her. The ic
touch of his fingers brought back fragments of the nightmare
She shuddered, a hot blush of shame scalding her cheeks a
she remembered.

"You are going to be part of *my* fantasy now, princess. I'v
been part of yours long enough. Come on, into the hip bath
Careful . . . there, isn't that luxurious? Here, let me fasten u
your hair."

She felt as though she were floating above her body, lookin
down on her own nakedness in the copper tub. Flower petal
drifted lanquidly on the surface of the fragrant water. Lucie
picked up a sponge and squeezed it over her shoulders. He ha
a dish of soft green soap and dipped his fingers into it, soapin
her neck, shoulders and arms. When his hand moved to he
breasts, she tried to push him away. She was trembling vio
lently. "Lucien, I don't understand . . . what do you want o
me?"

"You don't understand? But it's all so clear." His voice ha
become a soft purr, unlike any tone she had ever heard hin
use. The sense of unreality surely meant it was all a dream
The room kept receding, blurring. She felt weak, nauseated.

"How could you not have known?" he asked. "But of course
you don't understand why I worshiped you for three year
without ever letting you know. I shall explain. You woul
have used the knowledge to destroy me, my pet. I waited, s
patiently, for you to realize it was our destiny to be soulmates
to share a love that would soar to the heights of divinity. Bu
you were a creature of the flesh, just like all the others. S
distracted by the hormones surging in your blood that you wer
blind to true love—that unity of mind and spirit that transcend
mere lust."

When she tried to move, his fingers tightened about he

222

rm. He held her in a viselike grip that numbed her arm all
he way to her fingertips. Then his other hand slowly and
deliberately soaped her breasts, stomach, between her legs.
he gasped as she felt his bony fingers penetrate her.

"Even now, you are more aware of your body than your
mind." He released her so abruptly her head slammed back
gainst the high back of the tub.

"Lucien, for God's sake! Why are you doing this?" She
crambled out of the tub, dripping scented water. There was
towel on a carved wooden stool nearby, and she snatched
it up to wrap around her body.

"I built all of this for you, Clarissa. Come, get dressed and
'll show you the castle I built. I gave you a house by the sea,
ut it wasn't enough—you had to have the young men too.
Lucien was not enough for you—Lucien, who catered to your
very whim, spent his every minute feeling your pain, wanting
our happiness. So I built you a castle in the desert. Didn't
ve always joke that you had been deprived of a sandbox as
child? The beach was not the answer, so I give you the
esert."

With a dramatic flourish he unhooked a cord, and the velvet
raperies covering one wall fell open. The room was circular,
tower with windows curving out above the most incredible
iew Madeleine had ever seen.

A flat plain, dotted with growths of creosote bush, mes-
uite, and golden gardens of cholla cactus, rose to meet a
oulder-strewn mesa. Beyond the flat top of the mesa towered
urple mountains, gaunt, starkly simple, magnificent. The
esert sun slipped behind the mountains and disappeared as
he watched, leaving misty blue shadows to paint each canyon
nd crevice in sharp relief.

Looking down, she saw a courtyard surrounded by a high
vall of rocks. The house—or castle, as Lucien evidently con-
idered it—was built of the rock and granite natural to the
rea, but of medieval English design, with crenellated walls,
un embrasures, and a portcullis entrance. They were standing

in what appeared to be the main tower at the corner of t
structure.

"The view is superb," Madeleine said. "The house—ca
tle—is incredible. What do you call it?" Try to keep calm, s
told herself. He probably had had some kind of nervous brea
down— all of his work, all her own problems. Underneath
must still be her dear, kind Lucien. He wouldn't hurt her.

"Castle Cornell, of course. Our little place in the countr
my pet. Before you spoiled the dream, I had such plans. . ."
He stood close behind her; she could feel his cool breath
the back of her neck. She gripped the cold stone of the windo
ledge with shaking fingers, willing herself not to move.

"Lucien, I'm sorry. I had no idea you cared for me in th
way. I never meant to encourage you to believe—"

His hands were on her throat before she could finish. S
was spun around, crushed against him, gasping for breath. S
looked into eyes black and wild with despair, then his mou
came down on hers, hard, hungry, devouring. His breath w
icy in her throat. She could feel his bones beneath the silk
his coat, hard protrusions cutting into her flesh. His clo
enveloped her, drowning and suffocating, and his thighs we
pressed against hers. His hands slid from her throat, claspi
her face as his mouth consumed her lips.

When at last he released her she could only cling to hi
panting and gasping as dark waves of dizziness swept over h
again. His eyes glowed with tiny pinpricks of yellow flar
as she stared into them. From a great distance his voice can
to her, like the hollow echo in a cave. "We shall be lovers f
one night, Clarissa. One last night for you to wallow in tl
pleasures of the flesh."

He paused and there was a moment of heart-pounding s
lence. "And then, my princess, we shall be soulmates throug
all eternity."

CHAPTER 23

With teeth-rattling vibration, the rented jeep bounced over the rutted desert road and sent rocks flying from beneath the wheels. Wedged between Simon and Kevin Delaney, Sarita cried out as they hit a narrow wash and were airborne for an instant.

Sarita's hair spray had dissolved into a sticky glue, and pale friz framed a sweat-streaked face. Mascara and bright-green eyeshadow smudged her cheeks, blending with the remnants of her bruises. The crisp linen pantsuit in which she had started the journey was beginning to wrinkle and stick to her back. She let forth a stream of unladylike curses as the jeep bounced down again on the hard-packed gravel.

Kevin glanced at her admiringly. "Couldn't have expressed it better myself." He was rewarded with a narrow-eyed frown.

Sarita turned angrily to Simon. "Why are you doing this to me? I did save your life and I did all I could to help you. I told you where Madeleine is, and I gave you money—for damn little in return."

"You'll get your money back, as soon as I get my boat back in service. As to why I wanted the pleasure of your company, I had no intention of leaving you behind to phone Lucien and warn him we were coming."

Her lips curled in silent satisfaction, relishing the knowledge that Lucien had instructed her to tell Simon where the desert house was situated. Then the troublesome thought intruded that Lucien might be angry that she and Kevin Delaney had accompanied Simon, who was supposed to go after Madeleine alone.

Lucien had telephoned Sarita the previous evening. "Tomorrow morning you will find Simon Tanning on the beach. I want him to come out to the castle. Alone."

But Lucien had not mentioned there was a severance check and a note dismissing her awaiting her also. She found those on her desk along with the message to be sure to mail the script of *Deadly Lady*. And good old Sarita, her job finished, was supposed to quietly fade away. Much as she disliked the idea, she had no alternative but to help Simon. If Simon could take Madeleine away from Lucien, then Lucien would be hers. After all, Sarita knew enough to hang Lucien. Blackmailing him into marriage should pose no problem. She fanned herself futilely with the hat, which would not stay on her head in the hot wind.

They came to a stop in a cloud of dust on the top of a mesa. In the middle of the plain below was Lucien's castle, rising from the white sand like a mirage. The late-afternoon sun painted the walls with mellow light, but the stone fortress was coldly repelling, incongruous in its setting.

Simon and Kevin stared at the castle, fascinated, while Sarita tried to run a comb through her tangled hair.

"There's no way to get close without being seen, mate. He could take potshots at us as we went across that plain. And look at the height of those outer walls. How are you going to get in?"

"Let's pull back, out of sight." Simon said, throwing the jeep into reverse and backing up, to a wail of complaint from Sarita. Simon parked in the shelter of a giant boulder.

"How far away do you estimate it is?" Simon asked Kevin when they walked to the rim of the mesa.

"Probably ten miles—distances seem less than they really

226

are in this kind of country. See that clearing to the left, the long area with all of the cactus removed? Looks like a runway. No plane, though. Do you see a plane, Simon?"

"No. It could be hidden from view, behind the castle. Lord, I hate to wait until dark, but you're right, we would be seen in daylight."

"What kind of madman builds a castle in the desert? And what will he do to my little girl? I'm afraid for her, Simon. We should have brought the law with us."

"On what grounds? We haven't anything to accuse him of, and for all we know Madeleine went with him of her own free will."

"Stop worrying about her," Sarita put in, exasperated. "Lucien thinks he's in love with her. Will you please give me some water now?" She sat down in the shade of a towering rock and managed to look like a human sacrifice at the foot of a pagan god. Kevin Delaney's eyes rarely left her, straying frequently to the unbuttoned shirt that revealed an incredible cleavage.

Simon walked over to her, dangling a canteen of water in his hand. "I need a little more information, Sarita. You'll get your water when I know everything you know about Cornell."

She looked at him as innocently as she could. "I've told you all I know."

"I think not. Now here's the situation. You're miles from the nearest town. You couldn't possibly reach it on foot. You could hike ten miles to Lucien's castle, though I don't know how happy he'll be to see you—especially after I tell him it was you who hired Tony Waring to take Madeleine away from him. Blackmail is a double-edged sword, my friend." Simon let the canteen swing back and forth on its carrying strap.

Sarita licked her parched lips. They had been in the jeep over four hours and had not stopped en route. "What do you want to know?"

"Did Cornell know that Lola was not Madeleine's mother?"

Sarita nodded. "He made a complete investigation of Madeleine. I'll never understand what she did to him. She bewitched him from the first moment he saw her. He was on the balcony of his house and she was swimming in the sea below. She came walking out of the surf in that stately proud way of hers. He said something about Venus rising. He had me hire a detective agency that very day to get a full report on her."

"It was Lucien who planted the idea in her head that she was suffering from—what the hell did he call it?—dissociative neurosis, the existence of another personality. How did he do it? Nightmare-inducing drugs? Hallucinogens?"

Sarita was staring longingly at the canteen. "I don't know what he gave her, but he put something in her wine and something in the iron supplement she had to take. Not at first . . . but right after the Tony Waring episode and again after Dean Jennings. Before that he used hypnosis, though she didn't know it because he worked on her while she was asleep. Between times he kept planting the seed that insanity is hereditary, and that she'd end up like her mother unless she stayed with him."

"But people can't be made to do something under hypnosis they wouldn't do while awake," Simon said. "How did he get her to smash the studio, destroy her own paintings, and do all of the other things the mythical Madge was supposed to have done?"

"Madeleine didn't do any of those things. Lucien gave her a powerful sedative the night he smashed the studio. He carried her down to the beach where she stayed while he did the job. Lucien was also responsible for breaking Josefa's jaw. He was furious because she had accidentally come into the bedroom while we were in the middle of one of our games. That was the same day that Madeleine slipped Nurse Williams a mickey and took off to see Lola. I thought it was a neat way to use an unexpected incident for his own advantage."

"What became of Josefa?"

Sarita shrugged. "She and Ramón were both deported. The nice thing about hiring illegals is that they're very easy to dispose of. They certainly won't go to the law, will they?"

"What about the art teacher, Antoine?"

228

"What about him?"

"He had one of Madeleine's paintings in his gallery, when supposedly they were all destroyed."

"Lucien saved one from among those he destroyed because it was the same stretch of beach where he first saw Madeleine. There was another like it hanging over her fireplace. Lucien wanted the second one for his sand castle, so he gave it to Antoine to keep for him where Madeleine wouldn't see it. Antoine doesn't know anything."

Simon handed her the canteen, and she drank greedily.

"One last question. Did Lucien have the house bugged? Is that how he knew what I'd said to her?"

Sarita nodded. She wiped her mouth with the back of her hand and remembered Lucien's rage when they had listened to Simon making love to Madeleine that night. Lucien had systematically smashed every glass in the bar and every break-able ornament in his office and then had turned on Sarita in fury. For a moment she had been afraid he would go too far when he began to beat her, but she had summoned the courage to fight back, knowing that nothing aroused Lucien's sexual desire more than resistance.

The sun disappeared behind the mountains, and shadows moved swiftly to cloak the desert. There was no twilight. Day ended and night began. With it came cold air and the soft scampering of nocturnal animals. A pack of coyotes howled on a distant ridge. Sarita whimpered in fright.

Simon studied the plans of the castle which Sarita had provided. His flashlight went again around the outside wall. "You're sure that's where the door is, and it won't be locked?"

"I told you before, the front gate is electronically controlled. But there is an escape route that Lucien had built for emergency use. There is a passage that connects to a rear door concealed by a rock formation. The passage leads to a storeroom where you'll find yourself inside a crate. One side of the crate is hinged. See . . . here. Then go into this hall. These steps lead to the main hall, and the others go down to the dungeons."

"Dungeons?" Kevin repeated in disbelief. He was preparing

their meal, adding hot water from a flask to dehydrated camping dinners.

"The castle is built on a flat bed of rock with several natural caves. For effect he threw in a couple of cells with iron bars and manacles on the walls. He had a collection of medieval torture instruments, so he set them up in a display."

"Didn't all of this worry you?" Simon asked. "Didn't you ever question Lucien's sanity? You say he indulged in weird fantasies, and could become so enraged that he would smash everything in sight . . . and now you say he collected torture equipment."

"Plenty of men—and women too—are into sadomasochism," Sarita said. "Lucien likes to fantasize that he is living in the past. He's even written some stories that his publisher refused on the grounds that they were too bizarre."

"In what way?"

"Strange love scenes, particularly gory death scenes, and various taboos. Necrophilia, for one."

A chill went down Simon's spine. "I've got to get going, Kevin, if I'm not back in two hours, drive to the nearest ranger station for help."

"What does that word mean . . . that necrophilia?" Kevin asked.

"It means," Simon said in a frozen voice, "making love to a corpse."

CHAPTER 24

The scent of musk was everywhere. In her nostrils, on her eyelids, her fingertips. Her skin felt clammy and she was shivering, yet her body burned as though probed by electric needles. Struggling to escape the twilight stupor that engulfed her, she rose unsteadily from the four-poster bed, groping with shaking hands to find a way through the smothering velvet curtains. Her eyelids drooped, no matter how hard she tried to concentrate. There . . . an opening in the curtains.

Everything was gray, blurred, muted. Looking down at the dress she wore, she saw only misty muslin, without color. Yet she knew the dress was pale blue. The draperies covering the bay windows of the tower were deep blood red, she was sure, yet they now appeared a murky brownish black. It was as though the color had been switched off a film screen, leaving only black-and-white images.

There was a dining table at the far end of the room. She could see pewter dishes and goblets. She tried to remember if they had dined there. She was alone in the room, but the sense of unseen menace was everywhere. Where is Lucien? Must get out of here. He's having a nervous breakdown. Must go for help. The door . . . *where is the door?* She spun around wildly, panic lending her strength. There was no door in the room.

Stumbling to the nearest wall, she spread her hands on the cold stone, trailing her fingers as she made her way slowly around the room. She was looking for a hidden door, but found none.

The room was circular, its blank walls broken only by a window. She tripped over the torn hem of her dress in her haste to reach it. Then steadying herself on the rough stone ledge, she examined the window. It was made of small leaded panes which did not open. And even if they did open there was no possible escape. There was a sheer drop to the courtyard below.

Turning away, she took several steps and collided with the dining table. Decanters of wine . . . no food. No, she shouldn't drink the wine. Had she already drunk some? Her mouth was dry . . . she felt weak, disoriented. Dinner . . . she had had dinner with Lucien. He had worn eighteenth-century dress.

"We are acting out my fantasy, Clarissa. Nothing sinister about it. An adult game, nothing more. Don't look at me like that, as though I were mad. What a child you are. I waited for you to grow up, meet me on that plane where we would be one. We will meet there, Clarissa. Never fear. Drink your wine, my sweet, and I shall give you carnal delights like none you've ever known."

He stood in front of her, hands on her breasts, his mouth taking hers brutally. His kiss was so intense, tongue finding the far corners of her mouth, throbbing, pulsing. She was being drawn into the mouth of hell itself. He was the devil, Satan incarnate, and his kiss was sucking her up into a vortex of searing sensuality. She was weightless, floating, her only sensations in her mouth and between her legs, her only thought the gratification of her flesh. She was about to climax from a mere kiss. She hovered breathlessly on the brink of fulfillment, then he released her mouth, laughing again, devilishly, triumphantly. Lucien. Fiend. Controlling, tormenting, sadistic monster.

232

"Drink the wine," he ordered. His fingers dug deep into her flesh, bruising, icy.

She gulped the wine. Lights exploded in her head.

Descent into madness. But who was she—Madeleine or Madge? Lucien was not mad, Lucien was in control.

Portrait of a woman going slowly out of her mind. Clarissa of the portrait . . . no, that was poor demented Lola who killed her twin for love of a man and then went mad. Or did she? No, Simon said . . . Simon said . . .

Simon says, let's make love on a boat. The boat rides over the swells, sensually. Erotic movement . . . lazily, gliding, drawing nearer. Oh, yes, yes, Simon. Do that to me. Do it again.

Cold. So cold. Burning with the cold.

Something hard. Cold and hard. In her fingers, between her breasts, in her mouth. Musk. Everywhere the scent of musk.

No . . . the rough wood of the table beneath her fingers. *This isn't happening now.* This was a memory of what happened earlier. She had to get hold of herself. Think. He was not here now. *No door in the room—but he comes and goes. Must be a way out.* Her eyes drifted around the room. The bed, set on a dais behind heavy curtains. Marble-topped washstand, massive carved wardrobe, dining set, two or three chairs, the fireplace. Wall sconces holding candles. Two metal rings attached to another wall . . . manacles?

She collapsed weakly into a high-backed chair. Something she must remember. What? The novel—that was it, *Deadly Lady.* Lucien's book. Lucien's last chapter . . . oh, God! Clarissa's lover was with her and Sir Giles caught them. Sir Stephen was drugged, chained to a wall, and branded with a red-hot poker. Thumbscrew. An iron mask, through which he was forced to watch Sir Giles make love to Clarissa—and kill her. Then Sir Giles leaped to his own death from a parapet with Clarissa in his arms.

All at once Madeleine was glad Simon was not here. He

could not play the part of Sir Stephen in Lucien's ghastly fantasy.

Lucien sat in a carved wooden chair, surveying the screen of a closed-circuit television. He smiled faintly as the image of the man cautiously stepping from the crate in the storeroom appeared on the screen. Simon looked about, then crossed the room and went into hall.

At Lucien's side, Sedgewick said, "I've locked the other two in the south tower. Shall I go and get him now?"

Lucien sighed, thinking about the foolish Sarita. "Little fool. There's no hurry, Sedge. Let Tanning roam around for a while seeking his lost love. After you've locked him up I want you to leave immediately. You are all ready aren't you, and you're sure you know exactly what to do when you get back to town?"

Sedgewick looked uneasy. "Yes. But I don't understand why you want me to make public all of your experiments and findings. There's a fortune in some of your discoveries, and I don't know why you didn't make them public years ago. What about the commercial pharmaceutical possibilities—the substitute for DDT, even a chance of a possible cancer drug? I don't understand, Lucien. When we started out together all those years ago I was sure you would be hailed as the chemist of the century. Why did you give it all up to write women's novels?"

Lucien was chuckling softly at the amazement clearly evident on Simon Tanning's face. The screen showed him in the great stone-flagged hall.

"You were a brilliant chemist, Lucien, and I had such hopes. We go back a long time, but I've been no more than a bodyguard to you the last few years."

"Sedgewick, old friend, I've never known you to be so talkative. Odd, isn't it—all the years I've known you I had no idea you stayed with me because you felt you were riding the tail of a comet you felt was bound to soar. Is it because you were a failed chemist yourself, do you suppose?" Lucien's lips curled cruelly over his teeth. His dark hypnotic eyes

234

flashed maliciously in the dimness of the chamber as he surveyed the nonentity who had done his bidding, maintained his secrets, and never before asked questions.

"I wasn't exactly a failed chemist, Lucien. I never had a degree, as you well know."

"My lab assistant, working his way through college. I remember. Why didn't you finish?"

"There were two reasons for my decision. Firstly, I was supporting my elderly parents, and then there was the excitement of working with you. I couldn't bear to go back to school that summer you were on the verge of breaking down the compounds in the toxic seaweed."

Lucien sighed regretfully. "Ah, yes. Asparagopsis. Unfortunately it had physiological effects. I began to experience blurred vision and brief blackouts while working with it."

"But you allowed yourself to be sidetracked with various bonding compounds. I was disappointed. You were destined to be more. Then you became chairman of the board, and gave up your research. Even the textbooks you wrote didn't hint of what you had really stumbled into. But the final waste of talent had to be the novels. Why did you do it?"

"Even the workhorse needs more from life than endless toil. I wanted an outlet for my imagination. I enjoyed the power of life and death over my fictional characters. I was fascinated by the slow unfolding of the motives of my characters—their loves and hates and desires, the building of a story out of thin air. They became more real to me than the real people in my life. Real people are such a mass of contradictions, Sedge. They are hopeless—inconsistent, cowardly. Ah, but fictional people must always exhibit the same character traits. They can be wholly fearless . . . totally depraved."

"It was Madeleine, though, wasn't it, who really changed you from chemist to storyteller?"

"How can I explain what I felt for her? Did I, originally, see myself as Svengali, Pygmalion? Perhaps even Professor Higgins? She was a girl when I found her, but with a quality that was at once elusive and haunting. Beneath the thrift-shop clothes and unadorned face and hair I could see eternal woman. I never had to teach her how to walk, you know, Sedge. That graceful way she moves is completely natural. There was always that look in her eyes that was both vulnerable and spiritually sensual. She was a little girl trying to cope with adult problems. She was supporting a catatonic woman, desperately wanting to be an artist, searching for her lost father. Oh, yes, I knew that was the role I would have to play, in the beginning. I taught her everything—how to dress, to handle every level of society, what to read, what to accept and what to discard. And like the others before me, I fell into the trap. I was in love with my own creation. I became obsessed with making her love me in return. She would have, if only I could have kept the spoilers away from her."

On the television screen Simon was approaching the dungeons. He looked, Lucien decided, like a bad actor playing the part of a reluctant private eye. Tanning was far too muscular to do anything with stealth, yet stealth was a prerequisite of his calling. Ah, there—he had seen the barred cells, was staring in horrified fascination at the rack and the wheel. He was approaching the table containing branding irons, thumbscrews, and face masks. He was putting his hand on the inside of the face mask, touching the iron points. "Yes, my friend, study it all carefully. When it comes time to play with my little toys, I want them to be familiar to you."

"Lucien," Sedge said, "you wouldn't really use them on him, would you? You said he killed the shrink. So why don't we just turn him over to the police? Look, Lucien, I've done a few things for you that bent the law—here, in England, and in Mexico. But I won't be a party to murder, even for you."

"Sedgewick, Sedgewick," Lucien sighed, his eyes still fixed on the screen. "I am merely going to frighten him into confessing he killed Regis Vaughan. As soon as he tells me where he hid the body, I shall call the police."

"And what about Dean Jennings, the man he came looking for? Do you swear you had nothing to do with his death?"

"He died of natural causes. The only bacteria the Mexican

coroner found were the natural bacteria that live on all human beings."

"A long time ago," Sedgewick said slowly, memory stirring persistently and naggingly, "there were rumors of a chemical that could be placed on the skin that would take the external bacteria into the body, where they would be fatal." He stopped, thinking of what he was supposed to do when he returned to town. "Lucien, you're not ill, are you? This elaborate plan to have me make public all of your work . . . sounds like the plan of a man getting ready to die."

Lucien raised his eyes and stared at Sedgewick, who felt the familiar sense of panic which arose whenever his employer fixed that particular look on him. "Go now," Lucien said softly. "Lock him up. Then you will go to the hangar and fly the plane back to L.A. First thing tomorrow you will call a press conference to announce the legacy I leave to the world."

"Legacy? Lucien, you *are* dying. Why didn't you tell me? How long have you known?"

Lucien rose, dark eyes hooded, intense. Sedgewick blinked once as Lucien's resonant voice began to speak. Aware of the instructions, but remotely, as though from a distance, Sedgewick was also aware of the blood flowing along his veins, pumping slowly into his heart. He could see Lucien's eyes, hear his voice, but everything else was blank.

Simon never knew what hit him. He was examining the rusted relics of medieval brutality when there was the slightest suggestion of sound behind him. He started to turn at the exact moment something pinged through the air and hit his shoulder. He never saw Sedgewick come out of the shadows with the tranquilizer gun. Before the man crossed the floor of the chamber, Simon slid to the floor, unconscious.

Moving like a robot in a business suit, Sedge dragged Simon's limp body into a cell, fastened the manacles about his wrists, then locked the door.

Watching the brief drama enacted on the television screen, Lucien nodded approvingly. "Good boy, Sedgewick. Off you go now. Good, good." Lucien stretched his sinuous body, flexing shoulders and back. He was proud of his body. It was the taut, lean body of a man half his age. He had not used the sunlamp recently, and since he disliked outdoor activity, his skin was returning to its normal waxy sheen. He really preferred the pallor, because it tended to sharpen the aristocratic cheekbones, aquiline nose, and haughty chin, and set off the brooding eyes. His long bony fingers strayed to his thighs, and he touched the skin-tight breeches which disappeared into knee-high leather boots. The cutaway jacket was an inspiration of the time, revealing as it did the strong lines of a man's anatomy. His neck was deeply lined, but that was concealed by the cravat he wore. It was still another convenient accessory of the era in which he should have lived. Women knew how to act like ladies in those days.

Lucien arose, without haste, and walked through the gas-lit corridors. His stride was long and easy. His former short imperious steps had been a manifestation of that other Lucien, the Lucien who spent his days engrossed in logical thought, rigidly controlling mind and emotion so as to hide from the world the real Lucien Cornell. He laughed under his breath. He thought of himself as a dashing rogue, but "rogue" was too insignificant a word. He was a ravisher of women, a formidable and uncompromising adversary to his enemies, a nemesis who would not hesitate to conjure evil powers to gain his ends.

He paused in the circular hall, glancing toward the steps that descended to the dungeon. No, Tanning would not have recovered his senses sufficiently yet. There was plenty of time. Nights were long in the desert this time of year. He went instead up the stone steps encircling the main tower. The staircase stopped abruptly just below the top of the tower, ending in a massive iron-studded door. Beyond was a small chamber, barely large enough to accommodate the opening and closing of two other doors. One door led to the outside parapet, a foot-wide ledge just below the windows, the second to the room occupied by the faithless Clarissa. On the other side of the door were glass panels outlined in lead, exactly like those of the windows. Thus the door appeared to be part of the window, especially since the velvet draperies further concealed its location, even when drawn back.

Lucien silently opened the door and stood behind the draperies.

She was systematically probing and pressing every inch of the mantelpiece. He smiled. The drug was beginning to wear off and she was looking for a way to escape. Brave, resourceful Clarissa, so spirited, so damned independent. It was a good thing Lucien had something on Antoine, or that idiot would have told her long ago how gifted an artist she was. Antoine had quickly backed away from the suggestion that an exhibition of her work be arranged when Lucien reminded him that a rising young district attorney, Antoine's son, would not want it widely known that his father was once arrested for indecent exposure.

Never fear, Clarissa—soon we shall be able to choose the time in which we live. Back, back into the past when women were chattels, subservient in every way by sheer virtue of their financial dependence and need.

Lucien slid the draperies aside and stepped into the room. She turned at once in response to the soft slap of his leather soles on the floor. Instantly she sprang toward the brass canister on the hearth and seized the heavy brass poker. She brandished it, glaring at him as he approached. The pupils of her eyes were only slightly dilated. The effects of the wine were fading fast.

"Stop right there, Lucien," she said, "or I swear I'll clobber you."

Lucien winced. "Slang is both offensive and out of character, Clarissa." He paused, regarding her with eyes like coals. "Put down the poker, my dear, while I direct your attention to the washstand. If you will open the small drawer on the right, you will find two buttons. Press the button on the right and I believe you will see something of supreme interest to you."

Madeleine hesitated, then, still brandishing the poker, moved to the washstand. The button caused a television picture to flash on the mirror above the marble stand. Madeleine tried to keep one eye on Lucien but gasped when she saw the two figures materialize on the screen. They were in a small bare room containing only a sanctuary bench. Slumped on the bench was Sarita, her hair a yellow mop. Pacing up and down angrily was Madeleine's father.

"The button on the left, Madeleine, will give you a different image."

She dropped the poker in horror as she looked at the manacled figure in the barred cell. Simon hung limply by his wrists, his head forward on his chest.

"Sir Stephen has arrived," Lucien announced with formal pleasure. "Let the festivities commence."

CHAPTER 25

Simon opened his eyes and looked at Madeleine, sitting beside him on a strange bed, a wet cloth in her hand. They were alone in the tower room. "Thank God you're all right," Madeleine breathed.

"How did I get in here?" There was a throbbing sore spot on his back near his shoulder, as though he'd been injected there, and his circulation was sluggish, but otherwise he appeared to be in one piece and functioning reasonably well.

"Lucien brought you. You were unconscious, and he carried you over his shoulder. I had no idea he was so strong. He just dumped you on the bed, gave me a diabolical smile, and left."

"He hasn't hurt you? Did he drug you? Madeleine, why in the name of all that's holy did you knock me out on the beach?"

"I didn't knock you out. It was Lucien. He came from nowhere. I didn't even see him with all the barking and scuffling of the sea lions. You were sprawled on the sand and he was shoving an awful-smelling cloth over my face. I don't even remember coming here."

"Who else is here? Sedgewick? How many people have you seen? Is Lucien armed?"

"I've seen no one but Lucien. He has a knife, and a dagger I think, in a scabbard attached to his belt. I heard a plane take off a while ago. Oh, yes, Sarita and my father are here, locked up somewhere."

Simon groaned. "Damn!" He glanced around the room. "Wait a minute." Jumping down from the bed, he went to the dining table and picked up a pewter mug and a silver platter. Returning to her side, he began to beat a tattoo on the platter. He leaned close and whispered in her ear, "Lucien had your house bugged. This room probably is too. Maybe the banging will muffle our voices. What is he up to, do you know?"

"He says it's just a fantasy we're acting out, but he's so irrational I think he's actually living the last chapter of the novel he's just completed." Madeleine went on to describe exactly what was to happen to them, omitting none of the ghastly details she had read. She began to shake violently, and Simon wrapped his arms about her, continuing to beat on the platter behind her back.

"In his story, Sir Giles brands Sir Stephen with a red-hot poker, then puts an iron mask over his face. The inside of the mask has iron points tipped with a slow-acting poison. Sir

Giles makes love to Clarissa while Sir Stephen is forced to watch through slits in the mask. In the end Sir Giles leaps to his death from the castle parapet with Clarissa in his arms."

Simon's beating of the platter stopped. "Methinks," he said softly, resuming the tattoo, "We'll get the hell out of here."

"The door is behind the window draperies somewhere. That's where Lucien came in, but I haven't been able to figure out how to open it from this side."

Simon motioned for her to follow as he went to examine the window. Several minutes later he shook his head. "It's no use. There's no way to open it from this side that I can see."

Sarita looked up fearfully as Lucien's face appeared in the small window of the door. "Sarita, my pet, I shall need you after all. Mr. Delaney, remain where you are." The door opened and the muzzle of a blunderbuss appeared, pointed at Kevin's chest.

"You bloody madman," Kevin growled as Sarita ran through the door.

"Lucien, I know I was just supposed to send Simon, but he made me come, I swear it."

"Stop babbling and come with me. Since you're here you might as well play a role in our little drama."

She followed him, thinking that the reality of the castle was even more grim and forbidding than the plans she had seen. If people had once lived like this she couldn't imagine why Lucien longed for the past. There was a little comfort in unyielding surfaces and damp chambers. He took her to what was apparently a bedchamber, and she brightened considerably. Clothes that would have been worn by a serving wench were lying on the bed.

"Put them on. And for Lucifer's sake, wash your face. You look as though you have been dragged backward through the mesquite. You will play the part of Lucinda, the serving wench who takes wine to the doomed lovers."

"Lucien . . ."

"Sir Giles, wench. How dare you address me in so familiar

a manner? You slut. Do you want to feel my whip on your soft skin?"

"Ah," Sarita said. "I see. We're playing games. What is the fantasy tonight?"

Lucien gave her a crafty smile. "Get dressed. I'll return in a few minutes."

Sarita giggled as her eyes dropped to the bulge in his skin-tight breeches. It was all just one of his games. She felt a thrill of excitement after he left, and she began to strip off her pantsuit. It was going to be a memorable night, with all four of them involved in the game. She cleaned the desert dust from her body as best she could with the cold water in a pitcher on the wash-stand, then pulled on the voluminous petticoats and skirt. She ignored the pantalets—they would be a needless encumbrance later. The blouse was tight. Good. She pulled the neckline low, baring shoulders and most of her perfectly rounded breasts. She barely had time to dab rouge on her nipples before Lucien appeared with a tray containing a wine decanter and glasses.

"I love the clothes, Lucien. Especially those breeches you're wearing."

He placed the tray down carefully, and his hand closed over her wrist, jerking her toward him. His kiss made her knees buckle. "Oh, Lucien," she breathed a moment later. "When you kiss me like that I'd do anything for you."

"You will take the wine upstairs. I'll show you the way. Serve them and remain in the chamber with them." Lucien described exactly where the escape door was hidden, but added, "Once our little fantasy begins we must all see it through to the end. Have a sip of wine, my pet, to get you in the mood."

"Lucien, love, you know I don't need an aphrodisiac. I'm always in the mood." She tried to creep back into his embrace, but he pushed her away.

"It will slow you down, not speed you up. There are all sorts of carnal pleasures in store for you tonight, insatiable doxy."

Sarita laughed breathlessly and dutifully took a sip of the wine. "But you've put an aphrodisiac in their wine, haven't you?"

"Of course." He smiled a satyr's smile. "You can hardly wait to seduce the muscular detective, can you, my sweet?"

Sarita shivered in delicious anticipation. "You know you are the only one I want, Lucien," she said carefully.

His face was just above hers, his eyes boring into her with the impact of a laser—probing, stupefying, two tiny pinpricks of light in the center of the dark pupils. Her head swam and all feeling drained from her body. She could hear his voice, distantly, telling her of the games they would play. She felt the hot moisture between her legs. She was brimming over, yet limp and relaxed at the same time.

"Come, Lucinda. Sir Stephen has been alone long enough with my faithless Clarissa."

The door closed behind her so rapidly that Sarita almost stumbled as she stepped into the room. She steadied the wine decanter on the tray with a muttered exclamation.

Simon and Madeleine were on the bed, wrapped in each other's arms. Simon swung his legs over the side of the bed and said, "We were expecting you, Sarita."

"Lucinda," she corrected. She looked at him with her best seductive smile. "I'm glad you've decided to play along. Lucien loves these games and fantasies, and they don't do any harm. Although—" She broke off, concealing her unease by pouring the wine. She had been about to say that of late some of Lucien's wilder fantasies frightened her. They had been moving steadily into a realm of erotic mysticism that seemed to demand a macabre zenith. Lost in her own frenzied passion, Sarita did not heed the warning voice that said they were on a precipice and the slightest move in the wrong direction would send them crashing over the edge.

She handed the wineglass to Madeleine, whose eyes met hers unblinkingly. Lucien probably hypnotized her, Sarita thought. From the look of her she won't be much use to either of them. No matter, I can handle all of them.

"You look very fetching in your peasant blouse," Simon said, taking the offered wineglass. He slipped his arm around Sarita's waist, turning her toward the small decorative mirror on the top of the wardrobe door, which he had decided was probably a television camera.

He kept Sarita between him and the camera, his hand busy with the laces of her bodice to distract the watching Lucien. Behind her blond head he brought the wineglass to his lips, hoping the television camera would record that he'd drained the glass, not that he'd poured it into his shirt.

The cool liquid trickled slowly down his chest as he nuzzled the back of Sarita's neck. She squirmed and giggled, excited that he couldn't wait to get his hands on her, despite Madeleine's presence.

Sarita turned to face him, and he quickly stepped backward. If she touched him, she would feel the wet shirt. The room was illuminated only by candles in wall sconces, and he hoped she would not see the red stain soaking through his garment. As she reached for him he placed the empty wineglass in her hand. "What's next, Sarita? I mean, Lucinda?"

"We could improvise while we're waiting for Sir Giles," she said huskily.

Simon's knees wobbled, and he collapsed onto the bed. "Son of a gun . . . I feel . . . sort of . . . drowsy. . . ."

"Damn," Sarita said.

Madeleine watched, stone-faced and silent.

Simon toppled slowly backward and lay sprawled at the foot of the bed. Instantly Madeleine came to life, pulling the bedcurtains closed and grabbing Sarita to pull her inside with them. Sarita saw now that Madeleine was naked beneath the sheet, but was pulling a pale-blue muslin dress from under the pillow. Her voice hissed in Sarita's ear. "Put it on, quickly. I don't want Lucien to make love to me. I'll be Lucinda and you can be Clarissa."

Miraculously, Simon was suddenly wide awake. "Do as she says. We're rewriting the script." He too moved close to her ear to whisper. His breath was exciting. Sarita lost no time in tearing off the maid's clothes and donning the blue muslin dress. Her mind was fuzzy. She was trying to remember something that eluded her, something she should beware of. But it was difficult to think about anything but her burning needs and inflamed senses.

The moment Madeleine was dressed as a serving maid, she opened the bedcurtains and Simon assumed his drugged sprawl. Madeleine sped about the room, extinguishing the candles in the wall sconces. There were only two left, flickering their feeble light, when Lucien stepped into the room. Protruding from beneath his cape was the muzzle of an ancient blunderbuss.

"You can stop pretending, Sir Stephen," he said coldly. "I know you didn't drink the wine."

Simon got up slowly, his eyes fixed on the flaring muzzle of the gun.

"It will blow a very large hole in your chest," Lucien confirmed. "But I don't want our little play to end in that manner. Therefore, if one of you wenches will kindly fasten Sir Stephen's wrists to the manacles on the wall over there, we shall proceed as planned." He appeared unaware that it was Madeleine in the serving wench's clothes who moved to Simon's side as he stretched up his arms to the wall manacles.

Lucien went to the fireplace and plunged the brass poker into the glowing embers. "Light some more candles, Lucinda. It's too dark in here."

Madeleine fumbled with Simon's manacles. If she approached the fireplace to pick up a taper to light candles, would Lucien realize she had switched clothes with Sarita? Sarita was still behind the bedcurtains, dressing. Madeleine moved toward the hearth, where a smaller brass canister contained tapers.

Lucien straightened up, glanced at Simon's wrists in the manacles, then carefully leaned the blunderbuss against the wall. As Madeleine bent to take a taper, Lucien grabbed her from behind. She felt his lips on her back of her neck, pushing aside her hair, then tongue and teeth. She bit back a cry of disgust. "Oh, Sir Giles, how could you!" she wailed in a shrill voice. "Trying to kiss a serving girl with milady in the room."

Surprised, Lucien released her as Sarita came gliding toward them, holding up the hem of the too-long blue muslin dress.

"Her ladyship," Madeleine whispered urgently. "Sir Giles . . . your wife." *Look at the dress, look at the golden hair—Clarissa has golden hair,* Madeleine thought frantically. Her heart was pounding with fear. One false move, one misplaced word, and Lucien would slip over the edge into insanity. It was written in his eyes, wild, staring, and in the tension she felt in his bony frame as he touched her.

Lucien hesitated, glancing from one woman to the other. Of course, golden hair . . . the serving wench had dark hair.

Holding his breath, Simon watched for his opportunity. Madeleine had fumbled with the manacles, but his wrists actually were free; he merely held them in the open rings. The blunderbuss was inches from Lucien's side, while Simon was across the room.

Sarita's voice was slurred. "Sir Giles . . . here I am, your lovely wife."

Lucien's head jerked upright. "Clarissa, my darling. You will be my soulmate through all eternity. Come to me, my dear, and together we shall experience the ultimate."

Sarita tripped over her gown, which had been made for the taller Madeleine. She crashed into Lucien as she fell. At the same moment Simon leaped across the room. He closed with Lucien just before Lucien shook Sarita free and reached for the gun. Madeleine found herself caught between the fireplace and the scuffling men.

A log flared to life, filling the room with dancing light, and Madeleine saw the gun on the other side of the fireplace. She felt the weakness creeping over her again. Sarita was whimpering somewhere, in the shadows. Simon's fist connected with Lucien's jaw, and Lucien staggered backward, his cape whirling and his silhouette an enormous grotesque bat against the flickering firelight.

Lucien seemed to have the strength of several men, despite

Simon's superior size. Fighting like a man possessed, Lucien managed to catch Simon off balance, and the two of them rolled to the floor. Now Lucien jerked his cape free and flung it over Simon's face. Madeleine felt a dry scream rise in her throat as Lucien pulled the red-hot poker from the fire.

Madeleine's feet felt like lead as she tried to throw herself between the glowing poker and Simon's defenseless body. She was screaming, and Lucien's maniacal laugh rang out as he lunged. Simon groaned, and there was a sickening sizzle of burning flesh as he deflected the tip of the poker with his hand, rolling over to escape the imprisoning cape. Simon grasped the barrel of the blunderbuss, swung it around to point at Lucien. "Drop the poker. The game just ended."

Lucien held the poker aloft for a second, then let it fall with a clatter to the stone-flagged hearth.

Madeleine helped Simon to his feet. He grimly held onto the heavy weapon, despite the burned hand. Lucien suddenly grabbed Sarita's arm and yanked her toward the window.

By the time Simon had stumbled across the room they were through the glass-paned door, and it was closed and bolted from the outside.

"Simon, look, Madeleine said. Turning to follow her gaze, Simon saw the two shadows move into view in front of the window.

"They're on the parapet outside," Madeleine said. "Look how her dress is blowing. The wind must be fierce out there."

"I'll smash the window," Simon said through gritted teeth, not sure how long he could remain conscious between the pain in his hand and the dizziness from a blow to his head. "Perhaps I can hang onto them until we get some help. Take that gun and blast a hole in the door, then find your father and get him up here."

Simon picked up a chair and rammed it into the window, several feet from where Lucien stood, his arms tightly around Sarita.

Shards of glass cascaded in all directions as the wind howled into the room. Lucien turned at the sound of breaking glass, shouted something that was lost in the wind, and, arms around Sarita, plunged from the ledge.

CHAPTER 26

The sea lions barked a noisy welcome as Dan appeared. Madeleine was feeding them while Simon, his hand encased in a bandage, watched. Shiny black bodies ignored the fish and joyfully charged Dan's bare legs. Dan grinned and looked across the writhing mass at Madeleine and Simon.

"Welcome home," Simon said.

Dan dropped his knapsack. "Did you kids spend your whole time playing on the beach while I've been gone—or did I miss anything?"

Madeleine smiled and slipped her hand through Simon's arm. "We wouldn't have dreamed of getting married without you. Simon wants you to be best man."

Dan thumped Simon on the back. "Congratulations. When's the happy day?"

"Oh, I dunno," Simon said, considering. "How about in ten minutes?"

They both laughed at Dan's startled expression and dismayed glance at his lifeguard's red trunks. Simon said, "You can dress if you must. We have to wait for Madeleine's father to get here, then we thought we'd drive up to the Wayside Chapel overlooking the sea at Portugese Bend."

"If you two will excuse me," Madeleine said, "I'll go and change into my wedding dress. See you at the apartment?"

Simon nodded and kissed her lightly on the lips. He watched as she went up the beach to where the Volkswagen bug was parked.

Dan said, "I take it she's moved out of the beach house. I haven't seen a paper since I left. What's been happening?"

Reluctantly Simon tore his gaze from Madeleine's retreating back. "Lucien Cornell probably killed Dean Jennings and Regis Vaughan. We'll never know for sure, because Cornell is dead too." Simon briefly told Dan what had happened, adding that Sarita had somehow fallen on top of Lucien and wasn't killed, though she'd be crippled for life.

Dan digested the news silently for a moment, then asked, "Wasn't Vaughan the psychiatrist treating Madeleine? What happened to him?"

"We found his body in a shallow grave in the courtyard of the castle. There was a knife wound in his chest, but a postmortem revealed he was dying before he was stabbed. Bacteria that normally live on the human skin had somehow gained entry to his bloodstream. If it hadn't been for Sedgewick, Cornell's assistant, and Bruno—a small-time hood who hasn't stopped talking since the police picked him up—there would have been a lot of holes in the story. After Cornell jumped to his death, Sedgewick came forward and told the police he had disposed of Jennings' body. Apparently he posed as Jennings' next of kin and got a Mexican doctor to sign a death certificate and release the body to him. He buried it in the desert. The rangers couldn't find it in the place he directed them to look, because evidently the coyotes had dug it up."

Dan whistled as the awful irony hit him. "*Coyotes*—isn't that the name given to the scum who smuggle illegal aliens across the border for a price?"

Simon nodded. "Lucien convinced Sedgewick that Jennings died a natural death, and the Mexican doctor couldn't find any evidence of anything but sudden heart failure. Sedgewick believed he was merely saving Lucien the embarrassment of the news getting out that 'Penelope Marsh' was in Mexico with Jennings. You see, Sedgewick had been ordered to follow her wherever she went. He was on her tail all the way to Ensenada. He phoned Lucien when they checked into the motel there.

"Lucien immediately flew to Mexico with Bruno. According to Bruno, it was dark by the time they reached the motel. The surf was pounding on the rocks and covered the sound of their forced entry. Jennings was in a drunken sleep, but Madeleine was awake, crying, with her face buried in her hands. Bruno says that Lucien immediately said something strange and foreign-sounding. Apparently it was a command used during hypnosis, and Madeleine had been conditioned to fall into a trancelike sleep. Sarita told us that Lucien had begun by giving Madeleine small quantities of sedatives, and while she was half asleep, half awake, had begun to lead her into hypnotic trances, something in the manner of sleep-teaching. No doubt the nightmares she experienced were actually visitations by Lucien."

"And what about Jennings? What did they do to him?"

"Bruno says Lucien poured something from a small vial onto Jennings' bare skin. Madeleine was then given an injection and placed on the bed beside him. Bruno says they were in and out of the motel room in a matter of minutes. The injection was probably a powerful sedative that would keep her asleep while the chemical on Jennings' skin took effect. Lucien wanted to teach her a lesson by having her wake up beside the corpse."

"And what about the other man—the one in England?"

"Sedgewick also told Lucien that Madeleine had applied for a passport to go to England, so Lucien knew their plans before they left. We believe he arranged for a business trip for himself, then arrived in England almost the same time Madeleine and Waring did. The chances are that Waring picked up the salmonella bug before he left the United States, since Madeleine wasn't affected. So Waring's death was accidental.

In fact, it might have given Lucien the idea of staging a repeat performance with Jennings. Still, I can't help but wonder. There was evidence of an injection on Waring's body—the so-called vitamin shot. So there's a possibility that Lucien could have injected him with salmonella, but we'll never know now. Madeleine was never sure how long she had been in the room with Waring. In fact, she was often confused about the passage of time. What she thought were memory lapses were probably hypnotic trances, or posthypnotic suggestions planted by Lucien.

"Between her childhood trauma, the financial strain of keeping Lola in a sanitarium, and the masquerade as Penelope Marsh, it's remarkable that Madeleine didn't have a real breakdown. She was certainly susceptible enough to accept the alter personality invented by Lucien. It wouldn't have been difficult to convince her that there was another personality, because she was convinced she had killed two men even before Vaughan died."

"But why did Lucien kill Vaughan?"

"Madeleine says she regarded Vaughan as a father figure. She had embraced him a couple of times out of gratitude for his help, and Lucien saw them. Perhaps he misunderstood the gesture, and thought that Vaughan was making a pass. Or perhaps Lucien was afraid Vaughan would be able to prove to Madeleine there was no Madge and that she had been drugged and hypnotized. We'll never know for sure."

"It's true then," Dan commented, shaking his head, "that genius is close to madness."

"In Cornell's case, it seems so. He'd never wanted anything he couldn't have . . . until Madeleine. Funny thing about Sedgewick—he was so cooperative and freely admitted his part in everything, as well as telling us that he felt Lucien could have made an important contribution to the world of science. Sedgewick went to Lucien's house and destroyed all of his files. Years of research and the results of countless experiments went up in smoke. We'll never know why."

"Perhaps Cornell's records would have turned up something

incriminating about Sedgewick—or maybe he felt the exact components of that lethal chemical shouldn't be made public," Dan suggested. "What about Madeleine's father, and his wife in the sanitarium?"

"Kevin is going to stick around. At least he doesn't intend to go back to Australia immediately. He went to the sanitarium to see Lola, and the doctors feel she may have recognized him. Apparently her eyes filled up with tears, and it was the first emotion she's shown in all the years she's been there."

"And your friend Myron?"

"He's going to make it. He isn't out of the hospital yet, but he's in a general ward now. It was Bruno, carrying out Lucien's orders, who rigged the explosive device in the jeep. Lucien told Sarita to leave the book on explosives in Madeleine's studio, so she would believe 'Madge' did it. Bruno also broke into my apartment and laced my leftovers with poison. Sarita knew Lucien had ordered this, because she drove Bruno over that day, and couldn't resist leaving the piece of paint-smeared denim in the screen door to incriminate Madeleine."

Simon was silent, thinking that the prison Sarita had fashioned for herself was worse than anything the law could have inflicted.

"So you and Madeleine will get married and sail off into the sunset?" Dan asked, somewhat wistfully.

Simon threw the rest of the fish to the sea lions. "I'll have to rebuild my boat first, and Madeleine is anxious to get back to her painting. But we'll take a honeymoon cruise soon. We'll both be doing what we really want to do, and we'll be together."

Dan envied him silently as they walked up the beach. It was going to be one of those balmy winter days with a golden sun hanging lazily over the palm trees and the ocean calm under a cloudless sky. A perfect day for a wedding.

Great Adventures in Reading

EAST OF JAMAICA   14309 $2.50
by Kaye Wilson Klem

She was a titian-haired New Englander who had fled to the lush, volcanic island of Martinique. She never dreamed she would be forced to become a pleasure toy for the island's women-hungry planters.

THE EMERALD EMBRACE   14316 $2.50
by Diane du Pont

Beautiful Liberty Moore sought refuge at sea in the arms of a handsome stranger, unaware that he was the naval hero Stephen Delaplane, unaware that she would be taken from him and forced to become the bride of the most powerful ruler in the East.

KINGLEY'S EMPIRE   14324 $2.50
by Michael Jahn

Here is the story of a great shipping dynasty built on the ashes of a shore pirate's wiles and with the fire of an heiress's beauty.

FAWCETT GOLD MEDAL BOOKS

Buy them at your local bookstore or use this handy coupon for ordering.

This offer expires 1 April 81   8100-1

Great Adventures in Reading

THE GREEN RIPPER   14345 $2.50
by John D. MacDonald

Gretel, the one girl the hard-boiled Travis McGee had actually fallen for—dead of a "mysterious illness." McGee calls it murder. This time he's out for blood.

SCANDAL OF FALCONHURST   14334 $2.50
by Ashley Carter

Ellen, the lovely mustee, through a trick of fate marries into the wealthiest family in New Orleans. But she must somehow free the man she really loves, the son of a white plantation owner, sold to die as a slave. In the exciting tradition of MANDINGO.

WINGED PRIESTESS   14329 $2.50
by Joyce Verrette

The slave: Ilbaya, of noble birth, in love with his master's concubine. He risks death with each encounter. The Queen: beautiful Nefrytatanen. To keep the love of her husband she must undergo the dangerous ritual that will make her the "winged" priestess—or destroy her! An epic of ancient Egypt.

FAWCETT GOLD MEDAL BOOKS

JOHN D. MACDONALD

"The king of the adventure novel" John D. MacDonald is
one of the world's most popular authors of mystery and
suspense. Here he is at his bestselling best.

CONDOMINIUM	23525	$2.2
ALL THESE CONDEMNED	14239	$1.5
APRIL EVIL	14128	$1.7
BALLROOM OF THE SKIES	14143	$1.7
THE BEACH GIRLS	14081	$1.7
THE BRASS CUPCAKE	14141	$1.7
A BULLET FOR CINDERELLA	14106	$1.7
CANCEL ALL OUR VOWS	13764	$1.7
CLEMMIE	14015	$1.7
CONTRARY PLEASURE	14104	$1.7
THE CROSSROADS	14033	$1.7
DEADLOW TIDE	14166	$1.7
DEADLY WELCOME	13682	$1.5
DEATH TRAP	13557	$1.5
THE DECEIVERS	14016	$1.7
THE DROWNERS	13582	$1.7
THE EMPTY TRAP	14185	$1.7
THE END OF THE NIGHT	14192	$1.7
THE LAST ONE LEFT	13958	$1.9

8004-

Buy them at your local bookstore or use this handy coupon for ordering.

This offer expires 1/24/81